Praise for Martha Wel
the Books of the Rak

The Cloud Roads

"[Wells' Raksura books] are dense, and complex, with truly amazing world building, and non-human characters who are quite genuinely alien, yet still comprehensible and sympathetic. The characters, particularly the protagonist, Moon, are compelling and flawed and likable. The plots are solid and fast moving. But it's the world that . . . just, wow! There is a depth and breadth and sheer alienness here that I have rarely seen in any novel. Shape-shifters, flying ships, city-trees, six kazillion sentient races, floating islands, and on and on and on."

—Kelly McCullough, author of the WebMage series and
the Fallen Blade novels

"*The Cloud Roads* has wildly original worldbuilding, diverse and engaging characters, and a thrilling adventure plot. It's that rarest of fantasies: fresh and surprising, with a story that doesn't go where ten thousand others have gone before. I can't wait for my next chance to visit the Three Worlds!"

—N. K. Jemisin, author of *The Hundred Thousand Kingdoms*

"Filled with vivid action and memorable characters, *The Cloud Roads* is a terrific science fiction adventure story with a heart. I read it eagerly and look forward to its sequel with great anticipation."

—Sarah Prineas, author of *The Magic Thief*

"It reminds me of the SF/F fantasy I read as a teen, long before YA was categorized. Those books explored adult concepts without 'adult content'; the complexity of morality and the potential, uncaring harshness of life. This story's conclusion satisfies on all those counts as well as leaving me eager for the sequel."

—Juliet E. McKenna, *Interzone*

"There's so much to like here: multiple sapient species sharing a world (or NOT sharing) with complex gender roles, wildly differing societies, and varying technologies. This is rigorous fantasy without the trappings of European medievalism. And most of all, it's riveting storytelling."

—Steven Gould, author of *Jumper* and *7th Sigma*

"Martha Wells' books always make me remember why I love to read. In *The Cloud Roads*, she invents yet another rich and astonishingly detailed setting, where many races and cultures uneasily coexist in a world constantly threatened by soulless predators. But the vivid worldbuilding and nonstop action really serve as a backdrop for the heart of the novel—the universal human themes of loneliness, loss, and the powerful drive to find somewhere to belong."

—Sharon Shinn, author of *Troubled Waters*

"Wells . . . has created a new world of dragonlike shapeshifters and human tribes that could serve as the background for future novels in this exotic setting. Concise storytelling and believable characters make this a good addition to most fantasy collections."

—*Library Journal*

"A rousing tale of a lost boy who finds his way home and discovers that he has a role to play in saving the world. High-octane fight scenes nicely contrast with Moon's emotional growth and developing romance. Genre fans looking for something different will find this just what they needed."

—*School Library Journal Blog*

"I loved this book. This has Wells' signature worldbuilding and wholly real character development, and her wry voice shines through. I can't even explain how real the world felt, in which each race and city and culture had such well-drawn back story that they lived on even outside the main plot."

—Patrice Sarath, author of *Gordath Wood* and *Red Gold Bridge*

"*The Cloud Roads* is a terrific fantasy novel that stands out due to imaginative worldbuilding, accomplished writing and engaging storytelling. For everyone else, *The Cloud Roads* is a proud example of what the genre is capable of producing . . ."

—*Fantasy Book Critic*

"First off, the world revealed within this story is nothing short of amazingly detailed and intriguing. . . . you'll find this an imaginative and engaging novel."

—John Vogt, *Examiner.com*

The Serpent Sea

"Using its alien protagonist to explore the politics of gender and belonging, this is a fascinating read for SF readers looking for something out of the ordinary."

—*Publishers Weekly*

"*The Serpent Sea* is a wonderful and spellbinding sequel to *The Cloud Roads*, which was one of the best fantasy books of 2011. It gloriously continues the saga of the shapeshifting Raksura."

—*RisingShadow.net*

"With these books Wells is writing at the top of her game, and given their breadth, originality, and complexity, this series is showing indications it could become one of the landmark series of the genre."

—*Adventures Fantastic*

"I loved *The Serpent Sea*. It's extraordinary story telling with engaging characters in an enchanting world I want to visit."

—Diana Pharaoh Francis, author of the Path and Crosspointe series

"Another excellent and wonderful view into the universe of the Three Worlds and its fascinating inhabitants."

—*SF Signal*

"Moon is a delightful character and a great focal point for the story. The world the author has created is wonderfully complex and vivid and has wonderful layers of characters, cultures and creatures. . . . Reading this series is a choice [readers] will not regret."

—*Portland Book Review*

"Wells remains a compelling storyteller whose clear prose, goal-driven plotting, and witty, companionable characters should win her fans among those who enjoy the works of writers such as John Scalzi and Lois McMaster Bujold."

—Matt Denault, *Strange Horizons*

"*The Serpent Sea* is a worthy sequel to *The Cloud Roads* and it features all of the strengths (fantastic world-building, great story, awesome characters) of that first novel. It is so easy to fall in love with this series and the reasons are manifold."

—*The Book Smugglers*

The Siren Depths

"I really loved Book 3, which wound up as my favorite book of the trilogy. [. . .] I'll be pushing it on everybody who loves great writing, ornate worlds and wonderfully-drawn nonhuman characters. And I am also looking up Martha Wells' backlist, right now."

—Rachel Neumeier, author of *Lord of the Changing Winds* and *Black Dog*

"This is the type of Fantasy series I absolutely love—and highly recommend as a worthwhile series to read and fall in love with. [. . .] *The Siren Depths* closes the series really well."

—*The Book Smugglers*

"The first two books, *The Cloud Roads* and *The Serpent Sea*, were excellent, but in my opinion *The Siren Depths* is an even better and more satisfying book, because it takes the series to a whole new level of depth."

—*RisingShadow.net*

"*The Siren Depths* has more of what I've come to love about the Books of the Raksura—a compelling story, great world-building in a unique setting, and lovable characters with very realistic problems. In my opinion, it's also the most satisfying installment in the series."

—*Fantasy Café*

"Truly inventive and stunningly imaginative worldbuilding perfectly melded with vivid, engaging characters make the Books of the Raksura one of my all-time favorite science-fiction series."

—Kate Elliott, author of The Spiritwalker Trilogy

"Martha Wells writes fantasy the way it was meant to be—poignant, evocative, and astonishing. Prepare to be captivated 'til the sun comes up."

—Kameron Hurley, author of *God's War*, *Infidel*, and *Rapture*

Stories of the Raksura: Volume One

"Wells is adept at suggesting a long, complex history for her world with economy . . . Longtime fans and new readers alike will enjoy Wells' deft touch with characterization and the fantastic."

—*Publishers Weekly*

"An excellent collection of Raksura stories . . . demonstrates that there are plenty of intriguing stories to tell of the Raksura and the Three Worlds."

—*RisingShadow.net*

"The worldbuilding and characters in these stories are as wonderful as the novels and I had no difficulty immersing myself into Wells' world and societies again."

—*SF Signal*

STORIES

of the

RAKSURA

Other books by Martha Wells:

The Element of Fire
City of Bones
The Death of the Necromancer
Wheel of the Infinite

Fall of Ile-Rien Trilogy:
    The Wizard Hunters
    The Ships of Air
    The Gate of Gods

The Books of the Raksura
    The Cloud Roads
    The Serpent Sea
    The Siren Depths
    Stories of the Raksura Volume One:
        The Falling World + The Tale of
        Indigo and Cloud

Stargate: Atlantis
    SGA: Reliquary
    SGA: Entanglement

Emilie and the Hollow World
Emile and the Sky World

Star Wars: Razor's Edge

STORIES

of the

RAKSURA

VOLUME TWO: THE DEAD CITY & THE DARK EARTH BELOW

MARTHA WELLS

NIGHT SHADE BOOKS
NEW YORK

Night Shade books may be purchased in bulk at special discounts for sales promotion, corporate gifts, fund-raising, or educational purposes. Special editions can also be created to specifications. For details, contact the Special Sales Department, Night Shade Books, 307 West 36th Street, 11th Floor, New York, NY 10018 or info@skyhorsepublishing.com.

Night Shade Books™ is a trademark of Skyhorse Publishing, Inc.®, a Delaware corporation.

Visit our website at www.nightshadebooks.com.

10 9 8 7 6 5 4 3 2 1

Library of Congress Cataloging-in-Publication Data

Wells, Martha.
  [Novels. Selections]
  Stories of the Raksura. Volume two / Martha Wells.
    pages ; cm
  ISBN 978-1-59780-537-7 (softcover : acid-free paper)
  I. Wells, Martha. Dead city. II. Wells, Martha. Dark Earth below. III. Title. IV. Title: Dead city. V. Title: Dark Earth below.
  PS3573.E4932A6 2015
  813'.54--dc23
                                    2015006847

Edited by Jeremy Lassen
Cover art by Matthew Stewart
Cover design by Claudia Noble

Print ISBN: 978-1-59780-537-7

Printed in the United States of America

CONTENTS

THE DEAD CITY

This novella takes place some turns before the events of The Cloud Roads, *before Moon came to the Indigo Cloud Court . . .*

Moon had lost track of the days he had traveled from Saraseil.

The sun was setting as the grassland below gradually turned to marsh. The salt-tinged wind told him that there was a sea somewhere to the south, and he had just enough sense left to avoid it. He had been flying low, following a rough track that was beaten through the sweet-scented grass by turns and turns of groundling feet. It was recent, and nothing like the ancient but still functional stone roads he had encountered often enough.

Anyone else might have been looking for a place to die; he was so indifferent as to what happened to him next that there seemed little point in anything, even dying.

The track stopped at the edge of a shallow lake, with stands of reeds and floating purple and white flowers. Big delicate insects with wings like shards of glass flitted over it. The far shore rose up into hills cloaked with heavy jungle.

Moon circled and landed on the soft ground, his claws sinking into it. There was no dock, but there was a pile of long narrow boats, made by weaving the dried reeds together. A limp and tattered traders' flag hung on a pole nearby. It was dull gold with a stripe, and meant the boats were free to use but not to be kept. It also meant that there was something on the other side of the lake, maybe a settlement, maybe just another track through the dirt. Mist rose over the water and the boats seemed to beckon. He had been going forward so long he didn't want to stop.

There might be people nearby, so he shifted to groundling. The shock of his exhaustion dropped him to his knees. He closed his eyes and felt the world swing around him. Maybe he had been flying too long. Maybe he was dying from contact with the Fell, as if even their skin was poisonous. After a moment the world subsided back into place, and he shook his head and pushed to his feet.

Whatever it was, Moon couldn't face shifting back to his other form. He pulled a boat off the pile, and found a pole for it, and pushed it into the water. The dry reeds cracked when he stepped onto it, but the weaving held together. As tiny crabs and little green-silver fish fled, he poled the boat forward.

The last of the evening light gradually failed but the moon was half-full and the sky was clear, a dark bowl of starlight. There was a steady buzz and chirp from the insects, soft splashing and plops from the small shelled creatures living among the flowers. Every so often a muted light source glowed from under the water, a faint white light that illuminated the bugs skating on the surface. The light might be from the cities of tiny waterlings, or a plant, or a kind of water creature, using its natural illumination to attract insects to eat.

After a short time, Moon saw he had been right to shift to groundling; there were lamps in the distance, reflecting off the water.

The lights were steady, and the glow was white and clear, like the light beneath the lake's surface. As he drew closer he saw the owners stood on two wide flat boats, and were drawing nets through the shallow water. He could tell they were bipedal groundlings, and not much else. He slid silently past them.

Moon wasn't sure how much time had gone by when he spotted another white light ahead. Closer, and he saw it hung from a pole with another trader flag attached, marking a dock. It lay at the base of the heavy jungle, which sloped upward to the dark shapes of the hills.

The dock was part of a ruin, a stone statue several times as tall as Moon. It sat in a kneeling position at the edge of the lake, a platform sloping out from it into the water. It would have been even taller, but the head had been knocked off at some distant time. As he pulled the boat up the platform and out of the water, Moon saw there was weather-worn carving on the body that might have been meant to represent scaled skin. Before Saraseil, that would have been intriguing, a possibility to be explored. Moon had never known what he was, had never seen anyone else like him since his mother and siblings had been killed, so many turns ago. Wherever he had gone, he had always looked for signs of people like him. Now . . . Now he just dragged the boat past the statue and left it in the grass next to the others.

More boats were tied up along the shore, round ones and a few flat square rafts, more evidence that there was a settlement somewhere near.

The track to it lay beyond the statue, marked by another flag, and he followed it up the slope through the trees. The jungle was a mix of giant ferns and hardwoods festooned with moss so thick it was like they were wearing cloaks, and their leaves blocked all the starlight. It would have been difficult for a groundling without good night vision, but Moon picked his way up it lightly and almost soundlessly, relying on his perception of shapes and a sense that told him what was a shadow and what was a solid object. The air was heavily scented by the moss and wet earth.

At a bend in the trail Moon started to track movement not far away, paralleling him. It was a big body, whatever it was, sliding through the moss, brushing curtains of it aside, grass and small ferns crunching underfoot. Stalking him. He paused and growled, "Come and get me." It came out deep and rough, in his other voice, though he hadn't shifted.

The movement stopped abruptly, was silent for several considering moments, then it changed direction and headed away.

Moon hissed in frustration and continued up the trail. A few moments later he realized there had been no predator scent, and he wasn't certain if he had hallucinated the encounter or not.

After a time he saw more lights ahead, and then the trees gave way to a clearing. There was a structure but it was hard to make out in the darkness. He could see enough to tell it was made out of reeds, woven into big basket-like shapes, hanging from or braced against a tree or some other structure he couldn't make out. From the lights hanging in the triangular windows, it went up at least four uneven levels, and it was draped with vines. There were caravanserai flags on a pole in front of it, the ones meaning that accommodation and food were available.

Voices came from inside, and he followed the path up to the opening in the lowest level.

There wasn't a door, just a short reed-woven tunnel. The scent of the cut reeds was heady and faintly sweet, and made even more intense by the damp air. Moon stepped quietly, finding a doorway into a big open chamber. White lights hung from ropes strung across the curved ceiling, and the hearth was in a big metal ball on a stand, a grill around the middle keeping the coals from rolling out onto the reed floor. There were a dozen or so groundlings having a loud conversation in a mix of Altanic and at least one other language he didn't know.

Most of them were large and burly, covered with what looked like gray-green forest floor moss but might be tightly curled wiry fur, good for repelling water and stinging insects. It obscured their bodies and faces so it was hard to make out any other detail. They wore rough skirts made of woven leaves hardened with lacquer, and carried knives at their belts, but they were the sort of knives more used for fish-scaling than stabbing. They weren't the only type of groundlings in the room but none of the others looked remotely like Moon's groundling form. There was no possibility of blending in, but Moon stepped into the room anyway.

Some glanced at him but went back to their argument. But one of the green-gray-furred ones shouted and shoved back through the others.

He grabbed Moon by the throat. Moon felt the blunt claws dig into his skin and two things went through him: a wave of rage and the realization that he was ravenously hungry.

The spark of self-preservation that had brought him here flared just enough to keep him from shifting. The groundling was saying, "This is our house now. What have you got to pay for—" when Moon took his hand and bent it back at the wrist. He twisted the arm around and put the groundling on the floor.

He expected the others to attack him, but when he looked up they were all standing around watching, some concerned, others resentful. One, a short groundling with dark leathery skin and long white hair, said, "It's not your house, Ventl. You, stranger, did you come here to trade?"

Moon said, "I'm traveling. The flags said this was a caravanserai." His voice came out rough and thick; when he had growled at the movement in the brush, it had been the first time he had spoken in days.

The others muttered in a language that wasn't Altanic. The one Moon was standing on who was apparently called Ventl said, "It's for trade."

The white-haired one said, "You shut your face, Ventl." He added to Moon, "It's a caravanserai."

Moon released Ventl and stepped back. Ventl leapt to his feet and snarled, but kept carefully out of arm's reach. He said, apparently not to Moon, "One traveler doesn't make this a caravanserai, Ghatli!"

Ghatli told him, "Take your stupid face and your stupid relatives and get out, Ventl. Go back to your camp before the miners eat you."

Ventl snarled again and made menacing grabbing gestures at Ghatli. Moon felt a growl building in his throat and managed to swallow it back; Ventl was just posturing, trying to save his pride. Some of the other furred ones urged him away, and the whole group moved toward the door. Other green-furred ones stayed, wandering off now that the fight was over.

Ghatli watched them go, narrow-eyed. Looking at him more closely, Moon realized he was actually female, or some gender close to female. The dark color and roughened texture of her skin made detail hard to see, but there were breasts under the clumps of white hair trailing down her chest and shoulders. Her fingers didn't have the blunt claws of the others, but were long and delicate. She wore the same kind of loose wrap kilt, with decorative bits of polished shell sewn on fabric that looked as if it might be made from pounded reed. She turned to Moon and looked him up and down. "You've come a long way?"

Being reticent about where you came from was never a good idea, and Moon answered automatically, "From Saraseil. Going toward Kish."

"Ah." The hair tufts above Ghatli's ears twitched. "We've had word of refugees."

One of the others said, "They said terrible things happened there. That it was the Fell. Is it true?"

Moon conquered the impulse to shift and tear his way out through the wall but managed to make himself just step back instead. He didn't want to talk about Saraseil. "Is it a caravanserai or not?"

"That is actually a long story—" Ghatli paused, squinted at him and continued, "Perhaps later. You want food?"

Yes, Moon wanted food.

☾

When Moon woke he lay there for a time, sensing the change in the air that told him the sun had risen over the hills, feeling the faint vibrations through the reed floors and walls as the other inhabitants moved around in the rooms below. He felt more than heard their voices, and the mix of their scents blended with the sweet reeds in the damp air. His head was clear, or at least more clear than it had been last night. He just had no idea what he was going to do now.

He had slept unevenly, all his dreams too close to the surface. He had heard Fell voices on the wind, over and over again, and woke in a flush of panic to find the night outside calm and filled with nothing but the chorus of insects and frogs and treelings. He knew the Fell could do things to the minds of groundlings; he had seen the horrific results at close quarters. And he knew Liheas, the Fell ruler who had captured him, had been able to affect him to some extent. He had thought he had broken free of it when he had broken Liheas' neck, but maybe some influence still lingered.

It was lucky he had found the caravanserai, a relatively safe and private place to have his nightmares. Maybe some day when Moon could appreciate still being alive he would feel grateful for that.

After the encounter with Ventl, he hadn't expected anything to be easy, but Ghatli had been surprisingly hospitable and no one else in the place had seemed hostile. Moon had still had a small bag of agate chips, which Saraseil had used for currency, and Ghatli had taken half of them in exchange for a pan of a rice mixture with nuts and pieces of fish that had been warming in another metal ball oven in the next room. Moon had eaten it standing beside the oven and wasn't really aware of anything else until Ghatli handed him another pan. It was enough to take the edge off, though Moon was going to have to hunt soon. He wasn't entirely sure why he hadn't stopped to hunt before reaching the shallow lake, but then he wasn't entirely sure how long he had been traveling.

He had followed Ghatli through another roomful of groundlings who were having some earnest discussion about something and to a winding ladder that led up to the sleeping rooms, which were just small but private cubbies stacked on the third and fourth levels of the structure. Moon had stayed awake long enough after Ghatli left to find an emergency way out, an opening in the roof at the top of the ladderwell meant for ventilation. He had also stopped to look at the lights, and saw they were made of some very thin clear bladder-like substance with a little glowing mass inside that looked like coral. It must be harvested from whatever caused the occasional glowing spots in the lake.

When he had finally retreated to his cubby he was so exhausted he didn't even unroll the blanket, just curled up around it and sank into sleep.

Now he sighed and rubbed his face. He knew what he should do, what he always did. Leave the caravanserai and keep going . . . whichever direction he had been going. North, towards Kish? He was definitely west of what was left of the city of Saraseil. Maybe one day he would travel far enough and find a place that had never heard of the Fell, and where shapeshifters weren't regarded as vicious predators. Since every shapeshifter he had encountered other than his own family had been a vicious predator, this seemed unlikely.

Even more unlikely now that he had seen the Fell for himself. At least now he knew why groundlings always mistook his shifted form for one. When he shifted, his body grew taller and his shoulders broader. He was stronger but much lighter, and his skin grew overlapping matte black scales with an under sheen of bronze. He grew retractable claws on his hands and feet and a long tail, and a mane of flexible frills and spines around his head that ran down to his lower back. He didn't look exactly like a Fell ruler, but it was more than close enough for terrified groundlings.

Moon dragged himself out of the too-warm cubby. Ghatli had said last night that there was a latrine and bathing area on the lowest level of the house. He climbed down to the main level and wandered through, ignoring the curious looks from the groundlings who either lived here or seemed to use this place as a general gathering area.

Most were similar in shape and color to the green-gray-furred ones he had seen last night, but there was also a party of more unusual ones clearly preparing to leave. They were about waist-high to Moon and had heavy armored shells, rounded over where their heads should be, multiple dark eyes peering out from under a rim implanted with polished stones. They had tied their packs in front around their middles, so very little of the rest of them was visible, but they had several arms and large arrays of delicate fingers. Ghatli was speaking to them in a language Moon didn't understand, but she seemed to be trying to convince them to stay.

Moon found the half-ladder half-stair down near the front entrance. The latrine and separate bathing room had been dug out of the hill and there were several small basins, a large round metal bath with a pump to fill it, a stove with a supply of wood to warm the water, oily soap, and old blanket remnants to use as towels. The stove had a banked fire that must be from use earlier this morning. There was no one else here now, and Moon thought the gray-furred groundlings who seemed to congregate here probably had no need for it. Their fur looked like it was water-resistant and they would have other ways to clean themselves. The bath would probably be for Ghatli and any groundling travelers who preferred water for washing.

Moon built the fire up and was able to wash enough to feel vaguely awake again. He kept checking himself for wounds and not finding any; his dark bronze skin was smooth and unmarked. He hadn't been hurt during his escape from Saraseil, but some part of his brain was still convinced he was covered with burns or deep tears and punctures from claws.

When he was trying to get the ground-in dirt of the past several days out of his skin and scalp, the scent of smoke filled his lungs. It was memory, not a real lingering scent, and he stuck his head under the warm water until lack of air forced it away.

He made himself think about practical matters. He had taken nothing with him when he left Saraseil, except the clothes he was wearing and the agate chips which had been in a bag in his pocket. It was part of the magic of shifting that he could take fabric and a few other objects with him between forms, but he hadn't been paying attention over the last few days and it was just lucky he hadn't lost them. The light material of the shirt and pants had been fine for city living but had gotten increasingly stained the few times he had had to shift to his groundling form to sleep. But he wasn't committed enough to washing them to bother finding out if the groundlings here would care if he was naked while they dried. And he didn't want to stay here that long.

He went back up to the main level, where Ghatli stood in the outer door watching the short armored groundlings trundle away across the caravanserai's yard. They were heading down the path toward the lake. The sky was overcast and it made the ferns and heavy foliage around the clearing look an even deeper green than they already were.

Ghatli saw Moon and said, with a sigh, "Even the Agun-teil are afraid."

"Of the Fell?" Moon said, the words out before he could stop them.

"Ah!" Ghatli shuddered, making her sparse fur shake. "No, not the Fell. Not yet. Not ever, please." She made a complicated gesture which might be a ward against bad luck, or death, or Fell, or anything in general. "No, it's the miners. They have been attacking anyone who tries to go along the hill trade route. They haven't come down to the shore yet, but they've already frightened off a great many traders."

Moon considered leaving. The conversation, the caravanserai. If it wasn't the Fell, he didn't care. But it was a habit and an ingrained survival skill to pretend to show interest in things that groundlings were interested in, so he said, "The what?"

"You haven't heard of the miners? You must not have stopped at any of the trade camps along the Lacessian Way, I thought the word had spread—" She eyed him again. "Well, I suppose you didn't. The miners appeared here three cycles ago. We call them miners because they dig into the hills."

A vague spark of real interest stirred and Moon squinted up at the rising terrain behind the caravanserai. It was all heavily cloaked in jungle. It looked more like hunting country, or a good spot for gathering fruit and roots. "What are they mining?"

"We have no idea. No one lives up there. It's good country, and the trade route is right there, but there's been no settlements, as far as the fishers can remember. Of course there are tales of ghosts, but there always are, in empty places." Ghatli moved her shoulders uneasily. "There is obviously something the miners want up there, but we don't know if it is something natural, like metal ore or gemstone, or something buried under the ground." She lowered her voice. "Perhaps something left by some ancient species."

Moon nodded absently. One thing that had become obvious in his travels was that the Three Worlds had been home to many and varied peoples over uncounted turns. The hills and the jungle might conceal anything; there were a great many things the miners could be digging for.

Ghatli had apparently been hoping for a reaction of astonishment because she drooped a little. "We thought it a good theory. It's at least the most interesting theory."

Moon shrugged, noncommittal.

"Anyway, this place is a major route for the trade along the Lacessian and the Vaganian, which cross on the other side of the heights, but the miners have frightened almost everyone off, and the trader caravans are taking other routes." She scuffed at the dirt with the horny pads of one foot. "That's Ventl's problem. He and the other fishers can't get anyone to cart his reeds and the traders aren't here to buy their fish anymore, and it's made him angry, and he thinks taking over the caravanserai from me will somehow . . ." She sighed. "We are friends, still, I hope. But he's afraid and it's made him strange."

It took Moon a moment to remember that Ventl was the one who had tried to attack him when he had arrived. It hadn't been much of an attack. Moon's lack of interest in the trading difficulties of strange groundlings was in danger of overcoming him, but Ghatli said, "We can't even talk to the miners. Trader caravans don't want to mine, they want to trade. Fishers want to fish. The miners have no reason to think anyone here might impinge on . . . whatever it is they're doing."

"They speak a different language?" Moon asked, looking toward the jungle again. He needed to hunt, and he could hear more groundlings plodding and stamping up the path from the lake. This place was getting crowded.

"They don't speak anything, at least not to us. The fishers who went up into the hills to try to talk to them disappeared." Ghatli quivered, a mix of anger and disgust. "We think they ate them."

Moon swallowed the urge to hiss. "They usually do," he said, bitterly.

"It's a common problem?" Ghatli asked, startled, "Because—Oh, joy, here's Ventl again."

Ventl was coming up the path from the lake. With him were a couple of his green-gray-furred cronies and a new group of groundlings. They were taller and broader than the stocky fishers and had boney square skulls. They wore light leather armor and carried heavy metal weapons: javelins and sickle-like curved blades slung across their backs. That was always a bad sign, in Moon's experience. Ghatli's too, evidently, as she muttered, "I hope they don't want rooms. They'll go right through the floors."

The first armored one strode up to them and looked between Moon and Ghatli, as if equally dissatisfied with both Moon's tattered half-starved look and Ghatli's appearance in general. Ghatli gave a frustrated twitch and said, "What is this, Ventl? I didn't know you knew any Cedar-rin."

Ventl moved his big flat head in a way Moon interpreted as embarrassment or reluctance. He said, "They want to see the miners."

Ghatli's ears lifted. "See them in what sense?"

"That's our concern," the Cedar-rin said, his voice deep and grating. The skin of his face was oddly pale, but it caught the light as he turned his head and Moon saw it was coated with small pearly scales, and must be as tough as lizard-hide, though not as thick as Moon's scales in his other form. There was a distinct resemblance to the scales on the broken statue at the old lake dock.

From this angle Moon saw the leader had horns curling out from the back of his skull and the others didn't. They were all a little smaller, their heads not as large and boney. They might be female, or another gender, or even a variant of the species. The horned Cedar-rin said, "Why is this one here?"

He was talking about Moon. Moon didn't answer, just continued to stare unblinking at him. Normally he believed in being more circumspect, but his patience for it seemed to have stayed behind when he left Saraseil.

Ghatli said, "He's just a lodger. If you want to see the miners, just go up that road—" She turned to point toward the wide path that curved up the hill at the far end of the clearing.

The Cedar-rin reached to grab her arm and his hand bounced off Moon's chest. Moon had stepped in front of Ghatli almost before he knew he was going to do it. He had no idea why, except that the Cedar-rin was large and Ghatli was small, even if she did seem tough and wiry. He looked into the Cedar-rin's little pale eyes and said, "Tell her what you want. Don't touch her."

The Cedar-rin stared, emotion hard to read on its boney face. The others drew their sickles. Ventl came up on the balls of his big feet and Moon could hear reeds creak as the inhabitants of the caravanserai crowded out the doorway.

His voice calm and a little curious, the big Cedar-rin said, "You're brave for a soft-skin. Do you think you can best us?"

Soft-skin, Moon thought, feeling his upper lip curl. He knew he could best them. He also knew Ghatli and the others wouldn't much care for him after they saw him do it. His back fangs itched and his fingertips hurt and his pulse pounded through his body with the urge to shift.

Ghatli peered out from behind his elbow. She said, "We're all friends here, hey? My good friend Ventl brought you here, didn't he?" The look she directed Ventl's way must have been poisonous because he rocked back on his heels from the force of it. "Do as my friend here says, and tell me what you want of us."

The Cedar-rin considered it, then finally said, "Take us to the excavation."

"It's easy to find," Ghatli said. "You take the path there up through the hills to the trade route—"

The Cedar-rin grabbed Ventl by the back of his head, drew a knife curved into a half-circle, and held it to the fur at Ventl's throat. Ghatli flinched and the other groundlings in the caravanserai gasped in dismay.

If that was as fast as the Cedar-rin could move, Moon wasn't impressed. But he would have to shift to stop them and he didn't want to do that yet. He thought they would probably end up leading the Cedar-rin into the hills and it was best to get on with it.

Ghatli held up her hands. "There is no reason to get violent! Of course I'll take you."

☾

The Cedar-rin made them go first up the path into the jungle. It was Ghatli, Ventl, the other two fishers who had come with him, and Moon. The Cedar-rin had ignored the other fishers and groundlings inside the caravanserai, and Ghatli had signaled them to stand aside and not try to intervene.

The path was wide and had been well-traveled, but clumps of fast-growing grasses were already sprouting in the packed dirt. The tall fern-trees shaded it, along with moss-draped spiral trees and something that had multiple trunks that branched up and wound around in tight curls. It was warmer here, the scents thick and rich, but the insects, birds, and treelings were oddly quiet. There were a great many low flowering bushes and vines that obscured the ground.

Ventl had tried to walk next to Ghatli but she had told him, "You, you I'm not speaking to. Now shoo." He followed glumly with his two companions as Ghatli walked beside Moon. Now she muttered, "I hate people who use pejoratives. 'Soft-skin.' What does that even mean? He's made it up himself, like a badly mannered child."

Moon had heard it used before, but just asked, "What are Cedar-rin?"

"They come from west of the lake shore. They have big stone cities over there, very uncomfortable, I should think. I've not seen much of them here. I think the talky one is a male and the others are drones." She added, "They aren't traders, at least not on these routes."

If they were mercenaries hired to drive the miners away from the trade route, they could have said so and been welcomed by the groundlings at the caravanserai with open arms. That they hadn't didn't bode well. "You don't know what they might want, then."

"No. Perhaps the same thing the miners want? It's a mystery, as no one has ever wanted anything here before except honest trading." She looked up at him. "I think we are to be friends. What is your name?"

Moon wasn't willing to commit to friendship anymore. It had proved too painful in the long run. Often in the short run, too. But there was no reason to be rude to Ghatli. "Moon."

"Ah." She was still looking at him. "And what are you, Moon? You don't look like the traders I have seen from Saraseil."

"I'm from . . ." East, he used to say. Always east of where he was now. "I'm not going to tell you," he finished.

"Well, fair enough." Ghatli made the gesture of flicking something away, apparently dismissing the subject. After a moment, she sighed. "Now I have to talk to stupid Ventl."

Ventl, who had clearly been listening the entire time, stepped forward and said, low-voiced, "I don't know what they want. I met them on the Lacessian Way at the far shore, and I thought they were the escort of a big caravan, and I told them of the miners." Ventl shook his furry head. "I thought they'd fight them to clear the way for trade, but now it seems they want what the miners are digging for."

"It seems that, does it?" Ghatli made a derisive noise.

Ventl threw an awkward look over his shoulder, having to turn the upper half of his over-muscled body to do it. "But we could work with them, perhaps. Maybe we want what the miners are here for too—"

"You don't," Moon said. He thought it was obvious. "The miners will kill to keep it, the Cedar-rin will kill the miners to get it, someone will kill you to take it."

Ventl went silent. From behind them, one of his companions whispered, "I told you so."

Ghatli muttered, "I just hope no one kills us before we have a chance to say we don't want it, whatever it is."

Ventl said, grimly, "Here we are."

The path had been sloping upward and curving around, and now it met a wider track large enough to be called a road. It had been cut into the side of the hill and was heavily packed down, and lined with half-buried water rock. A stelae beside the edge of the path displayed a couple of flags indicating the presence of the caravanserai towards the lakeshore. Ghatli explained, "The hill route. This is as far as anyone's gone and come back."

There was a pause where Ventl tried to convince the lead Cedar-rin that this was as far as he needed to be guided and got a clout across the skull and another death threat for his trouble. Moon figured Ventl had it coming, so he didn't intervene.

They continued on along the trade route. The jungle wasn't any darker but seemed even more silent. They passed a spring that trickled down the hill through the trees and had been bridged with large flat stones where it crossed the road. A small stone basin had been installed to one side, to collect water for travelers and their grasseaters, and it was obvious this had been a well-traveled and comfortable route before the miners had arrived. Moon tried to taste the air without being obvious about it. The scents of the plants and wet earth still dominated. Unless the miners were unusually rank, he doubted he would be able to . . . There was movement ahead.

He said to Ghatli and Ventl, "Get ready to run."

"What?" Ghatli was startled, but Ventl tugged on her arm.

Behind them, the lead Cedar-rin snapped an order and the drones all drew their sickles. Ferns and branches crashed ahead, a frenzy of waving greenery as whatever it was gave up the effort to be stealthy. The Cedar-rin charged forward, roaring. Moon swept Ghatli off the road as Ventl and his friends scrambled out of the way. Moon shouted, "Run!" and Ghatli jumped back onto the road to comply, but one drone had stayed behind to block them. It lifted its sickle menacingly and Moon dove for its legs and knocked it off the road.

He heard Ghatli yell, "Come on, Moon!" and her lighter footsteps merged with the fishers' heavier thumps as they ran. Moon twisted away just as the drone brought its sickle down. Then he rolled into the heavy foliage and shifted.

Moon leapt upward into the branches before the confused drone could see anything but a dark blur. He swarmed up to the mid-layer of the canopy and leapt from branch to branch, trying to keep the disturbance to a minimum. He wanted a good look at these miners and what they were digging for.

He reached the upper part of the road again and saw the Cedar-rin fighting something big and white that moved too fast to see. Then whatever it was paused for an instant, and Moon got a good view.

It was spider-like, taller than the lead Cedar-rin, covered with long white fur, with a round body in the center and three broad legs on each side. He thought there were limbs under the round center part, and probably a mouth, judging by the drones' injuries, but he couldn't see it from here. It leapt at the drones again and Moon climbed further up the tree.

As the branches grew too thin to support him he pushed upward and snapped his wings out, and flapped to get high enough to catch the wind. He wasn't worried about being spotted; the jungle was too thick to allow for much visibility, and everyone was too busy to look up at the moment anyway.

It was good flying weather, the overcast breaking up toward the east and letting the sun gleam on the lake. There was a town along the shore, in a cove some distance down from the trading dock. The houses were built on stilts, standing in the shallows, boats docked beneath them, and there were berms fencing off shallow ponds for rice fields nearby. That must be the town of the fishers and reed-growers. Moon flew further up the rounded hills, able to spot the path by the lighter color of the fern trees that shaded it, and then to trace the more open channel of the trade route. But he didn't need to follow it very far; the excavation was obvious.

Not far ahead a series of hills like rounded cylinders surrounded a wide valley, and in it much of the trees and brush had been stripped away and lay in rotting piles. The white spidery miners were easy to spot, moving over the bare ground to and from a crevasse they were carving out near the center. Moon settled into a slow circle, high enough up that he could be mistaken for a large carrion bird.

They were transporting the dirt and rock by using a system of ropes strung across the valley, supported at intervals by scaffolds about ten paces or so high. Big slings or baskets were hauled up from the crevasse on the ropes, and then run along them to the edge of the valley and dumped. Then the empties were hauled back on a separate system. The rubble formed huge piles of debris at the edge of the jungle. The baskets moved smoothly along the ropes, as if they were on wheels, and it seemed to take little effort to push them along. *No, those aren't ropes*, Moon thought, circling again.

On the far side of the valley a group of miners were building a second system, probably because the debris piles at the end of the first one were growing too large. As Moon angled around he could see that they weren't stringing rope, but extruding it like a branchspider's web from somewhere beneath their bodies, and knitting it into place with their lower limbs. The stuff must be as slick as glass, and the big baskets and scaffolds were probably made from it as well.

The crevasse itself was about fifty paces long and growing, and he couldn't tell how deep it was. He also couldn't see anything of what they were digging for. They seemed to be discarding the rock and dirt and not even sorting through it, the way metal and gem miners did, so perhaps they hadn't uncovered what they were really looking for yet.

Which doesn't explain how the Cedar-rin knew what it was, Moon thought. No, as far as Ghatli knew, no one had seen the excavation and if they had, they hadn't survived long enough to talk about it. But the word from the fishers that a strange species they called miners was inexplicably digging in the hills had been enough to bring the Cedar-rin. There had to be more to it than that.

Moon judged that he had run out of time for sightseeing. He turned away, caught the wind again and arrowed back down to see if the Cedar-rin had killed the miner yet and how Ghatli and the others were doing.

He flew above the path until he saw rapid movement in the canopy, as something large—maybe two somethings—climbed through it. A little further down, faint twitches in the foliage told him something was running. The gap between the two spots was narrowing rapidly. *Uh oh*, Moon thought. He shot ahead and dove down into the upper canopy.

Moon climbed down the branches until he heard the pounding of running footsteps. He shifted to groundling and dropped out of the trees onto the edge of the path. Several figures came into view, Ghatli and Ventl, Ventl's two fisher friends, and two of the Cedar-rin drones bringing up the rear. One of the drones had its armor half-ripped off, bloody streaks torn through the flesh and clothing beneath. Moon yelled, "Don't stop! It's getting closer!"

"Moon!" Ghatli panted in protest as she passed him. She was pushing Ventl along; none of the fishers were particularly fast on their feet.

"Keep going," he told her. They passed him, the limping drone grimly determined to keep its wounded companion moving.

The fleeing groundlings pounded away, down the slope and out of sight. A moment later, two miners crashed into view. They didn't hesitate, but charged toward Moon. They knocked down small saplings and tore through the fern trees. Their motion was fast but odd, all six legs moving in a concert that was strangely not awkward.

Moon waited, thinking about distance and relative strength and how these things were supposed to be sentient and maybe a smart predator might have taken alarm by now. Or maybe they just assumed he was frozen with terror. The first one drew close enough to crouch and leap.

Moon had a moment to see the mouth, which was round and huge and lined with what must be hundreds of scissor-like projections. The two additional limbs to either side were long and slender, with at least six agile fingers.

Then he surged forward and shifted.

He sliced one arm off with the first sweep of the claws of his right hand, grabbed the other arm and used it to pull himself up and rip both sets of foot claws across the softer skin around the mouth. It happened too fast for the creature to know it was in pain; its teeth snapped at him as it tried to extend the musculature around the mouth. That was when its guts started to fall out.

Moon flipped up between one set of legs and landed on its back as the creature collapsed under him. The second miner was still coming at him though that was mostly momentum; it flared its legs to try to halt itself.

Curious about how to kill one from the top, Moon pounced onto its back and dug the disemboweling claws on his heels into its fur. The skin was tougher up here but his claws still sunk into it. The miner stood up on the three legs of its left side to try to bash him into a tree trunk. Moon sprang up onto one of its extended legs, wrapped himself around it, and twisted.

He felt the joint pop as the miner flipped around and grabbed for him. The creature realized a moment later why that wasn't a good idea as Moon ripped open its underbelly before it could extend its mouth.

As it collapsed into a steaming heap, Moon bounded up the path. He wanted to see where the other surviving Cedar-rin were.

He reached the road and slowed down as he neared the site of the initial attack, prepared to shift back to groundling if he sensed movement.

But bodies were scattered along the road and the torn-up ground to either side. Some were bitten nearly in half, some had limbs missing, blood pooling on the mossy ground and drawing clouds of buzzing carrion insects. There was only one dead miner; it lay to one side of the path, on its back with its vulnerable underbelly slashed open. The other two miners must have arrived unexpectedly, while the Cedar-rin were still busy with the first. Moon could tell from the way the bodies lay that they had been trying to retreat in order, but had become separated. Singly, they had been easy prey.

He found the male sprawled on his back across the body of the smallest drone, as if they had died back to back, or the leader had tried to protect it. Moon sat on his heels to check the drone trapped under him, hoping it was alive, but the torn flesh at its throat was already cooling.

He sat there for a time, twitching his spines to drive off the insects. He could have prevented this if he had shifted to fight the miners with them, but they would have turned on him next. He was fairly certain they would have. It was what had happened every time he had done something like that in the past.

He was tired of looking at dead groundlings, tired of feeling sorry for them. The Fell had hunted them through the streets of Saraseil, dug through the walls of their houses. There was a raw lump of emotion in his chest, boiling and expanding until it felt as if it was going to burst out through his scales.

He wanted to make somebody else feel sorry.

Moon sensed movement and lifted his head to see three more miners standing on the road, watching him. He bared his fangs and flicked his spines. "Just in time," he growled.

☾

Moon returned to the caravanserai a short while later, as the sun moved into afternoon somewhere behind the heavy clouds. He had had to take time to wash the blood off his scales in the stream, and he had caught a big flightless bird in a clearing and eaten it down to the bones. With his belly finally full, it was hard not to just find a good spot to curl up and sleep, but he wanted to know what was happening at the caravanserai.

He walked into the house to hear anxious voices and found the main room crowded with fishers and a scatter of other groundlings. The badly injured Cedar-rin drone lay on the floor on a bed of blankets, its bloody armor in a discarded pile and its wounds being tended by a green skinny groundling who looked like a stick insect, complete with large multi-faceted eyes. It had two sets of hands branching out from its forearms, more like feelers than fingers, delicate but adept.

The other drone sat nearby, its shoulders slumped in exhaustion. It was still wearing its battered armor, but had removed the shoulder and arm pieces on one side and was pressing a cloth to the ragged scratches there. Then Ghatli turned away from the round stove with a bowl of steaming water in her hands and nearly dropped it. "Moon!"

Everyone stared at him, startled. The upright drone made an abortive reach for its sickle, then just slumped in despair again. Ventl said, "We thought you were dead!"

Moon shook his head. "They chased me, but I lost them in the jungle." He stepped around a couple of gaping fishers and took a seat on a reed stool someone had just vacated. He nodded toward the Cedar-rin. "Did they say what they were after from the miners?"

"Not yet," Ghatli said. "Perhaps they will." She handed the bowl to the insect groundling and lightly touched Moon's forehead. "You're bleeding. Did you fight them?"

He managed not to flinch away. "No, I fell down a ravine trying to get away." He had cuts across his scalp, and bruises rising on his arms and legs and chest, blue-purple against the dark bronze, visible through the tears in his already ragged shirt and pants. Any injuries he suffered in his scaled form transferred to his groundling skin when he shifted. The damage was minor, but three of the creatures at once had been a bit of a challenge. Invigorating, but a challenge.

The insect groundling focused its glittering eyes on him, a concentrated stare that made his insides twitch and almost activated his prey reflex. In a deep buzzing voice, it said in Altanic, "You require aid?"

"No, thank you," he told it.

As the insect groundling turned back to the unconscious drone, Ghatli said, "Moon, that is Physician Iscre. And these two are An, and its relative Na, who are of the family Tskkall of the Rin of Cedar." An ducked its head, apparently embarrassed. Ghatli added, "Moon delayed the pursuit of the miners so we could all live. Perhaps An will tell us now what the miners are digging for that the Cedar-rin were so curious about. No one here will say where we heard it." She glanced around the room and got nods and various gestures of assent from the others.

In a voice lighter than the male Cedar-rin's, An said, "It doesn't matter if you tell anyone. My kin . . ." It hesitated, but then lifted a hand in despair. "We came to see if the miners were really digging in these hills.

I don't know why they want what is there. But it is the resting place of our ancestors."

Moon hadn't been expecting that. Neither had Ghatli, evidently, or anyone else. She said, "Your people are buried there? Since when?"

An said, "More than two hundred turns ago the Rin had a city there."

Everyone still stared in blank astonishment and disbelief. Ventl said, "Why don't you live there now?"

An betrayed a trace of annoyance. "It is a dead city. Do your people live atop graves?"

Ventl exchanged an uneasy look with one of the other fishers. He said, "Apparently we're as good as living atop your graves!"

"We pick fruit from the trees on those hills," one of the others said, shocked, and there were mutters of horror. "No wonder the traders tell stories of ghosts and strange voices."

Moon concentrated, remembering the landscape as he had seen it from the air. The uniformly rounded hills had formed a semi-circle around this side of the lake, centering on the same natural bay that the caravanserai was built above, the spot where the fishers had their dock for traders and travelers. The dock with the old statue that had had a Cedar-rin's scales carved on it. After so many turns, the jungle and grass and dirt might easily cover a large ruined city, but he was surprised the fishers had never encountered more traces of the foundations.

Ghatli's ear tufts were twitching. "There must be something buried with your ancestors that the miners want. Precious metals, or gems, or something. Is that it?"

The evasive expression that crossed An's face wasn't too obvious, but it was clear it didn't spend a lot of time lying and deceiving people when it was at home. It said, "I don't know. But it seems most likely."

An knew something but it obviously had no intention of telling them anything more. Which was understandable. Moon didn't think they would have gotten this far if the male Cedar-rin had still been alive. Moon asked, "Do you know anything about the miners? Where they came from? How they found out your dead were buried here?"

An frowned, the expression intensified on its square face. "I don't know how the miners found out. I don't think the primaries knew. Kall—" He stopped, swallowed, and went on. "Kall, the one who led us here, was our primary." He lifted his hand to gesture, winced, and set it carefully down on his knee again. "The location of our dead cities are not spoken of to anyone outside the Rin. And they aren't spoken of lightly within it.

I knew there was one near this shore of the lake, but not where, until we were sent to see if the rumors were true."

"But have you ever heard of a species like the miners before?" Moon persisted. He knew a great deal more about the miners' anatomy now, but he didn't think anyone could figure out their motives unless they knew how they lived and where they were from. "They're fairly distinctive."

"No," An admitted. "They sound like horror stories to entertain the pods."

Moon sat back. It was disappointing, but he was fairly sure An wasn't lying now. Ghatli let her breath out in a gusty sigh and said, "I assume other Cedar-rin will be coming to see what happened to you when you don't return."

An's mouth set in a thin line, as it debated how much to say. "Don't try to stop them, and they will leave you alone."

"Your primary Kall threatened us to get us to take him to the miners," Ghatli pointed out. "I could've given you a map. This is a caravanserai. We have maps to spare. Giving people directions is a large part of what we do every day."

Earnest now, An said, "He thought it might be the fishers themselves who were digging, and the miners were just a story." It looked down at the injured Na. With its armor removed, it was easier to tell they were drones. Na didn't have any nipples or anything else that looked like a sexual characteristic. The doctor-groundling Iscre had just finished spreading a waxy substance over the last of Na's wounds, and the substance hardened immediately, forming a tight bandage. An said, "Now we know the truth, and the others will read our anima and know it too."

"Read your anima, that's good," Ghatli said and pressed a hand to her head in frustration. "Hopefully they'll stop to do that before they decide we did for all your friends in some violent outburst." The other fishers muttered darkly.

"They won't—" An began, but footsteps creaking on the reed floor of the house's entrance interrupted it.

Three fishers crowded into the doorway. One said, "We found a dead miner!"

Someone said, "At least the Cedar-rin killed one of the pestilent creatures."

Annoyed, Ventl said, "We know, we were there! What were you doing so far up the hill route? I told you to stay away, it's dangerous."

"We weren't on the hill route, we were on the east curve path, not ten pad-lengths up it," one protested. "The miner's legs were there, laid out in a circle, but there was no middle."

Moon looked away to hide a wince. He probably shouldn't have done that. Ventl stared. Someone said, "A carrion predator must have done it, with a miner that the Cedar-rin killed."

Everyone looked relieved at this suggestion. Everyone but An, who frowned in doubt, and started to speak. Moon asked hurriedly, "When will the other Cedar-rin come after you?"

"Soon. They know what happened to us." The other drone Na stirred and whimpered and An reached down to take its hand.

Ghatli caught that. "What do you mean?"

An shrugged a little. "The primaries are all aware of each other. When our primary Kall . . . The others will know something is wrong and come for us."

Moon had wondered about that, with that comment about the Cedar-rin reading An's anima to know the truth of what had happened. "So they can . . . hear your thoughts from a distance?"

An tried to explain, "No, not like that. For drones it's just feelings, intuitions. But the primaries know more. It's hard to describe."

But Ghatli nodded. "I've heard of this before. Some species have mental connections, that let them communicate over long distances." She glanced at Moon. "There are rumors the Fell can do this. Did they know of it in Saraseil?"

"I don't know." Moon got up and stepped away. The mention of Saraseil was like a quick stab in the eye. "The people in Saraseil knew a lot of things about the Fell, but . . . some weren't true."

"Ah, well." The others were staring but Ghatli quickly said, "It means the Cedar-rin will be here by morning, at latest. The weather is so calm any trip across the lake will be quick and easy."

An seemed encouraged by this prospect but no one else did.

One of the fishers said, "Should you leave, Ghatli? If the miners and the Cedar-rin fight . . ."

"They haven't come down here yet," Ventl said, not looking at her. "But they might."

"They might have at any moment before now." Ghatli rubbed the wrinkled skin of her forehead. "I'm not leaving until I have to. I'll stay until the Cedar-rin come. Perhaps they can drive the miners away. If they can't . . . I'll go."

☾

Moon left the others while they were discussing setting guards and trying to convince Ghatli to flee. He climbed up to his cubby and lay there for a time, listening to the house calm down around him. He felt different. He had felt different since leaving the dying Saraseil behind him, but this was the first time he had let himself think about how.

Since he had first come out of the forests and tried to live as a groundling, there had been a wall between his real self and what he had pretended to be. He had still needed to be that other winged self, when he had to travel swiftly, to hunt, to explore places that were dangerous or difficult to get to. But for these past several turns, when he was pretending to be a groundling, it was like he had fooled himself more than anyone else. People had been suspicious of him, he had made mistakes, and he had resented it even more because in some part of him he really believed he wasn't lying.

When the Fell had come to Saraseil, that wall had come apart like the city's inadequate defenses. He had tried to get closer to the Fell because they had looked so much like him. He had been terrified that he was one of them. As soon as he had spoken to a ruler face to face, he had known this wasn't true, that whatever he was, he wasn't a Fell. But it had been too late by that point. And the effect seemed to be lingering.

His other self had felt so close to the surface today it was a shock that Ghatli and the others couldn't see scales and claws through his ever-thinning skin.

He should leave, fly past the hills and the valley and the miners and on into Kish, past the high mountain ranges full of skylings where rumor said the Fell didn't travel. Now, as the afternoon crept toward evening and the light lengthened, it would be a good time to go, to fly west into the sun with no one to see.

Except he didn't appear to be doing that.

(

Moon woke when he felt the sun drop behind the distant hills. He had slept more deeply this time, with no dreams frightening or vivid enough to wake him. Either killing miners had been somehow calming or the clean sweet scent of the reed walls was soothing; maybe a combination of both.

The house had quieted somewhat and he made his way back down to the main room. Many of the other groundlings had left, and the few who were still here were half-asleep. An and Na lay on the floor asleep on the blanket pallet. Moon could hear two more groundlings, probably fishers, out in the entrance area, who must be standing guard.

He found Ghatli and Ventl in the attached room that was for cooking and eating, both sitting near the big cylindrical stove. They were picking at a pan of cooked fish and rice. The shared danger of the day seemed to have led them to repair their relationship. "Aren't you hungry?" Ghatli asked Moon.

He was still full from the hunt but he took a pan from the stove anyway and sat on a stool nearby. Ghatli waited until he was settled, then said, "Ventl has a plan."

"Does he," Moon said, not enthusiastically. His short acquaintance with Ventl had done nothing to inspire confidence in Ventl's plans.

Ventl said, "He won't like it." He took an empty pan and dumped the fish bones in a pail near the stove. "He's the type."

Moon swallowed a piece of fish. "What type is that?"

"Not to like plans," Ventl said, darkly.

Ghatli said, "I don't like your plan, either." She told Moon, "He thinks he knows a way into the Cedar-rin's dead city."

Moon remembered to spit the bone out and not chew it. "That's a surprise, because up until this afternoon he didn't know the Cedar-rin had a dead city."

Ghatli cocked her head in assent. "That's what I said too, but I didn't use the word 'surprise.'" She added, more thoughtfully, "He thinks he knows where an entrance is hidden."

Moon eyed Ventl skeptically, but Ventl said, "This was turns and turns ago, when we were sprouts and the traders were clearing the hill route. I say 'clearing' because stretches of it were already there, paved with smooth stones, it just had to be dug out and connected up again. On the east side of Bowl Tower hill, a narrow piece of the road branched off and went down a ravine, and we followed it with the workers, and it went toward a cave in the side of the hill. The workers said it was too dangerous to go in, and it did stink of predators. They said that the cave was a coincidence, and the road so old it was there before the hill." Ventl shook a fishbone for emphasis. "But when you know those hills cover a city, I bet that cave was an old entrance to it. It might still lead into the streets, depending on how much filling in the Cedar-rin did when they abandoned it."

He could be right, but the cave might also dead-end in a wall of dirt. Moon said, "So you think someone could get in and attack the miners from inside the city."

Ventl said, "It's a good plan."

Moon had to point out, "Except the miners are probably even more dangerous underground, in narrow caves, than they are in the open."

Ghatli sighed. "I said that too. But he means to tell the Cedar-rin."

Moon ate another piece of fish and didn't comment. If the miners and the Cedar-rin fought each other to the death, it might be the best thing for the fishers and the traders. Except that the Cedar-rin seemed to have been peaceful up until this point, and no one knew what the miners meant to do with whatever they were digging for.

It was annoying that the Cedar-rin must know exactly what the miners wanted, it was just that An didn't want to tell anyone.

"Will you leave in the morning, Moon?" Ghatli asked him. She was watching him carefully, but it was hard to read her expression. "The hill route is blocked, but you could go along the lakeshore and find other places to wait until it's open again."

Moon shrugged, and absently stirred his fish bones. "I'll think about it."

"My thought is . . . You are the only one here who isn't afraid."

Moon went still. The sense of being caught made his heart stutter. He forced himself take a breath, to keep poking at his food, as if looking for fish pieces among the rice.

But Ghatli continued, "I know it's because of . . . the place you have just come from and what must have happened there. This must all seem like not much trouble at all, compared to that."

Ventl whispered to her, "What place?" and she elbowed him to silence.

Relief ran through Moon's skin, like cold water. Ghatli thought the horror of his experience in Saraseil had left him in shock, and numb to the danger the miners and the Cedar-rin represented. He decided she probably wasn't entirely wrong. He said, again, "I'll think about it."

Ghatli's mouth twisted in dissatisfaction and she picked up a stick to poke at the fire in the stove. "I feel we're all being foolish and we should all pick up and leave."

"And go where?" Ventl said wearily. "Who would have us?"

There wasn't much to say after that.

☾

Moon took a turn at watch with the other fishers, but nothing came near the caravanserai under the cover of darkness. Ventl was worried about the fisher town, but it had a large gong that clocked the hours and acted as a weather alarm for lake travelers. The distant echo of it rang at the right intervals through the night.

It sounded out of turn just before dawn, nearly half an hour off by the gears of the caravanserai's water clock, a subtle way of giving the alarm. Ghatli climbed up through the house and out the little trapdoor in the roof to try to see what was wrong. Moon went with her, mentally chafing at the necessity, when he could have been aloft and back down with a report already. His bruises and cuts had already mostly healed, but that wasn't a characteristic groundlings usually associated with shapeshifters, so he wasn't too worried anyone would notice.

The bundles of reeds that formed the roof were easy to balance on, and over the tree canopy they had a view of the edge of the stilt town where it curved into the cove. And the longboats that were crossing the water toward the caravanserai's dock.

Ghatli swore in dismay. There were two boats visible and Moon counted thirty Cedar-rin or so aboard each. He said, "We need to get An and the other one out there."

Ghatli turned and lunged for the trap door, shouting, *"Ventl!"*

☾

Moon waited outside with Ghatli and Ventl while a couple of fishers helped An down from the doorway. An moved stiffly, more so than it had yesterday. While Na was judged still too hurt to move, it was alert and able to speak and had taken some food earlier. If the Cedar-rin faulted the way their wounded had been treated, then they were so unreasonable that there would be no talking to them.

There might be no talking to them anyway, Moon thought, watching the path with narrowed eyes.

The first of the boats must have landed before they got down from the roof, because Moon sensed movement in the jungle. "Here they come," he told Ghatli and Ventl.

A few moments later three of the larger Cedar-rin that An had called primaries appeared, followed by a few dozen drones. Moon knew there were more off the path, hidden in the foliage, stealthily approaching.

The primaries stopped when they saw An, and all the drones, including the ones Moon could hear in the jungle, froze.

An stepped away from Ghatli and limped toward its people. The first primary came to meet it. Moon thought this primary was probably female, just from the shape of its body under the light armor. She was just as large as the one yesterday, but her square skull was more angled back, the lines of the large bones and the shape of her horns more elegant. She reached out and put her hand on An's cheek. As if they were in the middle of a conversation, An said, "As you see. But we tried—"

"All you could," the primary said. She looked toward Ghatli, then at Ventl and Moon. "We mean not to harm you. I am Eikenn, primary of the family Tskeikenn of the Rin of Cedar. I see you are not our enemies."

Ghatli made a noise of pure relief. "That's good." And then after an awkward pause, "Can I ask what you mean to do?"

Eikenn hesitated, and Moon wondered if she was somehow consulting the others. Then Eikenn said, "No."

"Fair enough." Ghatli exchanged a look with Ventl. "We have information you may want."

Moon winced inwardly. He had been hoping they had changed their minds about telling the Cedar-rin about the cave Ventl had seen. As a way to get rid of the Cedar-rin more quickly, he didn't think it would work.

Eikenn just stared at Ghatli, apparently waiting for the information. Then one of the Cedar-rin cried out in shock.

Moon turned with everyone else and looked toward the top of the clearing where the path curved down from the jungle. A Cedar-rin primary walked down that way, ducking past the fern fronds that extended over the . . . It wasn't just a Cedar-rin primary, it was Kall, the Cedar-rin primary who had come here yesterday. Kall, who was dead. *That's . . . different*, Moon thought. Horrible and different.

"Kall," An whispered, its expression turning from shock to horror. "He . . . I can't . . . It's his body, but his mind is not there . . . "

Eikenn's face worked, her lips drew back in a grimace of fury; it was the first real expression Moon had seen her make. "This is impossible. This is an abomination."

Following Kall was a fisher Moon didn't recognize. But Ventl and the fishers with Ghatli did. One started toward him, calling out, "Benl! We thought you were dead—"

Moon caught the fisher by the wiry fur on the back of his neck before he took another step. "He is dead." Moon could smell the corruption that drifted toward them on the damp air. "They both are." Moon had had to lift Kall to check the drone under him, and there had been no breath or pulse of life in his body.

"You're sure?" Ventl demanded. "Benl was the first one to go try to see what the miners were doing. Perhaps—"

"No, this is a trick," Ghatli muttered, aghast. "For them to appear at this moment—"

Yes, it's a trick, Moon thought. *But how did the miners do it?* The possibilities made his skin go cold.

The Cedar-rin stared in silence, their expressions horror-stricken or dumbfounded or blank with shock. They clearly knew Kall was dead, probably the same way Eikenn had known, through their mental connections, but the realization had frozen them in place.

Kall walked toward them slowly, his footing sure on the grassy mud of the clearing. He carried something that looked like a woven basket. The dead fisher, Benl, carried one too, and as he entered the clearing he turned toward Ventl and Ghatli and the others.

The nearest drones dropped back to form a half circle. An stayed where it was, as if it was rooted in place. Eikenn regained control of her face and voice, and said evenly, "Kall, what has been done to you? Your connection to us is severed. And your body is so damaged." Clearly she knew this was a trap, but she seemed more inclined to spring it than flee it.

Kall said, "I have word. They don't wish to fight." The Cedar-rin primaries didn't speak with much inflection anyway, so there was no real difference in his voice to Moon's ears. Kall held out the basket. "They want the being who killed their scouts yesterday. If you give it to them, they will leave the rest of us alone."

Moon hissed in dismay. He thought, *You idiot*. And how long would it be before Ghatli and everyone who was in the caravanserai realized that Moon was the only one who had been gone long enough, the only one who had been alone in the jungle, the one who had come back covered with minor injuries.

Ventl stared in confusion. "But that was the Cedar-rin, wasn't it? That Kall and the others. They killed the miners."

Ghatli shook her head, confused. "I don't . . . "

Benl still moved toward the astonished fishers. This close the basket he carried looked like it was made of some kind of webbing, and not straw or reed as Moon had first thought. Webbing. Like the webbing the miners extruded. One of the fishers called, "Benl, what happened? Where have you been?"

Another fisher caught her arm to draw her back. Sounding frightened, he said, "Moon is right, Benl's dead. I can smell it too now."

Moon's eye caught movement and he shoved a fisher aside and stepped forward. Yes, the basket was moving. He yelled, "Those things they're holding, that's the trap! Don't touch it! Get back!"

He didn't expect anyone except maybe Ghatli to listen to him but his conviction must have sounded in his voice. Fishers scattered away from Benl. Ghatli bolted for the house. And then the basket Kall held burst open.

It rained tiny white creatures in the air, glittering and spidery. Eikenn shouted, "Kill them! Don't let them touch you!"

Moon resigned himself to shifting. Benl's basket was a heartbeat from bursting and his scales might provide just enough protection from whatever was in it. But before he could shift, Ghatli yelled, "Moon!" and threw a metal bucket at his head.

Moon caught it and swung it, smacked Benl in the face and knocked him flat. The fisher let go of the basket as he fell and Moon pounced, slamming the bucket down on it.

He pinned it with his weight but the bucket jerked under him. The basket must have burst and the bucket was now full of whatever those things were. The drones had surged forward, two holding Kall while the others stamped and sliced at the white spider-like things. One ran past and Moon had a good look: it was a miniature miner, tiny and complete in every detail. Then a drone leapt to swing its sickle and sliced the creature in half.

The mini-miners inside the bucket surged again and Moon struggled to hold it down, thinking for a moment that he might have to shift anyway. Then Ventl ran up beside him and added his weight to Moon's. Ghatli arrived a moment later, waving over two fishers, who carried a large flat rock. She said, "Here, use this."

Moon and Ventl held the bucket by the sides as the fishers set the rock atop it. It sunk a little into the wet grass and stopped bucking, as if the inhabitants knew they were stuck now. It made Moon's skin creep. He looked toward Benl, who lay there as if dazed, and knew it was going to get worse.

Eikenn strode over. The drones circled around to check the packed dirt and grass for more of the creatures. Kall was surrounded by drones, but he hadn't moved. Eikenn said, "What is the purpose of this? What being do they speak of?"

"I don't know," Ghatli answered. She turned to look down at the unresponsive Benl, and shivered in dismay. This close, it was possible to see the fur was sunk in around his eyes and mouth, showing that the flesh beneath had begun to decay. "Some fishers found a dead miner last night, but we thought it must be one that died later, after your people fought them. I would rather know why two people we thought dead are—were—walking and talking." She crouched down to look more closely at Benl. Moon said, "Careful. Let me do it."

Ghatli stood and he stepped around her and used his foot to roll Benl over. Everyone but Eikenn flinched backward. Moon half-snarled.

Buried in the back of Benl's head was one of the miniature miners. The way it was sunk into his fur, its legs must extend down through his skull.

Ghatli made a choked noise. Ventl gasped, "These things meant to kill us and eat out our brains."

Moon wished that was an exaggeration but he was afraid Ventl was right for once.

Eikenn whipped around and snapped an order to the drones. One stepped behind the motionless Kall and used its sickle to slice his armor open. Moon didn't have a good view but he saw the moment when the drone grimaced in disgust. The miner must be buried in Kall's neck, below the curving horns that protected the back of his skull.

Ghatli and the fishers were locked in place, as if their bodies had turned to stone. Then Ventl said, "Kill it."

Moon figured later that what happened next would probably have happened anyway, no matter what they had done. The timing was just a coincidence. But as one of the fishers drew a scaling knife and stabbed it down into the thing buried in Benl's head, a dozen miners burst out of the upper slope of the jungle.

Fishers scattered in fear and drones surged forward. Moon shoved Ghatli and the nearest fisher toward the house and shouted, "Get inside!"

The miners went for the drones and the primaries first, but more drones poured up the path from the lake. A miner bounded toward the retreating fishers and Moon lunged into its path. It pounced on him, rictus jaw wide and arms reaching. Under the cover of its body Moon shifted and ripped with both feet and hand claws. Guts spilled out onto him and he shifted back to groundling and rolled out from under the miner as it collapsed. *This is going to be tricky*, he thought.

Miners tore across the clearing as drones slashed at their legs. Eikenn was on top of one, driving her sickle through a leg joint. Another miner darted at the house and Moon grabbed a rock and flung it. It bounced off the miner's back and the creature charged for him.

There were too many Cedar-rin and miners fighting in the jungle so he ran past the front of the house and around the corner. He ducked under a limb of the large tree that supported the structure and flattened himself against the reed wall.

The miner tried to outthink him by leaping onto the wall as it came around the corner, perhaps meaning to get above him. But it landed half atop Moon and he shifted and popped its leg joint. Three more miners followed it, and three more died in quick succession, with limbs torn off and guts ripped open. Moon was far more expert on killing miners after his rampage yesterday and not nearly as blind with anger; he was able to dispose of them far more efficiently.

He got tossed into the jungle at one point by a miner's death convulsion and was almost seen by a group of drones. Fortunately their backs were to him as they hacked at an upended miner and Moon was able to shift to groundling before anyone saw him. He ran back around the house to the clearing and saw the battle was nearly over.

Severed miner legs and a few arms were strewn across the grass and dirt. There were four dead miners still mostly whole, one on its back with a sickle buried deep in its open mouth. Dead drones also lay beside them, and one of the primaries sprawled unmoving. There weren't as many dead as Moon would have expected after seeing the aftermath of the battle yesterday. Clearly the Cedar-rin had learned from that encounter too, and An hadn't been exaggerating about their ability to rapidly and silently share knowledge.

Other drones huddled on the ground, alive but badly wounded. An had survived, Moon was glad to see, and was helping another wounded drone remove its torn armor. Eikenn was alive as well, striding across the clearing with her armor splashed with miner blood.

Ghatli charged out of the house's doorway and slid to an abrupt halt near Moon. She looked him up and down. "Are you hurt?" she demanded. "How are you alive?"

Moon shrugged. His clothes were wet and stinking with miner guts. It was an unfortunate consequence of shifting, that whatever was on his scales transferred to his skin and clothes whenever he changed forms. He couldn't say he had run away to avoid the fight this time, and the only other option was that he had tripped and somehow fallen inside a dead miner. He had learned from bitter experience that it was better not to try to explain unexplainable things. "I'm lucky."

The other fishers followed Ghatli out of the house more cautiously, and the Physician Iscre pushed past them, carrying a satchel of its medicines and tools. Ghatli pivoted, staring around the clearing, and said, "But where is Ventl?"

"Ventl?" Startled, Moon looked around. The only dead fisher in the clearing was Benl, whose body still lay undisturbed. The miners hadn't even bothered to overturn the bucket and rock holding down the miniature miners. "He wasn't with you?"

"He stayed out here to fight." Ghatli ran past him, scanning the clearing frantically. "He isn't here!"

Moon saw who else wasn't here: Kall was gone. Ghatli headed toward Eikenn, who stood with three other primaries. Ghatli said, "One of our people is missing! Did you see what happened?"

Eikenn turned toward her. "They have taken Kall—Kall's body, and seven of our drones who yet live. We go after them."

Ghatli said, "I'll go with you."

Moon hissed under his breath. "Ghatli, you can't—"

"I can," she said, and called to one of the fishers. "Get my weapon!"

Eikenn eyed Moon. "You have no weapon. How did you, a softskin, fight these creatures?"

"It's none of your shitting business!" Ghatli shouted at her, drawing the startled gaze of every drone in the clearing. "We must go after them now! If we hurry—"

"You will only slow us down," Eikenn said, betraying a trace of irritation. Considering how much emotion the primaries usually displayed, it probably meant she was furious.

Eikenn started to turn away, and Ghatli said, "I know a way into your ruined city." A fisher brought her a short metal spear with two prongs on the end. It was clearly for using on fish, and might be effective on a large lizard. Against the miners, it wasn't much better than a belt knife. Moon rubbed his forehead wearily and swore. Ghatli hefted the weapon and added, "I was going to draw a map but I'll take you there myself."

Eikenn stopped. Turning back to Ghatli, she said, "Very well. Lead us."

The fishers immediately protested, half of those gathered around wanting to accompany Ghatli and the others urging her not to go. Ghatli shook them all off and said, "No, stay here and help tend the wounded. And burn that mess!" She pointed at the bucket still covering the bundle of miniature miners. "I'll be back. With Ventl."

Eikenn didn't seem to need to give orders. She headed for the path upslope, all the primaries and most of the drones breaking off to follow her, leaving only a few behind to help the wounded. Ghatli hurried to catch up with her.

One of the fishers anxiously asked Moon, "What are you going to do?"

Moon let his breath out. This attack might have happened anyway, but his deliberate assault on the miners yesterday clearly hadn't helped. According to Kall, it was him they wanted. He said, "I'm going to do something stupid," and followed the Cedar-rin.

☾

Moon trailed after them long enough to see that Ghatli at least had no intention of leading the Cedar-rin straight up the path to the trade road. She took them to a narrower less-travelled way that branched off the main path and curved around the slope of one of the hills, then followed a ridge of rock upward. If Moon was guessing right, it would parallel the trade road as it curved to cross the valley, then turn off toward the cave Ventl had spoken of. If the cave proved to be a dead end, it would at least give the Cedar-rin a chance to come at the miners from a new direction.

Eikenn paused to send a primary and a group of drones up the main path, probably meaning them to be decoys, then followed Ghatli. The Cedar-rin were taking far more care, moving in groups with their weapons drawn, scouting through the jungle on both sides of the path. And they kept glancing at Moon, not quite suspiciously, but as if they were thinking of Eikenn's unanswered question about how he had survived the battle. It made it more difficult for him to slip away. Finally he seized an opportunity and stepped behind a large clump of fern, and waited for the nearest drones' footsteps to fade. Then he moved silently through the brush toward the closest tall tree.

He shifted, climbed it, and leapt into the air to flap steadily up toward the miner's valley.

Moon flew up to the hills and was in time to see a large group of miners cross the churned-up dirt of the flat and vanish inside the crevasse. He didn't see any sign of the prisoners or Kall, but they might already have been taken inside.

He did one high circle to check out the terrain. There were far fewer miners out in the valley, though the digging in the crevasse still continued. The second web system had been finished, though only four miners were using it to move dirt and rock, maybe the same ones who had been constructing it yesterday. There were still at least a dozen miners using the old web system to transport their baskets; the new one looked like a much better bet. It would have been easier to do this at night, but he didn't have a choice. Ventl would surely be dead by then, if he wasn't already.

Moon watched the miners long enough to memorize the pattern of their movements, then dropped behind the hill nearest the new web's smaller but growing debris piles. He jumped from tree to tree, until he could work his way down toward the edge of the jungle. It took him long enough that Ghatli and the Cedar-rin might have reached the cave by now, if it was where he thought it was.

As he drew closer to the jungle's edge the canopy thinned out and he went to the ground to creep between clumps of ferns and tall vegetation, tasting the air and listening for any hint of movement. Slipping out of that cover and into the gaps between the long piles of rock debris was tricky; fortunately his scales were nearly the same black as the freshly turned dirt. He made certain to get as much of that dirt as possible on him as he crawled between the piles; he hadn't seen any sign that the miners were scent-hunters, but since the dirt was convenient he might as well take advantage of it.

Moon crept to the last debris pile, making sure he was on the right side of it. He had watched the process of dumping the baskets enough to know this was just barely possible. It wouldn't have been, if the miners had their eyes on top of their bodies instead of between their front legs.

A miner pulled its basket closer. At this distance Moon could see the harness made of web that the miner used to haul the basket along and keep it steady. Moon flattened himself against the debris pile as the miner tipped the basket up, dirt and pebbles tumbling out. When the basket was between him and the miner, Moon scrambled lightly up the pile and rolled into the basket.

Unlike the other web-producing predators he had encountered, the miners' web was slick and hard, obviously meant to build things and not to trap prey. Moon lay flat to try to distribute his weight as evenly as possible. He was counting on the fact that the miners were enormously strong and Moon didn't weigh much compared to a basketful of rocks, especially in his lighter winged form. This one didn't seem to notice, and turned to haul the basket back toward the excavation.

The basket moved rapidly across the valley, jerking a little when it passed through the supporting scaffolds, and in moments it started to tip downward into the crevasse. Moon curled his legs under him and braced himself to leap out if he had to. Daylight faded as the basket moved faster and he caught glimpses of rough rock walls rising up. Then the other webs met in a junction and baskets slid and bumped along above him, but no miners appeared. Moon guessed they must tip the empty baskets into the shaft to slide down on their own, while the miners climbed down to get the filled ones and guide them up another branch of the web.

Shafts of bright light came from somewhere below him, and he had the sense of a much larger space than he had expected. This crevasse went a lot deeper than he had thought. That probably wasn't a good sign.

Moon had to get out now, before the basket dropped down to where the miners were filling them. He twisted around and dug his claws into the bottom of the basket and ripped open a slit. He pulled it open enough to see a slanted stone slope in the shadows below. That would have to do. Hoping he wasn't about to appear in front of an interested crowd of miners, he slipped out.

He landed on the steep slope and gripped it with his claws, finding purchase in what he realized was dressed stone, not smooth rock. The light was behind him and he twisted around to face it.

The bright shafts of illumination came from bundles of webbing that sparked and sizzled with light, as if they were burning without flames. Either the webbing itself was flammable or the miners had done something to it to cause this effect.

What the light was shining on made Moon just huddle there and stare.

The bundles of light cut through the shadow to reveal a city that should have been collapsed under tons of dirt. This should be a buried ruin, with miner tunnels drilled through the remnants. Instead it was all still here, the valley floor a roof over a section of a carefully preserved city.

The open space was ringed by tall, narrow pyramids, hundreds and hundreds of paces high. Moon was perched on the enormous sloping wall of one, and dark gaps between them showed that the city went on for some distance. At the feet of the pyramids were smaller structures, all square and blocky, like small houses. They were clustered thickly, with only narrow pathways between them. In the center there was a square open plaza.

Following the strands of the web, visible where the light reflected off it, Moon saw it led down across the lower part of the city to vanish among the smaller structures. The ceiling overhead was a smooth dome, unbroken except for the jagged opening the miners had carved out. The dome must have been constructed to cover the city, then concealed by turns of dirt and grass and jungle.

This meant Ventl's tunnel might not be a dead end, but might lead deep enough into the ground to reach this city cavern, or at least its outskirts. Moon eased forward and started down the slope of the pyramid, his claws gripping the pitted stone. More empty baskets slid by on the webs overhead. A pyramid on the far side of the open area had a web system on its slope, with light bundles hanging from the strands and a few miners hauling up full baskets. But it was still too dark to spot any sign of the prisoners. Moon needed to get down to where those miners were digging; that was the only spot where he could see any activity.

As he climbed down the slope, Moon wondered, *But why did the Cedar-rin leave?* This still looked like a perfectly functional city, in far better shape than some places Moon had lived. And they had taken such care to bury it in a way that left it intact. *And what are the miners still digging for?* Was there something buried under the city? This place had been deserted and concealed long before the fishers had arrived, long enough ago for its existence to be nothing more than a rumor connected with the rebuilding of the trade road. It smelled of rock and earth and somewhere water, like a cavern; he didn't scent any rot. The Cedar-rin dead interred here must be nothing but dried bones.

Maybe the miners wanted the bones.

The shadows grew deeper as Moon climbed down to the street level. The slanted wall ended in a narrow path, barely four long paces wide, that led off through the blocky buildings. There was no room for wagons or draft animals and it would have been barely wide enough for two primaries to pass side by side. Moon followed it, feeling his way in the dark, heading across the cluster of houses toward the base of the pyramid where the webs had ended and the light bundles were concentrated. He heard sounds of digging, the grinding of rock, an occasional thump as something heavy was moved, but with the confusing echoes it was hard to tell the direction.

The buildings were all fairly small, with steps leading up to them, and doorways and windows blocked in by stone. It was impossible to say if they had been dwellings or places that sold goods or storehouses or what. It would make sense if this area was all some sort of market and the homes were in the pyramids, but he knew from experience that it was often hard to guess how groundlings or other species lived based on just their dwelling places. The truth was usually odder than anything he could imagine.

Moon reached the last house and cautiously peered around the corner. The path fed into a much wider avenue running along the base of the nearest pyramid. This was where most of the light bundles were, and the webs with their sliding baskets passed overhead and down into the space directly in front of the pyramid. It had a doorway, big and square and framed by heavy stone lintels and pillars. Until recently, it had been walled up by stone blocks, just like every other door Moon had seen. But now the blocks had been broken through until there was enough space for miners to walk in and out. They dragged out baskets of dirt and broken pavement, then attached them to the lower branch of the web system. It snaked away, supported by more of the glittering scaffolds, and ran down the avenue to disappear between the smaller structures. Two miners walked along it, hauling baskets of debris away from the pyramid.

Moon hissed, frustrated. At least ten miners were loading baskets, not counting those who had just left to haul their loads away. He tasted the air carefully. The miners didn't have much scent, and neither had the Cedar-rin, but he could just detect a more distinctive odor of fur. It was in the slight current of air coming from the doorway the miners had broken open. Ventl must be in there somewhere.

So Moon was going to have to get past the miners. But taking on ten at once wouldn't go well. And he had meant to try not to kill any; if the others found any ripped open bodies, they would know he was down here. If they had sent Kall and Benl, or what was left of Kall and Benl, after Moon, he must have made them angry enough that they might just drop everything and start looking for him. But he couldn't see any other way.

All the miners suddenly froze in place. Moon froze too, trying to blend into the wall of the little house. But he hadn't moved, they couldn't have heard him.

Then the miners dropped their baskets and charged across the avenue and into the maze of buildings. Moon flinched back against the wall, but they didn't come near him. They cut straight across the houses, climbing over the blocky roofs, squeezing through the narrow pathways. It was baffling, but at least it cleared the way through the broken doors for him.

Then he heard the clash of metal weapons. *The Cedar-rin*, he thought, exasperated. Somehow the miners had heard them enter the city.

Moon climbed the wall of the house to the flat roof. It gave him a better vantage point to watch the miners, but he couldn't see the Cedar-rin. Ventl's tunnel access must have led them through some passage on the far side of the city.

Moon struggled with indecision. He should look for the prisoners while he had the chance. But if Ghatli was still with the Cedar-rin . . . He didn't want to rescue Ventl only to find that he had let Ghatli be killed.

None of the miners seemed to be paying attention to anything but the Cedar-rin somewhere ahead of them. Moon dug his claws into the flat stone roof and extended his wings. He jumped up, used his wings for an extra boost, and landed on the roof of a house with a better view.

The Cedar-rin had just entered the plaza at the center of the city, spilling into it from one of the narrow pathways. The space was deeply shadowed but the Cedar-rin took advantage of its size as the miners charged in. They mobbed the first two miners and slashed at their legs. A primary rolled under one to stab it from beneath. More drones rushed to block a pathway, trapped the miners in it and forced them to climb the houses and leap down onto the Cedar-rin's sickles.

But how did the miners know they were here in the first place? Moon wondered. He hadn't heard or scented anything, and he hadn't spotted any miner sentries anywhere. If the miners knew the Cedar-rin were here, why hadn't they detected him?

More Cedar-rin ran through the plaza to attack the miners. Moon didn't see Ghatli, and hoped for an instant that she had wisely decided to stay outside once she had shown the Cedar-rin the tunnel. Then a small figure dodged around a group of drones and ran toward an open pathway. Ghatli. Moon half-groaned, half-snarled.

He leapt to the roof of the next house to keep her in sight. She reached the pathway and ran down it, then dodged down an intersection to avoid a knot of fighting. Then she stopped, looking around in desperate confusion.

She had obviously been hoping that the prisoners would be held in some easily spotted place, and the size and darkness of the strange city was a shock. Moon, perched some distance above her on the roof of a house, was also desperate. He was going to have to shift to talk to her, to tell her she had to get out of here. That was going to be a tricky conversation.

Then one of the miners turned into the pathway from the plaza and moved in Ghatli's direction. There was a house in the way, so it hadn't seen her yet, but as soon as it reached the next junction, it would spot her. Ghatli faced the other way, peering uncertainly toward the light that shone from the base of the pyramid ahead, clutching her fishing prong. Moon rolled his eyes. Well, at least that was settled.

Moon leapt off the house and landed on the miner's back, grabbed one of its legs and flipped himself under it. It flailed but he ripped his foot claws through its tender underside to spill its entrails. He shifted to groundling and shoved the dead body off him, and rolled to his feet in the junction just as Ghatli turned around. "What are you doing here?" she demanded, baffled. "You were behind us on the road!"

Moon hastily moved forward so she wouldn't see the very recently dead miner. There was no non-suspicious answer for her question, no way to really explain his presence. He said, "Ghatli, you need to leave. Turn back the way you came, go back down the tunnel—"

"I have to get Ventl!" Ghatli was clearly just as determined as she was terrified.

"I'll get him. That's why I came," Moon told her, trying to sound reassuring. He glanced behind him just as two miners and more Cedar-rin drones spilled into the pathway, fighting viciously.

"I can't go back that way," Ghatli said, jerking her fishing prong to emphasize the point. "Do you know where Ventl is?"

"This way." Moon caught her hand and pulled her along, down the path toward the avenue. He was going to find a hiding spot for her among the houses, then look for Ventl.

But as they got closer to the avenue, Moon caught movement overhead. He looked up in time to see several miners pass through a shaft of light as they climbed down the upper web system. They were coming down here to attack the Cedar-rin. And the sound of fighting was drawing closer as the miners on the city floor fell back and the Cedar-rin pursued them.

And Moon and Ghatli were now almost directly across from the temporarily unguarded entrance to the pyramid. There might not be another chance. Ghatli pointed. "There? Is that where they took Ventl?"

"I think so." Moon made his decision. It was probably a bad decision, but that was nothing new. "Come on."

Moon led the way across the avenue and through the piles of debris and discarded baskets, and up to the door of the pyramid. It was dark inside, lit only by the reflected glow of the light bundles behind them. A corridor with open doorways on each side led forward toward a large stairwell. The scent of fisher was a little stronger, carried on a faint breath of moving air. Moon stepped inside, an anxious Ghatli on his heels.

It was difficult to see, but as they went down the hall Moon could smell recently disturbed dry earth and traces of rot, mixed with more complex scents that he couldn't recognize. The last doorway at the far end had been made larger by the miners knocking the side pillars out. Past it was a large dark space, barely lit by one or two distant light bundles, and Moon waited for his eyes to adjust.

"How did you get here ahead of us?" Ghatli was still breathing hard, but sounded less panicky and far more focused.

There was still no good answer for that. Moon began to make out details in the cavernous chamber past the doorway. It seemed to span the width of the whole pyramid. Sections of the paving had been torn up, but instead of disturbed earth, it revealed small shallow chambers buried beneath the floor, each about four paces long and two wide. "These have to be the graves, the Cedar-rin graves," Moon said to Ghatli. But the ones he could see were empty. "The miners must have taken all the bodies."

Moon stepped away from the doorway. This was getting stranger and stranger. He spotted faint light coming down the stairwell from the level above. That was where that draft and the hints of fur scent were coming from. The stairwell was Cedar-rin-sized and hadn't been made wider by the miners. The scents and air drafts seemed to indicate that it was connected to the bigger grave chamber. "Let's try this way."

Keeping her voice carefully low, Ghatli said deliberately, "Moon, wait. Tell me. What are you?"

Moon turned to look at her in the meager light from the stairwell. It might have been better to seem bewildered at the question and say "what do you mean?" but somehow Moon just couldn't do that. With no mental wall between his real self and his groundling self, there was nothing for him to fall back on. If he couldn't pretend to himself that he was just another groundling, he couldn't pretend it to her. Not while she was looking at him like this.

If Ghatli had been unsure, his blank response had just made her all that more certain, had confirmed every suspicion. She said, "The one the miners wanted, the person who killed their scouts. That was you."

Moon couldn't even try to deny it. "Yes." His throat was so dry the word barely came out.

He saw Ghatli swallow back fear. "Moon, you don't even have a knife. You are strong and fast, surely, but—What are you?"

"When the Cedar-rin asked that question, you told them it wasn't their business."

"I didn't want them distracted. But now I'm asking it. What are you?"

Moon squeezed his eyes shut briefly. He should have known this was coming when he hadn't been able to convince her to leave. Maybe he had known it was coming. He didn't have much choice, if he still wanted to get Ventl free. And the heavy shadow in this corridor wasn't going to help. He said, "Remember I'm not a Fell."

She said, "What?" and then Moon shifted.

Ghatli clapped a hand over her mouth and made a strangled noise. He shifted back to his groundling form and she fell back a step, made more choking noises, then started to swear in her own language. "*Mova getta, bazada, dis'tril de—*" The only good sign was that she seemed more outraged than afraid. Possibly after the close calls with the miners, she had used up most of her fear already. She finally managed to say in Altanic, "You're a Fell! You slept in my house!"

"I'm not a Fell." Caught between that familiar bitter resentment and despair, Moon added, "And I also used your bathtub."

"Stop that! Stop, implying that I . . . That's not what I meant! I don't turn people away because of how they look . . . You . . ." Furious and confused, Ghatli shook her head, her white hair flying, her ears twitching. She brought herself under control with effort, and lifted her hands helplessly. "You really look like a Fell, Moon."

"No, I look like the descriptions of what Fell look like." He took a deep breath. This wasn't the first time he had had this conversation. Or tried to have it. He didn't usually get this far. And even if occasionally one person believed him, the others in their settlement or tribe or group didn't, and it wasn't worth their life to defend him. In any other situation, he would give up and fly away, but this wasn't any other situation. "If I was a Fell, you wouldn't be able to say these things to me. Fell rulers can make people believe anything they want. If I was one, it would never occur to you to be suspicious. Anything I did, whatever I did, you'd find an excuse for it."

Ghatli shook her head again. "But then what are you?"

A few other conversations had gotten this far, but this was where they usually fell apart. "I don't know."

Ghatli grimaced in disbelief. "How can you not know? Who doesn't know what they are?"

"When you're the only one." Moon rubbed his forehead. He felt sick and exposed. "I had a mother, brothers and a sister, and they were all killed. Turns and turns ago. They were the only ones like me I ever saw. The first time I saw the Fell, it was in Saraseil. I'm not one of them." He was very sure of that. Besides his own gut instinct, Moon had had time to examine Liheas' body in detail, before and after killing him, and there were just too many differences.

Somewhere outside the pyramid, he heard movement, the distinctive scrabble of miners' claws on stone. They had run out of time for this.

"They're coming back, Ghatli. I'm going to rescue Ventl, and then leave; do you want to come with me?"

Ghatli almost growled with frustration, but then said, "Right, yes. One more question. Why are you helping us?"

"Because you let me sleep in your house." That wasn't the reason. Moon didn't know what the reason was. He was just tired of looking at dead groundlings.

He led the way up the steps and Ghatli hurriedly followed him. They reached the top where a wide corridor stretched away. It had floor to ceiling windows on each side, separated by large blocky pillars, that looked out on the cavernous chamber that seemed to form the rest of the pyramid's interior. Moon could hear more movement below now, miners and the scrape of feet on stone. He moved to the nearest pillar and whispered, "Get over here, they're coming."

At least Ghatli didn't hesitate to step into concealment behind him. Moon was still less scary than the miners, which he supposed was a good sign.

Below, light blazed across the big chamber. It was a miner carrying a small web-light bundle like a lantern. Then more miners moved into view, crossing the disturbed pavement. They were herding several injured Cedar-rin drones, and one tall primary, prodding them over and around the open graves in the floor. All the Cedar-rin were disarmed, their armor bloody. "Surely they didn't kill all the others," Ghatli whispered.

Moon doubted it. He was willing to bet many of the surviving Cedar-rin had fallen back to the tunnel. They had a way in now, and they had a better idea of how many miners they were dealing with. Retreating and sending for reinforcements was the only sensible act. Of course, that didn't mean the Cedar-rin would do it.

The miners took their prisoners further into the pyramid. Moon waited until the group was well past before he stepped away from the pillar and slipped quietly down the bridge to follow them. Ghatli crept along behind him.

The miners passed by a tall pile of debris and Moon didn't realize it was made up of jumbled bones from the graves until the drones cried out. The primary said something, a short command, and all the drones quieted. Ghatli whispered, "Not many bones for all these open graves. Maybe they eat the dead, not the living."

Moon wasn't so sure. *If they live off carrion, even the carrion of sentients . . .* Except this wasn't carrion, it was dried bones. That just didn't seem like a practical food source for a whole species. There couldn't be that many mass graves like this. At least he hoped not. "That can't be it. It has to be something else."

"At least the dead are dead, and don't know anything about it," Ghatli added. "It's not so terrible that way."

The miners headed toward a square structure at the far end of the chamber, and Moon stopped in the cover of the next pillar to watch. The structure was set back at an angle in the shadows, and as the miners drew closer with their light Moon saw it had open walls, and was just a set of pillars with a roof atop them. It could be a mortuary temple, set here in the middle of this room of graves . . .

There was movement inside it. And the light caught lines of webbing, forming bars. The miners had turned it into a cage for their prisoners. "We may have found Ventl," he whispered, and Ghatli made a quiet noise of relief.

The miners reached the makeshift cage, and one did something to a section of webbing. It swung aside and the new prisoners were forced to enter.

The webbing was reattached and the miners retreated, moving rapidly across the disturbed ground now that they weren't hampered by slower-moving bipeds. Moon said to Ghatli, "I'm going to go let them out." Then they would have to make their way back to the tunnel where the Cedar-rin had come in. That was the part he was mostly worried about.

"I'll come with you," Ghatli said.

Moon turned to face her. "I'm not going to walk."

"What?" She hurriedly stepped back as he shifted and extended his wings. "Oh."

"I'm going to land on top of it, and start cutting the web." He was hoping to avoid showing himself to the Cedar-rin. It would be easier if he and Ghatli could just grab Ventl and let the Cedar-rin make their way out on their own. "Once I let them out, I'll come back and get you."

Ghatli shook her head, determined. "I want to go with you. I can climb down from here and go across, while you're—"

"If you come too, you have to fly over there with me." Moon thought that would be a deal-breaker.

Instead, Ghatli lifted her chin. "Very well, let's go."

Moon swallowed back a hiss. He should probably just stop trying to figure out groundlings. He said, "All right, I'm going to pick you up."

He leaned down and lifted her. Her little body was more solid than it looked. "You can hold onto that ridge of bone around my neck." She gripped his collar flange. "Like that."

"What do we tell them about you?" Ghatli said, a little breathless, probably from fear and shock at her own daring, "When they see you—"

"They'll try to kill me. We'll worry about it later."

As he crouched to leap, Ghatli said, "I think you're helping us because you have a deathwish."

"I don't know." Maybe. He knew he didn't have a lifewish.

Moon chose an angle where the prisoners wouldn't be able to see him approach. Two flaps and a long jump took him across the chamber. He landed on the flat roof of the temple and set Ghatli on her feet. He didn't hear any exclamations of surprise from the inhabitants and guessed the stone was so thick that his landing had been silent. This close the cage smelled like urine and feces and very dirty fisher. The web was anchored around a short pediment along the front. Ghatli went to the edge and leaned over to look inside, dangling her head down. "Ventl?"

Ventl's voice said, "Ghatli!" Now there were startled exclamations.

"Quiet!" Ghatli turned to Moon. "Help me get down."

"Just be careful," he told her, and caught her arm to lower her over the pediment and down the front of the structure. He didn't like letting her out of arm's reach, but she needed to be able to get the prisoners organized for their escape.

Ghatli dropped the last pace or so and landed on the pavement in front of the cage. She peered through the web. "Disl! Meryl! We thought you were dead! Are all of you here?"

Moon bared his teeth in annoyance. With other fishers than just Ventl in the cage, his vague plan wouldn't work. Once they were free, he was going to have to fly ahead and try to clear the way for them. He pried at the web, but it was harder and thicker than the type that made up the baskets. Moon pried at it, then sawed at it with his claws. It hurt; his claws had obviously not been designed for cutting through glass-like substances, more for clinging to branches.

"All but Denin and poor Benl," Ventl told Ghatli. "The others have been trapped here for days, without much food or water. But at least the miners didn't stick those brain-eating things in them."

"Who is out there with you?" Eikenn's voice demanded.

"It's Moon." Ghatli, wisely, gave no further details. "We'll get you out." She added, "Tell me, Eikenn of Cedar-rin. Why is this happening? What do the miners want with your dead?"

Eikenn didn't answer, and Ghatli swore in frustration. "Tell me, or we won't help you."

Moon, to add verisimilitude, stopped cutting the web.

Maybe Eikenn really believed Ghatli would abandon the fishers, or maybe she just didn't see a reason to conceal it anymore. "An told you our species can communicate to a certain extent at a distance, without sound or gesture."

"Yes."

"When we die, this does not stop."

Ghatli was silent. It took Moon a moment to remember to keep cutting the web. The fishers had mentioned stories of ghosts associated with this area. Apparently they weren't just stories. Eikenn continued, "There is no consciousness that can be spoken to by the living, but our dead continue to . . . not speak, but make sound. They sing to each other in their eternal sleep. After a time, when there are so many dead that the sound begins to drown out the living, we seal the city and leave it to them, and go to found another."

"Oh." Ghatli sounded blank. After a moment, she added, "So your dead are not quite . . . And the miners are . . . This seems very horrible. I understand your anger."

Moon understood it too. This was far more horrific than it had seemed. He hoped the dead weren't aware of what had happened to them. To lie there in your grave and listen to the digging . . . He twitched his spines, the skin under his scales creeping at the thought of it.

Eikenn's armor creaked as she moved. "We do not know what benefit the miners derive from ingesting our dead. But I suspect they must communicate in a way similar to our silent exchanges. There must be some connection."

Moon bet that was it. The miners must be able to hear the Cedar-rin dead too, and maybe they could hear the live Cedar-rin as well. That would explain how they had known the Cedar-rin had entered the cavern.

Ghatli said, "Ah. That does make more sense. I thought perhaps—" Moon practically heard her reconsider telling the Cedar-rin that she had thought the miners were using their dead as just a food source. "Never mind."

Moon felt the web bar snap under his claws. The slight sound made one of the fishers curse in alarm, and the others shushed him. Moon leaned on the web and twisted, and the whole section quivered.

The echo of rock clinking warned him just in time. Moon sat up and squinted toward the far end of the chamber. Yes, there was light moving down there. He leaned over the pediment and whispered harshly, "Ghatli, they're coming! Find somewhere to hide."

Cursing softly, Ghatli scrambled to get away, the fishers inside urging her to hurry. Moon watched her fling herself into an open grave behind the temple and then flattened himself below the pediment. If the miners saw that the web was loose, hopefully they would think it was just a natural break. But if one came up here to fix it, he was in trouble.

After a short, nervous time, Moon heard the crunch of miners moving across the broken pavement. A fisher whispered, "They're coming."

Ventl, Eikenn, and a mixture of other voices hushed him.

The light grew brighter and the sounds louder and closer. Then a voice said, "We would speak."

Moon tensed. It was Kall's voice, or the voice of Kall's reanimated body. Below him, Eikenn said, "You want to speak? You destroy our sacred dead, and mock us with the still-warm corpse of our brother. What do you have to speak of?"

"You have abandoned this place and the resources here. Why do you return?"

Moon had to see who was really doing the talking. He flattened his spines and pushed himself up just enough to see over the pediment.

Several miners stood at a short distance from the temple, one holding a light-bundle. But in front of them stood Kall, and something else. Moon supposed it must have been a miner too, but it was twice the size of the others. It had extra arms, or feelers, between each of its legs.

Kall said, "We have taken these resources for our own. I heard the power of this place echo through the rock, and I led the others here. It is ours now. You have no right to attack us." The miniature miner buried in Kall's back must be there as a translator, because it had to be the large miner standing by who was really speaking. Eikenn had been right, the miners did speak silently to each other, and couldn't communicate with other species without this extreme method. It didn't bode well. A species that couldn't talk to anyone unlike themselves without killing someone first would not have learned how to negotiate.

And if the miner's leader truly couldn't see any reason why the Cedar-rin might object to the miners breaking in here and digging up their ancestors to eat, then he didn't know how Eikenn was going to explain it.

Eikenn clearly didn't know either. She said, "This is our city, the resting place of our honored dead that you have desecrated, that you call resources. Now that we know how to fight you, the Rin will come here in as many numbers as it takes to destroy you utterly."

Another miner moved forward, as if it meant to speak through Kall too. Then the leader lifted one of its big legs and slapped it. It staggered back and its rear legs collapsed under it. Moon blinked, startled. It was the first time he had seen the miners interact except to work or fight as a team. The other miners skittered away, their rapid movements conveying a nervous tension. He hadn't seen that before either.

Kall said, "I need your dead to grow. They are dead, you have lost your claim on them."

Right, Moon thought, impatient, *arguing with these people is a waste of time.* Now if the miners would just give up and leave so they could finish the escape.

Eikenn said, "Our dead sing to us, we can hear them! You have no right to silence them, to use them—"

"I ingest them, I grow in power." There was a pause, and Kall added with stubborn persistence, "This place is no longer yours, I have taken it."

Eikenn's voice was eerily calm. "Then we must kill every one of you."

The leader wasn't saying "we" anymore, Moon noted. Maybe it was the only one eating the remains, getting the power. Some of the miners skittered forward again, and made darting motions at the leader. The one it had knocked down pushed itself up and just stood there, its fur trembling above what must be breathing orifices. It looked furious.

The leader rounded on the other miners and they retreated a little. The leader turned back and Kall said, "If you tell your people not to attack us, we will give you what you want."

Eikenn made a noise that might possibly be a bitter laugh. "There is nothing you can give us except to leave here, leave our dead, and never return."

The other miners quivered, skittered around, even more badly agitated. Moon wondered if they had ever fought anything capable of killing them before. He had thought the miners had sent Kall and Benl to the caravanserai as retaliation because they were angry at what he had done to their scouts. But maybe what they really were was afraid. And now they knew the Cedar-rin could kill them too, and would come down here after them to do it, and that there were many more on the way.

Obviously some of the miners didn't like that so much, and if the only reason they were down here at all was so their leader could become more powerful . . .

Kall began to say, "We are not done here. If you come, we will kill—"

The angry miner leapt on the leader's back. They rolled in a wild scramble, legs flailing, dust and debris flying. The others clustered around, darting in and out, so it was impossible to tell whose side they were on. The light-bundle fell, rolled a little distance away. Moon shoved himself upright and reached for the webbing again. They weren't going to have a better chance.

As he wrenched at the section of web, Ghatli ran around to the front of the cell. She grabbed at it and pulled, urging the prisoners, "Come on, push!"

Moon wrenched at the loosened sections and felt it break somewhere lower down. It ripped free of the stone as the prisoners pushed at it. Moon leaned down and told Ghatli, "Lead them out. I'll stop the miners if they come after you."

She waved an acknowledgement and Moon stepped back from the edge as Ventl, several fishers, and a number of Cedar-rin spilled out of the cell. It was hard to tell in the dark but it looked like Eikenn was the only primary. He wondered if she had let herself be caught, either to try to communicate with the miners or to collect information she might be able to pass on to the other Cedar-rin through their mental connection. A few drones looked back at the temple, trying to see who had been on the roof, and Moon crouched behind the pediment.

He heard their hurried steps over the debris-strewn pavement. It would have been quicker to go out via the bridge, but while the Cedar-rin might have been able to climb up to it, the fishers and Ghatli probably couldn't. He lifted up a little to check where they were, and saw in the illumination from the fallen light-bundle that Ghatli had swung wide to avoid the fighting miners. She jumped over the open graves and dodged around the piles of rock and broken pavement. The fishers followed her in a tight anxious group. Eikenn and the drones moved faster, but then Eikenn split off and ran toward the miners. No, not toward the miners. Toward Kall.

Moon jumped up and flapped hard, passing over the miners. He landed and crouched in the rubble. He could see Eikenn clearly from here as she ran into the lighted area around the struggling miners. Kall stood unmoving. She ran up behind him, scooped up a rock, and smashed it against the base of his neck.

All the miners froze, even the two who were locked in combat. Moon groaned to himself. He wished she hadn't done that. He understood why she couldn't leave Kall's body as an animate toy for the miners, but he still wished she hadn't.

Kall collapsed and Eikenn sprinted away. The leader shoved aside its miner opponent and lunged after her.

Moon craned his neck to try to see where Ghatli was, but the shadows were too thick. He could still hear running from that direction so they hadn't reached the passage out of the pyramid yet. He waited until Eikenn passed by, then leapt at the leader.

He landed atop it and raked his claws through its furry back. It flipped sideways to throw him off and he jumped away to land between two open graves. He turned in time to see a blaze of light streak toward him and dove sideways. Eyes dazzled, he realized one of the miners had thrown the light-bundle at him. He rolled to his feet and leapt upward. He felt something brush his foot-claws and knew he had had a very close call.

The leap gave him just enough time to get a sense of where the miners were; his eyes were still dazzled but he heard their big bodies move over the broken paving. He landed and went into a crouch, just as the leader leapt atop him. Moon slashed upward as the mouth and hands reached for him but his claws barely grazed what should be the soft underbelly. The leader wasn't only bigger, it was much tougher. A wiry hand grabbed for his face and he bit at it. As the creature tried to fold over on top of him, he shot out from under it.

The leader lunged at him and Moon leapt away, used his wings to propel himself a good fifty paces, then did it again. He spotted Eikenn running toward the big doorway at the far end of the chamber but the others had already vanished.

Moon reached the doorway just ahead of Eikenn. She stopped when she saw him, hefted the rock that she held. Moon guessed that his silhouette in the shadow and dim light was not reassuring, but he wasn't going to shift. He said, "Just keep running."

She threw a look back at the rapidly approaching miners and then darted through the doorway. Moon followed her through and out to the pyramid's entrance. In the avenue beyond, the drones had stopped to wait for Eikenn. Ghatli and the fishers had stopped with them, waiting uncertainly. Eikenn ran down the steps to the drones and Moon leapt into the air again to cross over the avenue and land on a roof in the first row of houses. This provoked some alarmed noises and hasty shushing from the fishers. The drones appeared to be waiting for Eikenn's verdict.

From here he had a better view, but the chamber seemed even darker than it had before. He caught movement among the shafts of light where the basket-moving web was, and saw miners climbing down the strands. But he couldn't see any miners waiting among the paths between the houses. "It's clear so far, but you've got to hurry," he called down to Ghatli. "They're not going to be far behind you."

"This way, this way," Ghatli whispered. "If the Cedar-rin won't come, leave them."

"Why are we following a monster?" one of the fishers whispered back.

"Shut up, Kenyl!" Ventl said.

They all plunged into the first pathway and hurried along it. After a moment of indecision, Eikenn followed with the drones.

Moon hopped two roofs over and caught a miner hiding between two houses. He dropped on it and ripped it apart before it had a chance to react.

The leader and his group of miners burst out of the pyramid into the avenue. The leader hesitated, its front legs waving in what might be uncertainty. More miners charged down the avenue and the leader started into the first pathway.

The groundlings aren't going to make it, Moon thought. *Not like this.* Eikenn seemed to know it too. She sent half the drones ahead and stopped in a junction that was minimally defensible. Moon looked frantically for anything that might help. In a path that led away from the plaza where the battle had taken place he spotted some fallen sickles and long knives. He scooped them up, jumped up to a roof again, and hopped back to drop them in the path of the Cedar-rin. Then he turned to catch up with the fishers.

They had just reached the plaza and bolted through it, dodging around the bloody bodies of the drones who had died in the first attack. Ghatli pointed ahead, for the fishers' benefit and for Moon's. "The tunnel is there, between those two slopes!"

She pointed to where two pyramids formed a junction just beyond the last cluster of houses. From his better vantage point, Moon hissed in irritation. There were at least a dozen miners in the open space in front of the junction, more working their way toward it from an open passage along the far end of the houses. They were guarding against the Cedar-rin who had retreated into the tunnel. *No, we're not going to make it*, Moon thought again. He hopped from one roof to the other, to get in front of the fishers. They stumbled to a startled halt as they saw him and he called down, "Ghatli, careful! It's blocked by miners."

Ventl peered up at him uncertainly, and Ghatli cursed again. She said, "What are we going to do?"

Moon looked around again and growled in despair. There was movement in the shadows and light shafts all over the cavern, the miners coming in from all sides. The Cedar-rin had fallen back to the plaza and fought the leader and its group of miners there. One miner stood to the side, just watching. From the gashes and wounds on its back, Moon guessed that was the one who had challenged the leader in the grave chamber. If he could just talk to it . . . But that was impossible, without someone's dead possessed body as a translator. He told Ghatli, "Just . . . be ready to move, if there's an opening."

Ghatli's expression clearly said she understood that meant there was little or no chance of escape. "All right."

Moon pushed off from the roof and flew back to the plaza. He could only think of one thing to do.

The leader hung back a little to let the other miners engage the Cedar-rin. A few more of the drones had managed to take fallen weapons from their dead comrades and they fought in a tight circle, surrounded by the miners.

Moon leapt straight up and then dove for the leader, landed on its back, and wrenched at the join of one of its left legs. He yanked, twisted it with all his weight, and stabbed his claws into the joint. It lifted up on its other set of legs and slammed Moon down on the pavement. It jolted him loose but half the leg came with him, swinging sideways as he rolled away. The leader charged at him and Moon struggled to push himself up. Then Eikenn lunged in front of him, slashed her sickle at the leader's wounded leg and sliced it the rest of the way off.

The leader jerked backward and staggered on its five remaining legs. Moon pushed himself upright and said to Eikenn, "I'll go high, you go low?" He just hoped the drones could keep all the others occupied.

She jerked her head in agreement. "Try to get another leg on that side."

The leader charged them again and Moon leapt for its back. He didn't think killing the leader would change anything, or give them a chance to escape. But if he was going to die down here, he was going to take this thing with him.

He landed on the leader's back and it spun to throw him off, but he dug his claws in and held on. Eikenn ducked in and got a good slash at the creature's underside. Then it flipped and slammed Moon down on the pavement. As it spun upright again he got a dazed view of Eikenn sprawled on the ground.

Then something flashed over Moon's head and another miner crashed into the leader.

Moon awkwardly scrambled away, his head ringing. Eikenn rolled to her feet and stumbled to stay upright. The miner was the same one who had challenged the leader inside the grave chamber, the one who had refused to take part in the battle. It had hit the leader between the two front legs and bowled it over, and now the two were locked underside to underside, as if they were having sex or trying to eat each other. Moon knew which one he thought more likely.

He threw a desperate look around. The other miners had stopped fighting and now skittered away from the drones to stand frozen in place. They watched the confrontation as if nothing else existed. He gasped to Eikenn, "Go, we need to go."

She glanced around and said, "These creatures . . . make no sense," and started toward the drones.

Moon felt you could say that about a lot of people. He managed to jump to the nearest rooftop, staggered but regained his balance, then leapt toward where he had left the fishers. Eikenn and the drones moved quickly into the pathways, carrying a few wounded. From up here Moon saw all the miners had frozen in place; they were everywhere among the pathways and houses now, where they had been converging on the plaza. The leader obviously didn't control them completely, or the other miner wouldn't have been able to attack it. But it clearly had some sort of connection to all the others, and they obeyed its orders. But it was as if the challenge by the other miner had suspended those orders until the matter was settled.

Moon found Ghatli and the fishers at the edge of the avenue, warily eyeing the miners who guarded the junction that led to the tunnel opening. More than a dozen stood in the open area between the two pyramids, unmoving, waiting. A light-bundle sat in the middle of the space, foiling any attempt at concealment in the shadows. But the miners just stood there.

Moon dropped off the roof next to Ghatli. All the fishers except Ventl scrambled back in alarm. Moon said, "I'm going to walk toward the tunnel. If they don't kill me, follow."

Ventl said, "Is that a good idea?"

Ghatli's ears twitched with nerves but she was still determined. "Our choice is to stay here and be killed, so . . . let's just get it over with."

That was how Moon usually felt, too. He started forward, every nerve jumping, his partially extended foot claws clicking on the stone. Behind him, the fishers anxiously whispered to each other.

Once out in the open area of the junction he could see the passage between the two pyramids was only a hundred or so paces long. It stretched back to a shadowy fold of the cavern wall, and Moon thought he could spot the tunnel opening at its base, but only because several miners were grouped near it. He understood how it might have gone unnoticed by the invading miners. It might have been a passage left open for the Cedar-rin who had buried their city to leave it for the last time.

He stepped cautiously close to the first miner, and looked for its eyes. The small dark orbs were glazed over with a white film. It was like the miners were in some sort of catatonic state. *Listening*, Moon thought. Or watching the dominance battle through the miners who were close enough to see it? He lifted a hand and motioned for Ghatli to follow.

Ghatli and the fishers sprinted into the open and Moon waited until they rushed past him before he followed. He stopped at the mouth of the passage, trying to watch all the miners at once. Presumably there were still Cedar-rin waiting in the tunnel. He hoped they didn't stop the fishers. Ghatli was going to have to handle that part; Moon's appearance there would just start another fight.

Ghatli and the others ran down the length of the passage. The fishers hurried to disappear into the shadow that marked the tunnel entrance, but Ghatli stopped. "Moon!" She whispered, and motioned frantically for him to follow.

"Go on," he told her, "I'm right behind you." Eikenn and the drones emerged from the path between the houses and started across the avenue. Moon meant to follow them through the tunnel. Hopefully the Cedar-rin inside intended to withdraw, and he would be able to get out without any violent confrontations.

The drones were too disciplined, and too occupied by helping the wounded, to do more than glance warily at Moon as they passed by. Eikenn followed, limping a little. Moon moved after her, backing away from the stationary miners.

The drones reached the tunnel and started in. Eikenn stopped to face the miners, waiting until the drones all filed inside. Moon waited too.

The last few drones slipped into the tunnel. Then the nearest miner twitched into motion. Moon hissed and flinched back, as Eikenn braced herself and lifted her sickle.

But the miner moved away toward the junction and the avenue beyond. The others moved too, and all headed in the same direction.

"Something changed," Moon said under his breath. He thought the fight must have come to a conclusion.

The pearly scales on Eikenn's brow furrowed in frustration. She said, "I have to see what's happened," and started after the miners.

Moon said, "Wait." She stopped and he leapt up the side of the pyramid and landed on the pitted stone slope. He hooked his claws into the gaps and cracks and climbed rapidly up to where he had a view of the cavern.

The larger shape of the leader was easy to spot. It lay on its back, five remaining legs in the air. Its opponent stood nearby. It looked unsteady and there were gaping tears in the fur across its back. The other miners moved toward it, all of them, from all over the cavern. As the nearest gathered around, Moon thought they might attack it. Instead, it moved away, taking a path between the houses, and the miners in the plaza followed. The others Moon could see changed their direction toward a point at the far end of the cavern.

Moon jumped, used his wings to slow his fall, and landed in a crouch. "The big one—the one you talked to—is dead. The others are following the one who killed it, all going toward the other end of the cavern."

Eikenn's expression hardened. "They are going to destroy more of our dead. We will have to return here with more drones."

"Maybe, maybe not." Moon looked toward the entrance of the passage. The last miner had vanished, leaving the light-bundle behind. Looking at this place now, he couldn't see it as a ruined city, just a giant tomb. "It didn't look like the others wanted to go to war with you. That was why that one attacked the—"

He sensed movement through the air just behind him. He flared his spines and twisted away, and the sickle that had been aimed at his head bit into his shoulder and glanced off his collar flange. Eikenn slashed at him again and Moon hooked the sickle in his claws and tore it out of her hand. He flung it away and she fell back a step.

Moon leapt away from her, up onto the slope of the pyramid. He snarled, "I helped you." He was surprised, and bitterly angry at himself for it. This is how it always happened, this was what he got for helping groundlings. He didn't know how he could let himself forget for one instant. As if that one encounter with the Fell had made him forget who he was.

If that was true, then this was a pointed reminder.

Eikenn backed away, watching him. "And why would a creature like you help us?"

"Because—" He stopped himself. *Because Ghatli asked me to*, he had been about to say. But she hadn't. Moon had inserted himself into this whole situation.

Eikenn said, "You are a Fell, one of their vanguard."

"Idiot. The rulers aren't the vanguard of the Fell, the major kethel are," Moon said. There was no point in protesting. And if she thought he was a Fell ruler, she wouldn't blame Ghatli or the fishers for his presence.

Eikenn backed away toward the tunnel. Moon turned and climbed further up the pyramid, until he had enough height to push off. He half-spread his wings and managed to leap to the next pyramid, then the next, until he was below the basket-web structure. It was abandoned now, the miners gone to the cavern floor for the ceremony or meeting or whatever it was they were doing.

Moon clung to the sloping wall just below it and took a deep breath to steady himself. Moisture trickled over his scales, but he could tell the cut wasn't deep. It just hurt. For more than the obvious reason.

He braced himself and leapt up to the web, and climbed back out of the crevasse.

(

Before Moon went to look for a resting spot, he flew over the hills until he saw Ghatli, the fishers, and the Cedar-rin leaving the tunnel and making their way down the trade route. The miners had all retreated into the crevasse and there was no sign of any attempt to pursue the Cedar-rin.

Weary and in pain, Moon went to ground on the roof of the caravanserai. He lay across the trapdoor, so the vibrations of anyone approaching it would wake him. There was no vantage point that overlooked it, and it was relatively safe from predators. He drowsed in his other form first, listening to movement in the house below, the quiet voices of the fishers and an occasional Cedar-rin. When he felt the cut stop bleeding, he shifted to his groundling form to sleep more deeply.

He woke when the sky was awash with a gold sunset. He flexed his shoulder cautiously, but the cut had continued to knit and was now scabbed over. There was more movement in the house below, but nothing that seemed urgent. He could smell cooking, fish and maybe some sort of sweet tuber.

He shifted to his winged form and eased up along the edge of the roof. In the clearing below, several drones and three Cedar-rin primaries sat. One of the primaries was Eikenn. They had some packs with them and there was some evidence that they had made a meal off of provisions they had brought with them. They weren't impeding access to the caravanserai;

as Moon watched, a group of a few fishers and other groundlings crossed the clearing and went inside, and two other fishers left, heading down the path for the shore. All the other groundlings circled widely around the Cedar-rin and watched them without favor, but they didn't seem afraid.

Moon squinted toward the lake and saw the Cedar-rin boats were now moored in the shallows near the fishers' stilt village. The fishers there were ignoring them, busying themselves with rolling up their nets for the night.

Moon sat for a time, watching the lights made from the glow plants gradually come to life in the clearing.

He wanted to stay here.

It was an idiotic impulse. Even if Ghatli had been the only one to see him, she didn't know him well enough to trust him. It wasn't a survival-conducive act for a groundling, or a skyling or a waterling for that matter, to let something like him into their home, among their unsuspecting friends. He didn't even know what he was. He wasn't a Fell, but he had killed a Fell ruler; maybe he was something worse.

Below, he saw Ghatli walk out of the caravanserai with Ventl, heading toward Eikenn.

Moon turned to the back of the roof and climbed down the tree that supported the structure. He slipped down along the side of the bathing room where it was half-buried in the roots and the hillside, and stopped when he could hear voices.

Eikenn was saying, "Our scouts report the miners are leaving our city."

Ghatli said, dryly, "We are overjoyed."

Eikenn didn't react. "They are moving away through the hills, presumably returning to where they came from. We will, naturally, remain here until we can confirm that they have left none of their number behind. And we will seal the city again."

"Good." That was Ventl.

Then Ghatli said, "Where is he?"

Eikenn didn't answer.

Ghatli continued, "I know you did something to him. I think he's dead in there, and when you seal the city, you will cover up evidence of your crime."

Eikenn said, "That is not true."

Ghatli's voice was almost as calm as Eikenn's. Except Moon could hear the anger under Ghatli's cool tone. "Then tell me what you did."

The silence stretched. Then Eikenn said, "I drove it away. It flew out through the opening to the surface."

Ghatli was apparently unsatisfied with that. "I call you a liar."

"Then I will speak to you no longer." Moon listened to Eikenn's quiet footsteps move away across the grass, then to Ghatli and Ventl entering the caravanserai, much less quietly.

Moon stayed where he was, concealed in the brush. He dozed off and on through the night, listening until the groundlings in the caravanserai gradually quieted. At some point before dawn, the Cedar-rin withdrew down toward the shore. He didn't think they were leaving, but he wondered if they were meeting reinforcements who had been sent to help make sure the city was secure.

He knew Ghatli got up before dawn, so it wasn't a surprise when he heard movement in the lower rooms of the structure. Then a few moments later someone came down the ladderwell into the bathing room. Moon climbed out of the brush and slipped around to the back of the building, and went in through the door used for cleaning the latrines.

Moon peeked through the passage into the bathing room to make sure it really was Ghatli in there. It was, and she was priming the pump for the bath. He stepped into the doorway, shifted to his groundling form, and whispered, "Ghatli."

"Gah!" She spun around. "Moon!"

"I just came to tell you I'm leaving," he said hurriedly, wanting her to know he didn't mean to make this any more difficult for either of them. "And that Eikenn stabbed me in the back. So . . . Keep that in mind, when you're dealing with her."

"Ah." Ghatli wrinkled her lips in distaste. "That doesn't surprise me." She watched him, her expression hard to read. "I'm glad you survived."

Moon shrugged. He was too, mostly. He supposed. He turned toward the door. "Keep Ventl out of trouble."

"Moon, wait. I thank you for everything you did for us. You saved our lives." Ghatli hesitated. "If I could ask you to stay—"

"I wouldn't stay." He shook his head immediately, relieving her of that burden. "I'm not looking for a place to stay." He had already gone over all the reasons remaining here was impossible. He would find another groundling town or settlement at some point, but it would be a place where no one knew what he was.

Ghatli didn't sound very relieved. "What are you looking for? Your people?"

He wasn't looking for anything in particular anymore. If there were any people like him, they had been left behind in the far east somewhere, long ago, and he wasn't sure they were anyone he wanted to know. But that wasn't what Ghatli wanted to hear. "Yes, that's what I'm looking for."

So with the last words he said to Ghatli a lie, Moon slipped out the door, and into the jungle.

MIMESIS

First published in The Other Half of the Sky, *edited by Athena Andreadis and Kay Holt, in April 2013, from Candlemark & Gleam Press. This story takes place three months after the end of* The Siren Depths.

Jade spotted Sand as he circled down from the forest canopy, a grasseater clutched in his talons. She said, "Finally." It would be nice to eat before dark, so they could clear the offal away from the camp without attracting the night scavengers.

It was Balm who said, "I don't see Fair."

Jade frowned, scanning the canopy again. They were standing in the deep grass of the platform they had chosen to camp on, and it was late afternoon in the suspended forest and getting difficult to hunt by sight. The open canyons under the heavy canopies of the immense mountain-trees were filled with green shadow. The breeze stirred jungles of foliage that grew on the platforms formed and supported by the immense intertwined tree branches. Raksuran eyes were designed to track movement, and between flocks of colorful birds, treelings, flying frogs and lizards, and the myriad of other life, the whole forest was moving. But after a heartbeat's concentration, Jade could see there was no one else flying anywhere near Sand.

She turned to Balm, lowering her voice so the other warriors wouldn't hear. "Why did I think it was a good idea to send them off together?"

"I thought it was a good idea, too." Balm shrugged her spines helplessly. "I just can't think why at the moment."

Jade growled in her throat and waited for Sand to land. She should have known something was wrong. Sand and Fair had been gone too long; Aura, Serene, and Balm had already had time to put together a lean-to for shelter on the platform where they had decided to camp. Now Serene and Aura sat by the fire pit in their soft-skinned groundling forms, watching Sand's solo approach with sour expressions. Aura muttered, "Male warriors shouldn't be allowed out of the court until they're old enough to know better."

Serene laughed. "When is that, exactly?"

Balm caught Jade's expression, then said to the other two warriors, "That's not helpful."

Serene and Aura subsided. Balm was Jade's clutchmate and they had been born within moments of each other; it gave her an authority over the other warriors, though Balm occasionally had to demonstrate her fighting ability to prove it.

Jade tried to keep her spines from bristling. If Fair and Sand had gotten into a fight, at least it had happened on the way back from their trading visit.

Fair was a warrior of Pearl's faction and Jade had brought him along because he was young and seemed less hard-headed than the usual run of male warriors who attached themselves to the reigning queen. She had wanted to give him a chance to spend time with warriors of her own faction. As sister queen, Jade had a soul-deep bond with every member of the court, though at her young age she didn't always feel it. It wasn't necessarily her duty to try to make the warriors all get along whether they liked it or not, but the Court of Indigo Cloud had become increasingly divided for the past few turns. Fighting off the Fell and moving to the new colony had forced them all to pull together for a while, and she wanted to encourage that to continue by making the warriors of the different factions interact more. It had seemed a good idea at the time. It still seemed a good idea.

Sand cupped his wings at the last moment, dropped the grasseater to the platform with a thud, and landed nearby. He folded his wings, shook his spines out, and looked around as if surprised everyone was staring pointedly at him. He said, "I got a nice fat grasseater."

Aura, before Jade could, said, "Where's Fair?"

Sand looked around again, his spines starting to flatten in dismay. "He's not here?"

Jade hissed. "No, you can see he's not here. Did you—" *Lose him somewhere and just fail to notice until now?* she started to say, but managed to hold it in. Acid sarcasm was Pearl's habit. Jade didn't think it was a good way to deal with the warriors, no matter how tempting it was at times. "—split up?"

"Yes. I mean, we didn't have a fight." Sand was genuinely upset, which did help calm Jade's urge to slap him senseless. "We saw a few different platforms with grasseaters, but all the herds were too small for both of us to hunt. Fair said he was going after the hoppers."

Jade saw the others' expressions turning from annoyance to real worry, and felt her own spines start to bristle. They had all assumed that Sand and Fair had had an argument and Fair had stopped somewhere to sulk and tend his wounds. Sand added, "It was just hoppers. Small ones, even, hardly bigger than us. That's not dangerous."

Balm glanced at Jade. "Maybe he missed a strike and got hurt."

Jade knew Balm was just saying it to calm Sand. And there was no point in overreacting until they found a body. Jade said, "Sand, show Balm and me where you saw him last."

Serene and Aura came to their feet and shifted to their winged forms, their scales in shades of green. As Aeriat Raksura, they all had retractable claws on hands and feet, long tails with a spade-shape on the end, and manes of spines and frills down their backs. Both were a half-head or so shorter than Jade; she found herself wishing she had brought along some of the older female warriors, who tended to be almost as large as young queens and vicious fighters. Serene said, "Shouldn't we all go?"

"No, stay here and wait." Jade stared them down, until she got reluctant nods from both. Though it warmed her a little to know that they were so willing to go after Fair. Their court might be plagued by factions and infighting, but at least no one wanted to see anybody eaten. "I'll send Sand if we need you."

Jade turned and leapt off the platform, snapped her wings out and flapped for altitude. Balm and Sand followed her. Jade kept her pace slow, so Sand could pull ahead of her and lead the way.

She found herself trying to remember who Fair's clutchmates were. *Oh, damn, I think one of them is Blossom.* Infertile warriors came from the clutches of queens and consorts, like Balm, or from the clutches of the wingless Arbora. Jade was sure Fair had come from the same clutch as the Arbora Blossom, who was a teacher and particularly well-liked by the court. When Jade clutched, she meant for Blossom to be one of those who would raise her fledglings.

Trying to put aside the vision of telling Blossom her mouthy but affectionate clutch-brother had been eaten by something horrible, Jade concentrated on her flying.

Sand led them between the multi-layered platforms of two towering mountain-trees, all supporting small forests of spirals and fern trees and other varieties. None of it was good territory for hunting grasseater herds. The Reaches and the suspended forest might be the ancestral home of the Raksura, but the Indigo Cloud court had only recently returned here. There were too many dangers here that they didn't know about yet.

They passed the heavily forested platforms and came out into a more open area that had formed around a larger mountain-tree. Its canopy was so heavy and extended so far, it had kept any other mountain-trees from forming around it. Falls of water gushed from several knotholes, falling down the hundreds of paces toward the dark of the forest floor. Mountain-trees drew so much water up through their roots, most of them had to expel the excess. In a Raksuran colony tree, the water would be used for drinking, bathing, irrigation.

Jade spotted the platform that held the scattered remnants of Sand's grasseater herd. They were big brown-furred creatures, obviously recently agitated by his hunting run. Most had taken cover in the sparse trees towards the far end of the platform. Some had started to cross one of the bridges formed by a larger branch, heading for another grassy platform that curved further around the mountain-tree's enormous trunk.

"Fair went this way!" Sand called, and slipped sideways and down, toward the lower platforms on the opposite side of the tree.

Most of the platforms to this side were smaller and overflowing with a thick jungle growth that might have hidden anything. It was bound to be unexpectedly deep; young male warriors could be feckless, but Jade couldn't imagine Fair thinking it was a good idea to land there. Then she spotted a lower platform, extending further out from the tree. It had formed atop the stump of a long dead mountain-tree, probably killed by the stronger roots of the larger one. The platform was covered with grass and trees, and its surface was rolling with small hills formed by the underlying branches of its parent tree and what must be the uneven surface of the dying stump below. "That one?" she called to Sand. There was no sign of hoppers now, but the platform had several branch-bridges dropping away to other platforms, so the herd might have fled.

"Maybe," Sand said. "I didn't see which one he was heading for."

Jade heard an annoyed hiss from Balm and had to squelch her own anger. *Little idiot warriors. If only Arbora could fly, we wouldn't have these problems*, she thought. *Find Fair first, then punish them both later.* She just hoped Fair was alive to be punished.

Jade gestured for Sand and Balm to stay back and surged ahead. She reached the platform, passed over, and then turned back to circle above it. There was high grass on the hills and a few stagnant ponds in the low spots between them, but much of the terrain was concealed by the feathery canopies of fern trees. In the open areas, she could see disturbed trails through the grass. It did look like a small herd of hoppers had dashed across the open area of the platform, heading toward the cover of the trees. But she didn't see any sign of Fair.

That wasn't good. If Fair had missed a strike and hurt his wing, or knocked himself out, he might have involuntarily shifted back to his groundling form. In that form, warriors had soft skin, and no wings, spines or claws; he would be vulnerable to a far larger number of predators.

She slowed, coming in over the platform, then cupped her wings and dropped to a landing atop one of the hills. The ground under her claws was soft, grass coming up past her knees. From here she could see under the fern trees, where the trails of flattened grass led. The birdsong and hum of insects was fainter, as if there had been a recent disturbance. She couldn't hear any treelings. She turned, eyes narrowed, looking for movement, a flattened spot in the grass that might be a body, anything. Then she hissed in dismay, waved an arm to signal Balm, and bounded down the hill and toward the trees.

The grass trails led under the round canopies of fern down to a hollow where a dark hole gaped in the dirt and grass of the platform. As she reached it she could see the disturbed dirt, the rips in the grass and underlying moss. Jagged parallel lines, clearly the marks of Raksuran claws, began a few feet from the opening and disappeared over the side. Cautiously, Jade stepped to the powdery dirt at the edge and crouched.

It led into the ground at an angle, a dark tunnel extending down toward the dead stump of the mountain-tree below the platform. She took a deep breath, tasting the air, and caught the rank odor of predator mixed with a trace of dead grasseater, and just a hint of Raksura.

The air stirred as Balm and Sand landed behind her. Sand made a noise of pure dismay. Balm moved to Jade's side and hissed under her breath. Jade said, "I'm going after him." She wasn't quite aware of having made the decision until she said the words. But once she had, it seemed obvious. There was nothing else she could do.

"No." Balm stared at her. "Jade—I should go."

Jade shook her head. Sending anyone else down there, let alone her clutchmate, was so out of the question it hadn't even occurred to her. "Wait here with Sand."

"Let me come with you, at least!"

Jade thought it was bad enough she was risking herself, she didn't want to risk her clutchmate too. "No, stay here."

Balm growled, real fear under it. "You can't do this."

Jade grabbed Balm's collar flange and pulled her close. She put all her authority as queen into the words: "Stay. Here." It wasn't just for Fair's sake, or the sake of Blossom and Fair's other clutchmates and friends, and it wasn't for dread of Pearl's reaction when she heard the only warrior Jade had lost was one of hers. *I don't want to be the kind of queen who leaves warriors to die.* Courts didn't follow queens who couldn't protect their own, and Indigo Cloud had enough trouble without losing faith in its sister queen.

Balm bared her teeth, but after a moment dropped her spines and muttered, "All right." Jade released her and Balm stepped back, but said, "If I come home without you, Moon will kill me."

Jade didn't want to think about her consort's reaction. Moon was a survivor; whatever happened, he could handle it. He was Jade's first consort, and first consort over the court; if she died, his place was assured and he wouldn't have to accept another queen unless he wanted to. Though the idea of another queen taking her place with him made her disemboweling claws itch. She just said, "I intend to come back with you."

Jade turned away from them and leapt down into the tunnel.

She moved cautiously, her mouth open to test the scents, her feet silent on the soft dirt. The light didn't last past the first twenty paces and then she was moving through pure darkness. She couldn't hear anything except the distant sounds of the birds and insects, and those faded as she went further down.

The predator scent was strong enough for her to tell it was nothing she had ever encountered before. *Oh good, something new,* she thought wryly. The one thing they had discovered about the suspended forest was that it was never dull. But it was confusing that it was mixed in with other predators' scents. She could still catch hints of Raksura in the still air, and at least it wasn't dead Raksura.

The dark began to weigh on her. Stepping into the tunnel had been easy; continuing to follow it grew harder with each step. *Some sort of lesson in that.* It would be nice to live long enough to discuss it with Balm.

Of course, the lesson might be that instead of the court losing one warrior it was about to lose a warrior and a sister queen, just because Jade didn't want to look like a coward. And maybe a predator's burrow wasn't a good place for an inner debate about responsibility and leadership.

Then her eyes found faint light ahead. It revealed the tunnel walls of dirt and rotten wood streaked with white mold, hung with webs of dead roots. As she drew closer the light was murky, but more distinct. She looked up to see the tunnel roof was riddled with cracks and fissures, leading to tiny holes that let in dim daylight; she must be all the way down into the mountain-tree stump.

Then the tunnel widened and twisted down, and Jade heard something ahead. A slight rustle, air movement, maybe. *Or maybe not.*

She eased forward, climbed down the twisted passage. The light grew measurably brighter, and she could hear distant birdsong again. It was the murky gray-green light of the lower part of the forest, below most of the platforms.

Then abruptly the wall to her right ended and she found herself looking out into a large open space.

She was in the top of the stump of the dead mountain-tree, and much of it had been rotted away by rain and wood-eating beetle swarms. The soft craggy wood left behind was permeated with holes, festooned with drapes of moss, with odd bulbous shapes of mold clinging to every crack and crevice. White tendrils of vine had grown all through it, winding throughout the space. They were strung across the hollowed-out arch of the top of the chamber like a web. Jade started to step forward, then she froze for a heartbeat, biting back a hiss.

Fair hung limply from a web-like net of the tendrils, suspended from the upper part of the web. He was in his groundling form, curled into a huddle, one bronze-skinned arm dangling down, his head tucked against his shoulder. He was unconscious, not dead, his breath making the tiny copper beads on his armband tremble.

Jade hissed, relief mixing with a strong sense of vindication. She had been right to come down here, she could still save Fair. *Save him from what is the question*, Jade thought, and carefully stepped forward. There were more openings on the far side of the chamber, leading down and away into the rest of the stump, though it was hard to tell if they were rotted holes or tunnels. But the predator had to be down there and she needed to get Fair and escape before it returned.

She picked her way through the chamber, careful not to touch the web of tendrils. The wood was brittle under her feet, and she could feel a myriad of tiny snaps and cracks as her weight came down on it. Her bones were light in her winged form, being mostly hollow, so hopefully she didn't weigh enough to fall through. Fissures in the delicate surface were large enough for her to see big white mushrooms feeding on the wood and mold lower down.

As she drew closer to Fair, she spotted more of the vine nets strung from the web above, many containing shriveled corpses. Most were large furry predators with wide fanged mouths and curving claws almost as big as Jade's. They were very like the predators that preyed on hoppers and other grasseaters on the platforms closer to the Indigo Cloud colony. Hanging next to Fair was a web holding a creature that was still intact, but it was curled up too and all she could tell about it was that it had slick dark green skin and a large knobby skull.

She passed its net and reached Fair. He was dangling about four paces above her head and she crouched to leap. A wordless cry stopped her in mid-lunge.

It wasn't Fair, it was a groundling, hanging in another tendril web-net twenty paces or so across the chamber. And it was staring at her with big, startled blue eyes.

Jade stared back, surprised she hadn't noticed it before. It was smaller than Fair's groundling form and had pale, almost luminescent skin, with dark blue hair or fur in a fuzz on its head and down its back. Its eyes were wide and round, nose flat and protected by an extra flap of skin, and mouth small. It wore a belt and a wrap woven of dark leaves around its narrow hips. She couldn't make a guess if it was male or female; its legs were folded under and tucked into the bottom of the net, hiding any genitalia. Its hands were large and clawless, the knuckles big and gnarled where it gripped the tendril net.

Jade had never seen a groundling like it before, but in the Reaches that didn't mean much. The Kek lived around the roots of colony trees, and there must be other civilized species occupying similar niches in the lower parts of the forest. But this groundling didn't seem to have ever seen anything like her before, despite the fact that Raksura had been native to the Reaches since time began.

Jade realized she must look like another predator, especially if Fair had shifted involuntarily when knocked unconscious and this groundling had never seen his winged form. She could shift, but queens didn't have the same groundling form as warriors. She would be without her wings and some of her spines, but not without her claws, scales, or any of the other things most soft-skinned species found intimidating. And she weighed more in her other form, and might just go right through the weakened wood beneath her feet. So she lifted her hands, palms out, claws retracted, in a gesture she hoped the groundling would recognize.

It blinked, as if it couldn't believe what it saw, and its eyes widened with an emotion that might have been hope. Jade sighed. Obviously, she would have to rescue it too. It would be pointlessly cruel to leave it here. She would free Fair first, then it.

She reached for Fair, but the groundling cried out again, waving at her frantically.

Jade stopped, baffled. The groundling twisted around and pointed urgently down. A tuber from one of the tendrils trapping it was attached to its pale skin. He pointed up and she traced the tuber up through the web, into the mass at the top of the chamber. A growl building in her throat, she looked to Fair, and spotted the pale shape of another tuber across his back, disappearing under his arm where it must be attached to his body. "It's feeding on you?" she said aloud, the words coming out in a low growl. Obviously, if she removed the tubers, the predator would know instantly.

She thought of going back to get Balm and Sand to help her, but her spines twitched at the thought of leaving. The thing was *eating* them while she stood here. She didn't know how long they had left. Keeping her voice low, she said, "This is going to be tricky."

The groundling stared worriedly at her. It said something in Kedaic that was so distorted, it took her a moment to realize the words had been, "I hope you understand, whatever you are."

Jade had spoken in the Raksuran language. She said in Kedaic, "Can you understand me?"

"Yes!" It twitched in surprise. "You speak—I didn't think—I mean—" It wiped its face wearily. "Forgive me, I have been trapped here with no hope and still half-think I am imagining you."

"You're not. How big is this thing?"

It waved one big hand in a helpless gesture. "Very big. Its body is down there, I think." It pointed back toward the openings on the far side of the chamber, and shuddered. "I only saw its limbs."

"Lovely." No, much as it pained her, she was going to have to go back up and get Balm. To make this work, they would have to free Fair and the groundling at the same time, and then flee. Two could do that better than one. "I'll have to go and get help. It won't take long."

She thought the groundling would protest, but it only nodded and said, "Yes, please, bring others! Hurry!"

As Jade turned, the green creature in the other net stirred and lifted its knobby head. Its face was wide and flat, eyes and nose and mouth just slits. Then its eyes opened wide and blinked at her in amazement. It gasped out words in a deep voice, in a language she didn't understand. So it wasn't dead, and it wasn't an animal. "I'll free you too," Jade said. "Just wait—"

It waved its webbed hands at her frantically, staring past her in terror, and spoke more urgently. She didn't understand any of the words it said, except for one. *Raksura. It said Raksura, it knows what I am.* It had a feeding tube attached to its chest, this one with a large sucker on the end, and the green skin around it was bruised dark and swelling with blood.

Jade realized three things simultaneously. It was odd that the other groundling had never seen Raksura before, when this creature clearly had. It was odd that the other groundling's feeding tube hadn't bruised its skin, when that skin appeared so pale and delicate. It was especially odd that the two trapped prey had been speaking so loudly and it hadn't brought the predator down on them.

She turned, meeting the groundling's blue eyes again. Was there something wrong with the expression in them, were they not quite focused on her? She said, "Before I go, show me your legs."

It stared at her for a moment more, then its mouth opened in a rictus and it lunged out of the net. By that point it wasn't a surprise to see that the whole lower part of its body was made up of the white tendrils.

Jade didn't wait to see what it would do. There were plenty of predators that had body parts that mimicked groundling forms in order to draw prey in, and obviously, this thing was one of them. The Raksuran ability to shift to a groundling-like form had originally been just that, a way to move unnoticed among groundling species and kill them. Some predators could even modify the appearance of their lures, adapting to whatever prey they were after.

Jade leapt for the web, flipped and hung by her foot-claws. She slashed open Fair's net prison and yanked the feeding tube free. She caught Fair before he could tumble out and tucked him under her arm.

The tendril predator took a swipe at her, wielding its decoy groundling body like a club. Jade let go with her feet and slammed into the net holding the green creature, the real groundling. She slashed through the tendrils and the feeding tube and with a desperate cry the green groundling lurched toward her and wrapped its arms around her neck. It was heavy, and Jade thought, *Good.* As the tendrils closed around her, she dropped to the brittle wood below, then bounced back up and flipped to push off from a projection of wood above. She shifted to her heavier Arbora body, then flung herself at the nearest fissure in the floor as hard as she could.

The rotted wood gave way with a crack and she smashed through. They fell through open air into the dark canyon of the main part of the stump. The whole space was covered with mushrooms, some of which were bigger than Jade. The real groundling shrieked as she shifted back to her winged form; she thought it might have cut its arms on her spines.

She snapped her wings out and flapped frantically to stay aloft, heading toward a hole in the far side of the stump. The groundling, looking back over her shoulder, keened an urgent warning. Jade flipped sideways as tendrils reached for her, slashed them with her foot claws, and dove down and away.

More tendrils pushed through the hole above, the decoy dangling from them and jerking around like a horrible toy. It shouted, "Don't go, you have to stay and rescue me! Bring more help, bring more help!"

The groundling in her arms whimpered and shuddered. Jade was running out of room to fly. She came around, making for the opening again. Tendrils snatched at her legs.

In the next heartbeat, Balm and Sand shot through the opening and passed Jade, snarling and slashing at the tendrils. The predator drew back in confusion, and Jade shouted, "Go, go now!" They all three dove for the way out.

Jade flew out into the slightly lighter dimness of the lower part of the forest, just after Balm and Sand. The platforms above cut off much of the dim green daylight that fell through the canopy, and the air was heavy with moisture and all the muddy scents of the ground far below, but it had never felt better to Jade. They spiraled down to the branch of a twisted mountain-tree sapling a good distance from the stump and landed.

"Are you all right?" Balm demanded.

Breathing hard, Jade handed her Fair's still-unconscious body. He didn't look well but he was breathing. "Yes. You heard this one screaming?" She patted the green groundling reassuringly. It let go of her shoulders and stumbled away a few steps to sit down heavily. It was bleeding sluggishly from the wound where the feeding tube had been, as was Fair.

Balm felt Fair's throat to make sure he was breathing, then handed him to Sand. "It echoed right up through that tunnel. We heard something crack and fall, and we thought you were coming out somewhere underneath the platform."

"I'm glad you did." Jade shook her spines out. The skin under her scales still itched with the feel of those tendrils. "Get Fair back to camp. I need to find out where to take this one." She gestured to the green groundling, who had propped itself up on its hands, still reeling.

Balm nodded, and gripped Jade's shoulder. She couldn't say anything for a moment, then muttered, "Next time, take me with you." Then she backed away and jumped off the branch. Sand followed with Fair, and the two flew back up toward the light.

Jade turned to the groundling, who was watching her worriedly. She said, "Now for the hard part. I have to figure out a way to talk to you."

(

After ascertaining that they had no language in common, not even the few words of Kek that Jade knew, she resorted to gestures and pantomime, and the green groundling tried scratching out symbols and drawings on the bark. Once it finally understood what she was asking, and she understood its answer, she was able to fly it down to the forest floor. On a lake a short distance away, almost impossible to see in the twilight dimness, she found a small island with complex structures made of hardened mud, and a large group of similar groundlings who were ecstatic to have their friend back. Jade deposited her relieved groundling, waved, and took off immediately. She was worried about Fair.

Darkness had fallen by the time she arrived back at their camp. The others had built a small fire to heat water, and Fair lay in the shelter, with Serene, Aura, and Sand sitting with him.

Balm was at the fire pit, and stood as Jade landed. She said, "I made tea."

Jade shifted to Arbora and shook her spines out. She wanted a bath, to scrub the memory of the predator off her scales, but that would have to wait until they returned to the colony. "Good."

She sat beside the fire pit with Balm and asked, "How is Fair?"

"He woke up for a bit and talked." Balm poured a cup of tea from the small kettle and handed it to Jade. "We cleaned the wound and put a poultice on it. And I'm glad the mentors insist on sending healing simples with us, because it looked terrible."

"We'll leave before dawn," Jade said, and sipped the tea. They needed to get Fair back to the colony as soon as possible. The tea took the memory of the acrid scents of the rotting stump out of her throat. She said, "I almost did something very stupid," and told Balm about the predator's decoy. "I think it must prey on other predators. I saw a lot of those things that go after grasseaters down there. Fair and the other groundling must have gotten close to it thinking it was an injured groundling." Dying while fighting off a predator was one thing, dying because she had almost fallen for a trick was another. "The damn thing even spoke to me."

Balm grimaced in disgust. "You should have let me come with you." Then she waved that away. "I'm sorry, I don't mean it like that, I'm not criticizing your decision."

"I know." Balm *was* criticizing her decision, but that's what clutchmates were for. Jade felt the whole encounter with the predator could definitely have gone better, but they were all alive at the end, including one helpful green groundling, and that was enough. Though when Pearl heard what happened, the reigning queen was sure to have some pithy words about it. "To make up for it, I'll let you tell Pearl."

Balm looked horrified, and Jade smiled and sipped her tea.

TRADING
LESSON

*This story takes place one month after
the end of "Mimesis."*

The trading party from Sunset Water arrived late in the evening. There were no queens along, just warriors and Arbora, so there was no reason for the royal Aeriat to greet them formally tonight. This meant Moon wouldn't have a chance to see them until the next day. Rushing down to the greeting hall and demanding to see everything they had brought immediately was just not done, Jade had told him. They would have a formal presentation late tomorrow morning, when everyone could be dignified and pretend not to be as interested as they actually were.

Moon would have been fine with this, or at most only a little impatient and annoyed, if Chime hadn't come up to the queens' level to tell them how exciting it all was.

"They have a groundling with them," Chime reported, practically bouncing as he sat beside the hearth in Jade's bower. "He's—I suppose it's a he; he hasn't really said one way or another—is from a species that lives in the southern Reaches. The ground between the mountain tree roots is very swampy there, and these layers of fungus grow about a hundred or so paces above the ground level. These groundlings build their towns inside the fungus, because of course there are so many dangerous predators in the swamps. But they trade with the other groundlings who live deeper into the swamps and also past the Reaches in the lakes to the south and he's been traveling from court to court, and—" Chime ran out of breath and waved his hands. "I can't wait to see what he's brought!"

Moon stared at Jade. She said, "Don't look at me like that. If we go down now, the Sunset Water Arbora will know how anxious we are and we'll give away our advantage."

Moon jerked his head toward Chime. "Right, because our Arbora and warriors aren't down there right now giving away our advantage."

"We are not!" Chime was outraged. "We're very experienced at this."

Past history led Moon to doubt that. "How many courts did you trade with at the old colony?"

"Just Sky Copper, mostly, and sometimes Wind Sun and once Star Aster," Chime admitted, "But they were very canny bargainers. One time I had to trade a dozen unworked onyx lumps for the herb cuttings I wanted."

Moon could tell where this was going. "How many herb cuttings?"

"Almost a double handful," Chime said. At Moon's expression, he added, "What?"

Moon just looked at Jade. He had lived in places where a dozen unworked onyx lumps would have bought enough food for a small village for half a turn. Jade shrugged and said, "Herbs are for simples and healing. Onyx is for baubles."

Moon sighed. "I know." Every species, every different community, had its own ideas about value and trade, but the Raksura's ideas were odder than anything Moon had ever encountered in any of his travels, and that was saying a lot.

"What?" Chime demanded again.

"Nothing."

☾

By mid-morning, no one could wait anymore, so the reigning queen Pearl, with her consort Ember and her favorite warriors in tow, wandered down to the greeting hall and pretended to be mildly surprised to encounter the trading party from Sunset Water. Jade and Moon followed, and things started to get underway.

Pearl established herself and her entourage at the bowl hearth set into the floor of the greeting hall near the waterfall, with seating cushions and the best tea set. There she made polite conversation with the oldest Arbora and the oldest female warrior from the Sunset Water party. Instead of setting up a rival camp, Jade strolled around the hall with Balm, which allowed Moon to wander around and get a look at everything.

The trading party was nine Arbora, with twenty warriors to transport them, their goods, and the groundling who had tagged along. The Sunset Water trade items were set out on grass mats on the floor of the greeting hall, and the Indigo Cloud Arbora hauled their items up from the lower levels of the colony tree. Everyone was in groundling form, except for a few warriors who were helping to carry things. The queens kept their wings, though, and didn't shift to Arbora.

Moon had always liked markets, though even when he had the means to trade, he had never been able to carry many possessions. He had never bought much of anything except food, and the few items necessary to pretend to be a groundling. He had still liked looking at all the wares, and seeing what other people bought. He just liked looking at other people's stuff; it was one of the best forms of free entertainment that groundling communities offered.

The Sunset Water traders had brought the seeds, bulbs, and plant cuttings that courts commonly traded, but they had also brought more unusual things. There were spices, including little red balls dotted with black spikes, that Blossom, hovering nearby, told Moon was a special peppery spice that was also good for upset stomachs. There were dark-colored cakes of tea and powdered minerals that could be used to make inks and dyes. There were also some bundles of paper wrapped in waxed leather sleeves, that were copies of books from the Sunset Water libraries. Heart, Merit, and the other mentors clustered around that mat, intently going through the books, asking occasional questions of the Arbora who had brought them. Moon saw Chime hover nearby for a moment, then shoulder in to look too. Heart didn't even glance up, just passed him one of the books.

More interesting to Moon were the raw lumps of various kinds of ore and some uncut lumps of gemstone, chiseled out of the outcrops on the forest floor, hundreds of paces below the platforms of the suspended forest. Gold and Merry and some of the other Arbora artisans were deep in whispered consultation over them.

The Indigo Cloud Arbora had retaliated with their own array of seeds and plant cuttings, polished snail shells, and some bolts of the dyed cloth made at the old colony. They had been reluctant to trade the cloth at first, but the Arbora had finally gotten the plants that were needed to make it to grow on one of the tree's largest platforms, and there were good indications that they could expect a harvest next turn. The Arbora were also experimenting with making bark cloth, which Moon thought was almost as fine.

But the groundling and his goods were obviously the real attraction. He had a mat to himself, and was setting out a number of small bags. His hairless skin was white mottled with gray and black, and his ears and nose were concealed behind heavy frills of delicate skin. Sucker-like pads sprouted from his cheeks, and continued down his arms and legs. His clothing was a loose tunic that looked like it had been woven from moss. Moon could believe his people lived in the layers of fungus that sometimes sprouted from the lower levels of the mountain-tree trunks. It sounded unpleasant, but it was probably much safer for them than the forest floor. The Kek lived on the ground among mountain-tree roots, but then their skinny bodies were practically made out of sticks, and few predators bothered with them.

And if the warriors of various Raksuran courts were willing to cart the groundling around from colony to colony, whatever he brought with him must be choice.

Arbora were already starting to gather around him, waiting impatiently. Moon joined the back of the crowd, easily able to see over the shorter Arbora. Stone wandered up beside him, and Moon asked, "Have you ever met a groundling like this before?"

"Probably." Stone shrugged. "His name's Iglen. He's not a talker, like Delin."

Their favorite Golden Islander had a wealth of information and stories. Moon had been hoping for something similar, but from Stone's lack of reaction, Iglen was either reticent or boring. "Were you down here last night?" he asked, aware it sounded accusing.

Stone gave him a look. "Believe me, it wasn't that exciting."

That was probably true. But Moon would have still preferred to be bored himself instead of hear secondhand about it. "Did he say what he had to trade?"

"No. He mostly talked about fungus."

Somehow Moon doubted that. But then Iglen pulled a bag out of his pack and emptied it onto the mat. The Arbora pressed closer, gasping in awe. Moon craned his neck to see.

Spilled across the mat were small smooth lumps that ranged in color from dark honey to a pure grass green. The Arbora stared, fascinated, the warriors edging closer to look over their shoulders. Stone made a disgruntled noise and wandered off. He had clearly been hoping for something better. Moon had been hoping for something better too, and he couldn't think why the others were so excited.

Jade stepped up beside Moon, and he said, "It's amber. They've seen amber before."

"Yes, but we never had that much." She was stretching to see too, though her expression held studied indifference. Moon shook his head. It was a good thing the groundling traders of the Abascene would be too terrified of Raksura to attempt the journey here. Raksura were lousy traders.

"It's hardened tree sap," Moon pointed out. "You can't walk across open country in some parts of Kish without tripping over it." He thought the lumps of ore from Sunset Water, dug out of the rock of the forest floor with great difficulty and yielding harder and brighter stones, were much more valuable.

Jade lowered her voice. "Yes, but it's pretty."

After a while, everyone had had a chance to admire the amber and most of them had wandered off to take care of their own trading. Jade had gone to see to the more important business of the seed and root stock trading. Moon had just turned to head back over to see if Chime and the others had been able to get any new books, when Rill edged through the last of the lingering warriors. She plunked down at the edge of the groundling's mat and upended a bag of small lumps of polished pearl.

Moon elbowed a few warriors aside and sat on his heels next to her. "Rill, what are you doing?"

"I'm trading my pearls for some of these stones," she said brightly.

Yes, that's what Moon had been afraid of. "Do you remember when we traded five pearls for the right to use the Golden Islander's flying boats?" He pointed at the amber. "That's not the same as a flying boat."

The groundling Iglen watched in disapproval. In passable Raksuran, he said, "I didn't know warriors took an interest in trade."

Rill turned to Iglen, tilting her head ominously. She didn't shift but the heavy muscles tensed under her brown skin and it was suddenly almost possible to see the ghost shapes of the scales, sharp fangs, and sickle claws of her other form. She said in a flat voice, "He's a consort."

Iglen sat back, holding up his hands. "I apologize!"

Moon managed not to roll his eyes in annoyance. Even fungus-dwelling groundlings had opinions on his lack of suitability as a consort. He said, "That's all right."

Rill regarded Iglen a moment more to make certain he was actually sorry, then turned back to Moon. "These are small ones, though, and those were big."

Moon held up one of the glossy lumps of pearl. "Rill, somebody had to swim out to a sea kingdom and risk drowning and being eaten by angry sea creatures to bargain for these. Who knows what they had to trade to get them. Stone could fly somewhere and get you all the amber you wanted, just by picking it up off the ground." Stone heard his name from across the hall and looked around, spotted Moon, and eyed him narrowly.

Rill snorted. "But Stone won't do that."

Moon ran his hand through the bag. Some of the pearls were a tawny color, some almost pink, and he had never seen anything like them. Rill could have started her own trading empire in any number of eastern cities just with this bag. "Because he doesn't need to, because what you have is better."

Iglen said, "In the other courts, the consorts did not take this much interest in trade."

"Moon is different," Rill told him. "He used to live with groundlings."

Iglen's frills lifted. "Oh?"

"Near Kish," Moon said, pointedly.

Iglen's frills drooped. "Oh."

That, more than anything else, convinced Moon that Iglen knew exactly what he was doing. Stone was over there encouraging Blossom to trade handfuls of sunstones for cakes of pressed tea leaves, but that was to another Arbora, who was just as likely to trade the sunstones for wooden beads, or seeds for an unusual kind of berry. Iglen would eventually take Rill's pearls outside the Reaches where they could probably be traded for all the available goods in a medium-sized groundling town. Moon asked Rill, "Where did you even get all of these?"

"I traded for them turns and turns ago from Wind Sun, to make jewelry for Pearl. But she doesn't like them. And they wouldn't look right on Jade, or Ember, or Stone." She held one up to Moon's face and squinted at the result. "Or you."

"Make something for yourself, or somebody else."

"I don't like them either," she admitted in a whisper. "They aren't very good to work with. And I want the pretty green amber."

"We'll get you the pretty green amber," Moon told her. He shook out a few of the lesser pearls, then tied up the rest in the bag.

"But consorts aren't supposed to trade—"

"You'll do the trading," Moon said. He fixed a pointed, meaningful gaze on Iglen. "I'll just sit here."

Iglen's ear-frills twitched in dismay.

☾

That evening the Arbora prepared a special meal in the greeting hall for the visitors, with baked spiced roots, fruit, and bread along with the usual raw grasseater meat. Moon sat with Jade, Chime, Balm, Heart, and a few other warriors and Arbora, sprawled on the cushions and currently stuffed with good food. Everyone seemed deeply satisfied with the trading, and both Indigo Cloud and Sunset Water seemed to feel they had come out the winner in the exchanges. Moon supposed they both had, by Raksuran standards.

"Everyone certainly got a lot of that amber," Chime said, gesturing around at the Arbora who were showing their trades to each other. "Even some of the warriors."

Balm nodded. "The leader of the Sunset Water Arbora told me that Iglen has never had to trade so much of his stock to get so little."

"Yes, it's funny how that worked out," Jade said, gazing thoughtfully at Moon.

Chime frowned at Moon. "And why were you over there all afternoon? I thought you didn't like amber."

Moon's attempt to appear innocent and only mildly interested was clearly failing, so he said, "I like amber fine. I don't like traders that take advantage of people." Iglen wasn't obligated to play fairly. But Moon wasn't obligated to let him get away with it, either.

Jade flicked a spine. "Well, when they make a lot of amber jewelry for you, you're just going to have to wear it."

THE ALMOST LAST VOYAGE OF THE WIND-SHIP *ESCARPMENT*

This story is set in another part of the Three Worlds, with a different cast of characters.

Jai had thought this job was a good idea for a number of reasons, but watching Flaren's face as they waited to meet with Canon Hain, she was no longer so sure. Flaren was grimly trying to contain any emotion, but his desperation was leaking out of him like he was a sieve.

Jai scratched her lip beneath the curve of her tusk, and said, as if to herself, "We could jump over the side, swim for it, until Kiev could pick us up." Foreigners and exiles were only permitted to set foot on the floating city of Issila at the trading platforms, so that was where they waited, the fresh salt-tempered wind pulling at their hair and clothes, the sun warm and bright.

The platform was on the far edge of the city, about a hundred long paces above the restless waves of the sea. Jai couldn't see much of the city from this angle, just a few gleaming copper roofs beyond the stairwell tower. The whole massive structure of wood and metal platforms, held together by hinged joints, rolled with the motion of the waves so it didn't break apart during the Ataran sea's mild storms.

She saw that Flaren did not much like her suggestion that they flee. The open stairwell tower that led up to the city's main gates was only a short distance away, and Canon Hain's party was already making their way down the long spiral. Flaren said, "It's a little late to leave."

Hain reached the bottom of the tower and started across the open platform toward them. He was older than Jai had expected, the wind whipping at his gray hair and the dark robes wrapping his body. The five others with him were dressed in light scale armor over dun-colored garments, and must be bodyguards.

Jai found the armor unnecessary, considering how well-defended Issila was and how few serious enemies the city had. Two of them even carried the long silver tubes of projectile weapons, uncommon in the archipelagos. The Issilans closely guarded the secrets needed to construct the weapons, and the minerals used to fire them were precious and rare. "You would think they go to war all the time," she muttered. "Like children playing dress-up."

"Will you stop it," Flaren said through gritted teeth.

"He can't hear me," Jai retorted. But it was better to present a cool united front to Canon Hain, not look as if they had been arguing like children. Especially if they had been arguing like children.

Hain stopped ten paces away, fixing his gaze on a point between them. "Which of you is the captain?" His voice sounded strained, pitched to carry over the sound of wind and sea.

The bodyguards were staring at Jai. She felt herself to be a striking figure by any standard, but she knew they were staring because she was kinet, from a mountain range on the mainland far to the east, and her people seldom came to this coast. She was tall and strong, with smooth brown skin like polished wood, thickened to protect against the harsh cold of the mountains. Her hair was all long wiry curls and no one but other kinet appreciated the red designs carved into the white tusks curving down either side of her nose. The guards seemed to barely notice Flaren beside her, with the same dark hair, dark eyes, and softer, dark gold skin as they had.

Jai eyed Canon Hain with disapproval. "You may address me as Captain." The kinet didn't organize themselves in a way that most other species, including Flaren, could understand, but Jai usually took the leader's role. She spread her hands, palms out, in a polite greeting. "I am Jainin dan Ethana, of the ship *Escarpment*, and this is my esteemed navigator, Flaren."

Hain didn't acknowledge the introduction. His small eyes still fixed on a point between them, he said, "You agree to carry the ransom to the savages who have captured our ship?"

"That is why we are standing here, yes." Jai couldn't help sounding dry, and Hain's gaze flicked toward her.

"We'll take it," Flaren said. His voice was harsh. The bodyguards might think it was anger, but Jai could hear that it was pure nerves. "We'll make sure the crew and passengers are released, and escort them back here."

The Canon looked at him directly for the first time, a brief glance tinged with dismay. He made a signal and the bodyguard on the right moved forward, holding out a chased metal box. As Flaren stepped up to take it, Hain said, "The box is spelled. If the lock is broken before it is delivered, the contents will be destroyed—"

Jai cut him off. "We are not thieves, so we are uninterested in the lock."

Hain pressed his lips together, stiff with annoyance. Jai wanted to roll her eyes, but managed not to. Issilans were touchy and deeply concerned with their own personal honor, which sometimes meant assuming that no one else had any.

Flaren said, "We need the location." Watching Hain, he added deliberately, "And our payment."

Hain nodded to another bodyguard, who pulled a small sack off his belt and stepped forward. He tried to hand it to Flaren; his arms were full so Jai reached for it. The man stared at her hands, the round blunt nails as thick as claws, then blinked and surrendered the bag.

Jai opened the sack, and briefly counted the trading disks inside. They were good currency at any civilized port along the coast or the islands, and the amount was right. They had agreed to a third of the payment now, the rest once the hostages were freed. There was also a folded sheet of paper and Jai fished it out, unfolding it to see a quickly sketched map and some directions.

"You can find it?" Hain asked.

"Yes. If we can't, we'll just have to come back for better instruction—" She looked up in time to see Hain turn so abruptly he startled the bodyguards. He started away across the platform.

"Father!" Flaren choked the word out as if he couldn't stop himself. Hain didn't hesitate, didn't look back. The bodyguards followed hurriedly, darting glances back at Flaren.

Jai looked at Flaren's stricken face, and felt her heart sink. A large and guilty part of her soul had been hoping for this sort of rebuff. She knew it was for the best, but that didn't make it any less painful for Flaren.

When the message had gone out for an itinerant crew to deliver a ransom, Hain had obviously not expected the ship that had given shelter to Flaren to answer the call. Hain was not going to accept his son back into his house, and nothing Flaren did or didn't do was going to change that. She thought Flaren had taken that to heart, and suggesting the situation might be otherwise was no act of friendship. But Jai couldn't stop herself from saying, "Perhaps it's guilt. He knows he was cruel and unjust—"

Flaren turned and took a few steps away, his shoulders as tight as wire. Cursing herself, Jai waved up at the *Escarpment*.

Kiev must have been watching carefully. The wind-ship had been circling about two hundred paces above the platform. It dropped immediately at her signal, the ropes dangling from the break in the railing. As the ropes lowered within reach, Jai caught them, sorted out the one that had a basket attached for lifting small quantities of supplies. Flaren joined her to tuck the box into the basket and tie the lid securely.

Jai eyed his set expression. "I'm sorry. I think it was me. I spoke to him too sharply and he took offense—"

"It wasn't you," Flaren said, and clipped a safety line to her harness.

Inwardly cursing her stupidity, Jai rendered further apologies in the time it took the *ilene*-powered winch to draw them back up to the *Escarpment*. So much so that when they stood on the boarding deck, after they detached their harnesses from the lines, Flaren took her shoulders and shook her, saying, "Enough. I accept your apology. All of your apologies. Please stop."

The kinet believed that if something was worth saying once, it was worth saying a few more times, but Jai had long recognized that this was not the way of other species. She promised, "I'll stop."

Flaren squeezed her shoulders, gave her a wry smile, and went forward to the steering cabin and the hatch that led below decks. "What have you done to him now?" Kiev asked, leaning over the rail of the small upper deck. He was also kinet, though small for a male, being barely Jai's height.

"I was rude to his judgmental bastard of a father." Jai untied the basket lid to take the ransom box out. It was heavy, the sides and sealed top ornamented with swirling designs in copper and silver. From the weight there were several heavy objects inside, probably lumps of gold or some other precious metal. She could feel a faint vibration through the surface, the outward evidence of whatever spell had been used to secure it.

Kiev lifted his furry brows. "Your plan is to sabotage his chance to return home?"

Jai hefted the box, looking up at him in exasperation. "It is not a plan. He has no chance to return home." Flaren knew that. Or she had assumed Flaren knew that. She was beginning to wonder about her judgment.

Still wondering, she crossed the small deck toward the cabin. The *Escarpment* had been built in a place called the Golden Isles, or at least that was what the man she had bought it from had told her. Flying islands were more numerous there, and the wind-ships were powered by a tiny piece of the mineral that lay at the heart of the islands, which kept them aloft and drew them along the lines of force which crisscrossed the Three Worlds. The *Escarpment* was a small example of its kind, only fifty paces long from bow to stern, with a hull constructed of a light lacquered wood fiber that was deceptively strong. Its only sail was a fan-shaped one that opened out from the single mast.

A wind-ship would not be much use in the harsh mountain winds of Jai's home, but was perfect for trading along the coast and the archipelagos of the calm Ataran Sea. Kiev, skilled in the manipulation of metal and heat that was well-known in their own mountain country, had added improvements using *ilene*, an energy-imbued mineral mined beneath their home city of Keres-gedin.

Jai ducked under the narrow doorway and went down the short set of steps to the living hold. The common room held the navigator's table where Flaren sat, comparing the map Hain had given them with one of their own charts. Latal and Shiri had gathered around, worriedly studying the results. Lining the walls were chests for storing the logbooks and records of their trades, Jai's small collection of books, and their money and valuables. There was also a rack that held the rolled leather tubes protecting their charts and maps. The hold was lit by squares of *ilene* in its non-crystallized form, tuned to give off light but no heat, another Keres-gedin innovation added to the ship. It was much safer than candles or oil lamps, especially in high winds. Eventually, perhaps by the next turn of the seasons, the energy in their carefully hoarded pieces of *ilene* would run out, leaving the mineral blocks cracked and dull, and they would have to return to the mountains to purchase more. Jai hoped to have enough funds by then to make the journey easy, and this job would come near to accomplishing that goal, and make them comfortable through the rest of the warm season. It was most of the reason they had decided to take it, the rest being Flaren's desire to torture himself by proximity to his betraying snake of a father and his horrid family.

Jai stowed the ransom box away in a chest, put the bag of trading disks in the ship's lockbox, then shouldered her way between Latal and Shiri. By that time Kiev had set their course and followed her down the stairs. Leaning on the table beside Flaren, Jai looked over the map. "Do we know this place we are going to?"

Flaren was frowning, his dark golden brow furrowed. "No. It's in the shallows, some distance off the Visicae archipelago where the Issilan ship was captured. Our charts don't show any notations for an island there."

"The shallows," Jai repeated. It was difficult for larger sailing ships to navigate through there without running into any of the stone shelves and reefs that lay just below the surface. "I wonder how the pirates managed this. Perhaps they use skiffs." Though from what she understood, the pirates had taken the ship when it had anchored for the night and towed it away from the shipping lanes. Skiffs would be hard put to tow even a modest Issilan vessel.

"Hopefully skiffs, and not airships," Kiev muttered. Kiev was a pessimist. "If they come after us, we can't win a race."

"We're faster than any airship," Latal said, stoutly loyal to their flying bucket. She was the youngest, and most enthusiastic, of their crew. Jai ruffled her hair fondly.

Before Kiev could retort that they were not faster than an airship, Shiri said, "These aren't just any raiders." Shiri was of a species native to the Ataran Sea, and was short, with gray-green skin and silvery gray hair, and gnarled wrinkled features that made him look old and wise when he was just as fluff-headed as the rest of them.

"Of course they aren't," Jai said. Nothing about this was going to be easy. She would be unsurprised to hear that the ransom demand stipulated that they deliver it naked and with air bladders tied to their heads. "What are they?"

Shiri rolled his narrow shoulders and looked uncomfortable. "The raiders in the shallows don't raid to sell cargo and ransom crews, like the fishers and traders that can't make their living and turn pirate. They're predators."

He had everyone's attention now. *Predators.* The Altanic word meant "people who subsist on other people." *Like Tath, or Ghobin or Setaret*, Jai thought. *Or Fell, may everything that's holy curse them and keep them far away from here.* She said, "But these raiders asked for ransom, therefore they are not predators."

Watching Shiri, Flaren asked, "Do you know what they look like?"

Shiri shook his head. "Just that the rumor says they come from an old sea kingdom."

"Rumor!" Latal made an impatient gesture. "Just because they're sealings, doesn't mean they're predators." Sealings were any species that lived in the water, and might be anything from the civilized inhabitants of the deep sea kingdoms to the packs of barely sentient predators that preyed on fishing vessels and other sealings.

"That'll be fun to fight in the water," Kiev said sourly.

"We're not going to fight them," Jai said. Latal was right; appearance was nothing to judge by. Flaren tensed to argue, but subsided when Jai added, "We'll deliver the ransom and escort the hostages away, as we've been asked to. That's all."

Flaren gave her a small smile, relieved and worried all at once. "Are you sure? I mean, I know it's dangerous—"

"I'm sure." And she was, really. Not only would they be rescuing people who were badly in need of rescuing, stuck-up Issilan nobles though they were, but the rest of the payment Canon Hain had promised was so large they couldn't afford to pass it up. "The pirates want their ransom, we want their hostages and our payment for freeing them. If it goes well, everyone gets what they want."

Everyone nodded, reassured, and Jai felt the tension ease. Then Shiri had to say darkly, "You hope that's all they want."

☽

It would take them the rest of the day and the night to make their way over the open sea to the coast of the first Visicae island, and then to navigate along the archipelago until they reached the raiders' lair. They each took a turn at the steering column, navigating via the compass and their charts. They kept the fansail folded, as the wind was in the wrong direction and would just push them away from the invisible force-current, slowing the little wind-ship's progress.

The day remained bright and nearly cloudless, the sea sparkling beneath them, and there wasn't much else to do while they traveled except sleep, read, fret, or talk. So when Jai finished her stint on watch she found herself loitering in the doorway of Flaren's small cabin, where she could both talk and fret.

Like all their living quarters, it had a narrow shelf for the bed, and cabinets with basket weave doors for the storage of personal belongings. Not that Flaren had many, except a little spare clothing and the few gifts Jai and the others had pressed on him. The wind-ship's hull creaked beneath her feet, a restful sound, though their conversation was anything but restful.

Flaren put his book down for the third time, sat up and punched his pillow. He said, "I should take the ransom in alone. It'll be safer."

They had been making plans and discarding them all evening, but this was the first time he had made this suggestion. Jai gave him a derisive snort. "You want to do that."

Flaren looked annoyed. "I want to do that slightly less than I want to jump off the *Escarpment*'s deck without a harness. But we're doing this for me. I should take the risk."

"We're doing it for the money," Jai reminded him. "You rubbing your father's face in the fact that you are alive and thriving despite his best efforts is a side benefit." She hoped that was how Flaren saw the situation.

But he shifted uncomfortably. "I know why you're doing it."

Guilt reared its pointed head, but not quite enough that Jai could hold her tongue. "What do you mean?"

Flaren said, "You want to help me go back home."

Jai fought the urge to bang her head against the wall. By home he meant Issila, back to the city and the family that had rejected him so thoroughly they had set him off in a small boat to die. If the *Escarpment* had not stumbled across him where his boat had run aground on a reef, he would have been as dead as if Canon Hain had stabbed him in the heart. More sharply than she meant to, she said, "You're my friend. I want you to make your home here."

"I can't." Flaren's expression was earnest. "While there's a chance to return, I have to take it."

Jai wanted to smack herself in the head. Or better, smack Flaren in the head. She had thought, or at least convinced herself, that he knew any hope of going back was a daydream and a fantasy. But maybe it was her hope that he saw the truth that was a daydream and a fantasy. "You saw the way your father looked at you. Do you truly think there is a chance to return?"

He glared at her, startled, angry, and clearly hurt. "He was testing me."

"People who love you do not require such tests!"

Flaren's stubborn jaw set. "I know you left your family because you had to. For you, it was the right thing to do. Not for me."

It was mildly infuriating that Flaren had characterized the situation that way. He had been exiled because he dared to argue with his father and an elder brother had persuaded Hain that Flaren meant to rebel against him. Jai's family had made it more than clear that they were disappointed in her personality and many faults, and that they might be indifferent to her continued existence, but they had never tried to kill her. "I left my family because I was bored with selling supplies to miners and wished to find adventure. I was selfish and willful. You did not leave your family, you were put out to die because they didn't trust you."

Flaren slammed the book down. "Then you shouldn't trust me either."

"Unlike your family, I am not a fool, or a betrayer, or the kind of foul creature who would discard a half-grown child who displeased me," Jai said.

They stared at each other. Jai thought, *Yes, I should probably have kept that to myself.* Flaren shoved to his feet. "You—My father—This is none of your business."

Jai said, stiffly, "Even I can tell when I have gone too far. I apologize. We will speak of this later."

Jai turned away from the door, and winced as she heard it slam behind her. She stomped back up on deck, too aware that she owed Flaren a dozen or so more apologies, which he would undoubtedly receive with increasing impatience.

She leaned on the railing. The wind was like warm silk and there were only a few drifts of cloud, the setting sun painting the open water a glittering gold. One of the minor Visicae islands lay in the distance, its tall cliffs overflowing with jungle greenery.

Over the past two turns Flaren had practically grown up before her eyes, turning from a sulky frightened adolescent to a trustworthy adult she called friend. She did not want to lose him, anymore than she wanted to lose Kiev or Shiri or Latal, all of whom she had known longer. *Maybe less*, she admitted privately. She loved the others like brothers and children, but Flaren had become her confidant, perhaps the closest to her in his habits of thought and sympathies.

Jai said, "Maybe I am being selfish. Maybe I want him to turn his back on these bastards because it will reinforce my own decision."

Kiev, who was leaning in the doorway of the steering cabin, shrugged. He had undoubtedly heard the argument. The wind-ship was built for lightness and its deck and inner walls were thin, something that became spectacularly obvious whenever anyone tried to have a private conversation, or when Kiev and Shiri had sex. "I think it's both. You're being selfish, but it's true that he's better off making his own way, with us or without us, than he is with those people."

"But if he doesn't believe it, it does no one any good, and he will pine about it until he does something foolish," Jai said. Dolorous Kiev didn't even try to argue with her.

☾

The raiders' lair wasn't what Jai had been expecting.

She had thought they would find a small island with a fishing village or town, abandoned or with a few inhabitants barely holding on, that had been temporarily taken over by the raiders. But these raiders had no island at all.

Outlined by the waves it created, a round stone ridge stood just below the surface, forming a great flooded cauldron. Jai couldn't tell if it had been built to stand in the water and had sunk or been flooded as the sea rose, or if it was some natural formation. A shelf stretched across about half the cauldron, forming a platform only a scant pace deep, then dropped away into impenetrably dark water. That had to be a cave entrance, possibly built by the sealings, probably a passage down into whatever structure lay further under the surface. It was an inhabited darkness that made her flesh creep.

And she saw why the Issilans had preferred an air-going craft to deliver the ransom.

The captured Issilan ship lay some distance from the outermost edge of the cauldron, and it was caught inside a giant ball-shaped net. Jai had seen a great many things in her time but nothing like that.

The ship was a sailer with a graceful ironwood hull and three masts, the sails now furled. A metal spine curved up from the water in front of the ship's prow, arched over it, and disappeared below the surface behind the stern. The mesh of the net attached to it was very fine. It must be impossible to cut or surely the crew would have freed themselves already. Jai saw the trap must have laid flat in the water and been brought into place beneath the ship where it sat at anchor. Then some mechanism had allowed it to spring up and enclose the ship, like a hunter's trap for a big land predator.

The crew and passengers had come out on deck at the sight of the *Escarpment*, calling out and waving. Jai saw they were all heavily armed, with tools, clubs, fishing spears, and swords. Several crew members held long metal projectile weapons.

Beside her, Flaren said, "So they trapped the ship in that thing, and then hauled it here. Have you ever heard of anything like that before?"

"Never." Jai leaned on the railing. The air between she and Flaren had been heavy with the memory of their argument, and they hadn't spoken this morning. But the sight of the trapped ship had swept all that away for the moment. She wished Canon Hain had seen fit to give them more information, and not sent them off expecting ordinary pirates. "But how did they haul this thing from Visicae to here? I see no ships of any kind." She shook her head. "Shiri is partly right, as much as I hate to say it. They must be sealings."

Latal said, "If they pulled it through the water themselves, there must be a lot of them."

"Or they are very strong," Jai said grimly. "Take us over that thing, Kiev."

"It's a stand-off," Flaren said, as Kiev guided them closer to the trapped ship. "The ship can't escape, but the crew is too well-armed for the pirates to get near it."

"Yes." Jai waved a distracted hand at Shiri, who interpreted the gesture and went to get the speaking tube from the steering cabin. "It would be nice if we could throw down a hook and haul it away, but we can't possibly pull it through the water." The *Escarpment* might be able to drag the sailer, but not the weight of the large mechanism that held it. And she would bet Shiri's share of the pay that the net device was securely anchored from below. Shiri brought the speaking tube, and Jai used it to call to the figures below, "Are you well?"

"For now!" One of the men below shouted up to her. "Were you sent to help us?"

"Yes, we have a ransom for you, sent from Issila! Have you tried to cut through that mesh?"

"We've tried! It's some sort of metal."

That was that. "Be patient! We will get you free!" Jai handed the tube back to Shiri and told Kiev. "Go to the cauldron."

The deck angled beneath their feet as Kiev turned the ship back toward the cauldron. Jai tapped her nails on the railing, thinking. This was going to be tricky.

"I still think I should deliver the ransom alone," Flaren said, his jaw set in a stubborn line.

"I still don't care what you think," Jai told him, and added to Latal, "Get two harness lines ready, just in case."

Latal lifted her brows. "Just in case?"

"I'm hoping we can do this the easy way." They were over the cauldron now, about a hundred paces above the surface. There wasn't much wind today, so it was fairly easy for Kiev to keep them in place. Jai took the speaking tube and leaned over the railing. She felt like a fool, talking to a bare circle of water, but there was nothing else to talk to. "We have come from Issila with your ransom. Let the captive ship leave, and we will lower it down to you."

She stood back to see all the others staring at her. She shrugged. "It's worth a try."

"No one's coming," Latal observed after a moment. "Maybe they can't hear you from under the water."

Flaren muttered, "They're probably laughing too hard."

Jai took the high road and ignored that. Time stretched on, and she tapped her fingers impatiently on the railing. She was supremely reluctant to simply drop the ransom box into the sea, with no idea whether the hostage ship would be released or not. Or if the pirates had grown tired of waiting, abandoned their captives aboard the trapped ship to starve to death, and left the area to look for easier prey.

"There," Flaren breathed, and a moment later Jai spotted movement in the water below. She leaned forward, staring.

Water churned in the center of the cauldron. Then a figure climbed up out of the foam onto the shelf that was just below the surface, standing knee-deep in the water.

It was a tall thin man with gray skin. Kiev nudged Jai's arm, handing her their distance glass. She took it, focusing the lenses on the figure. With the glass, she could see the man had scales, long tangled hair like green sea wrack, and clawed hands. He wore no clothing except for metal armbands. A sealing, obviously. "He doesn't look that frightening," Jai said aloud, not quite sure she believed it. There was something about the figure that gave her an uneasy feeling.

"From a distance," Shiri pointed out nervously.

The figure looked up at the *Escarpment*, and began to make motions with his hands.

After a belated moment, Jai realized what he was doing. "Shiri, what is he saying?"

Shiri leaned over the railing. The sign language was an old one, used by the myriad inhabitants of the Ataran coast and islands when common language failed them. Jai had never mastered more than the rudiments but fortunately Shiri was expert.

After a moment, Shiri reported, "He says we're to bring the ransom down to him, and he will release the ship."

It was as ridiculous as Jai's initial offer. She shook her head. "Tell him to release the ship, and we will give him the ransom."

The figure signed back, and Shiri looked surprised. "He says to bring the ransom halfway down, and he'll release the ship."

"That is . . . quite reasonable," Jai said, startled herself. She had expected a much longer negotiation.

"Too reasonable?" Latal whispered to Jai.

It was certainly an opinion shared by their pessimist Kiev, glaring suspiciously from the doorway of the steering cabin. "It's a trap," he hissed.

"How?" Flaren asked.

Kiev withdrew from the doorway.

Jai studied the cauldron, the sealing, the glittering but uninformative surface of the sea. The shelf of rock a step or so below the surface was visibly bare and innocent of any trap. The sealings seemed to want the ransom, as a substitute for the trapped ship they could not approach for fear of being shot. And she could not see how this could turn into a trap for a wind-ship. "I think we will have to do it anyway."

"I'll take the ransom down," Flaren said immediately, giving Jai a look she could only interpret as mutinous.

"We will do it together," Jai told him firmly, and sent Latal for the ransom box.

"Be careful," Shiri said, twitching with nerves as he watched Flaren and Jai put their climbing harnesses on.

Latal put the ransom box into the basket, securing the catch on the lid so it wouldn't fly open on the way down. Then she fetched two long fighting clubs from the steering cabin, used only when they docked at the rowdier ports. "Take these, just in case."

Jai fixed her club to her belt, made sure Flaren had done the same, then they secured their harnesses. Jai led the way though she had to elbow Flaren hard in the ribs to do so, stepping through the break in the railing and letting the ropes take her weight. Latal manned the *ilene*-powered winch, lowering Jai and Flaren down toward the water.

Jai watched the surface come closer. Over to her left, the dark stretch that marked the entrance to the underwater cave grew darker and colder the closer they approached it.

When they were about thirty paces above the surface, she called up to Latal, "Far enough!"

They jolted to a halt, and waited.

Time seemed to crawl. The sun was warm even on Jai's thick skin; she worried that Flaren would burn bright gold by the time this was over. The sealing waiting below them stood like a statue. She saw the crew of the ship watching, too far away to make out any detail or expression. "What are they waiting for?" Flaren said, keeping his voice low.

"Perhaps for us to give up and drop the ransom," Jai replied. She had no intention of doing so.

A loud clang made Jai jump, but it was only the metal trap around the Issilan ship releasing. *Finally*, she thought in relief. The mesh sides fell back into the water with a huge splash, creating a small wave that a few moments later rippled the water below her dangling feet. The crewmen climbed with frantic speed into the rigging, and the sails dropped and billowed.

They waited until the ship began to slowly move, its sails catching the wind, its progress helped along by the emergency oars that shot out of the portals below the railings. When it was well underway, Jai turned to the basket, pulling it toward her to get the ransom box. And then everything went to the cold-hells in a hamper.

Flaren yelped in pure alarm, his voice higher than she had ever heard it before. She whipped around, startled, just in time to see a giant brown object shoot up out of the deep water. It spread gracefully in the air, revealing itself to be a giant net. Then it struck the side of the *Escarpment*. The wind-ship jerked downward and dropped at the sudden weight, and Jai landed in the water with a tremendous splash.

Struggling to her feet in the thigh deep water, gasping a curse that was incoherent even to herself, Jai dragged the club off her belt.

Flaren staggered to his feet and struck the sealing as it lunged for him, but the club glanced off its thick skull. It grabbed him, sending him staggering back. Jai swung at it, aiming for the spine in the middle of its back rather than the head. The blow landed with a resounding crack, and the sealing jolted forward and knocked Flaren down into the water. Jai struggled to reach Flaren, and more sealings popped up from below the surface.

She laid about with the club, striking everything that reached for her, having some satisfaction in that these greedy creatures clearly did not expect her to be as strong as she was. Her harness tugged at her, pulling her across the stony shelf; she had no time to look up but feared it was the *Escarpment* being dragged down by the net. Whacking a sealing across the face, she caught a glimpse of cables stretching up from the water, drawn tight with the strain as the *Escarpment* fought to escape.

The last sealing fell before Jai and she sloshed forward to Flaren. He was down, splashing frantically as he wrestled a sealing determined to drown him. Jai grabbed the sealing by the fins on its shoulder blades, wrenched it back and away. Flaren flailed free and Jai had a chance to look up.

The *Escarpment* was heeled over, the net caught on the folded sail and the steering cabin drawn tight, dragging the ship to its doom. But Shiri and Latal, wearing climbing harnesses, cut at the cables with a big cross saw meant for severing fouled anchor lines. *We're not dead yet*, Jai thought, and shouted at Flaren, "Get up there and help them!"

Flaren shoved to his feet, and Jai reached for her harness, fumbling for Kiev's emergency trigger device which she swore by all that was holy she would never make fun of again. The trigger would activate the winch, drawing them up, and Kiev had been very proud of it even though they had never needed it before.

Both their lines dragged in the water, slack and limp as the *Escarpment* was forced further down, and she hoped the thing would still work. Then something struck her from behind, slamming her face-first down into the water. Sealing teeth crunched into her shoulder and ground against her leather harness strap. Jai shoved against the stone and managed to get her legs under her to push upward. The creature hung on, claws scraped at her skull, defeated for a moment by her harder bones. Then it went limp and she flung it off.

She turned to see Flaren stood bent over the creature's limp body, still holding his club. More sealings shot up from below the surface and charged toward them. Jai found the trigger-thing and told Flaren, "Go, hit your thing!"

It wasn't very coherent, but she knew he understood her. She knew because he held up the frayed end of his line, slashed apart by one of the sealing's claws. Jai cursed, grabbed his harness and said, "Hold on!"

He wrapped his arms around her and grabbed onto the back straps of her harness. Jai hit the trigger, and with relief, saw her line jerk and start to spool up toward the ship. It went tight and she felt her feet leave the stone, then the water. Flaren slid down to her waist but held on. And she made the mistake of thinking, *We're going to make it!*

Flaren gasped, and they jerked to a halt. His voice grating, he said, "They've got me." She looked down to see two sealings hanging off his legs. She heard the trigger mechanism whirring as it strained to lift the extra weight.

"Damn these persistent bastards," Jai said, racking her brain for a solution. She had lost her club, not that she could reach the sealings with it anyway.

"I'll let go," Flaren said. He didn't sound as if it was the fondest wish of his heart, but she felt his hands loosen on the straps.

Jai tightened her hold on his harness. "If you let go, I will come down there and beat you like a drum."

He glared up at her. "There's nothing else we can do!"

Jai was damn tired of being the only optimist on this crew. "Shut up and let me think!" She looked up at the ship, which was alarmingly close to them, only about twenty paces above her head. Latal and Shiri had managed to saw through one of the cables attached to the net and were at work on a second but three others still held. The deck angled toward her and she saw the winch, the *ilene* sparking in the grip of its case—And remembered what happened when *ilene* touched water. "Latal," she screamed at the top of her lungs. "Throw the lamps in the water! The *ilene*!"

Latal almost dropped her end of the saw, looked down, her face a desperate mask of terror and resolve. Jai knew she must look much the same.

Latal shoved away from the railing, shouting to Kiev. Leaving Shiri to saw at the cable as best he could, she scrambled up the deck and into the steering cabin.

The sealings were trying to climb Flaren's body like he was a ladder, even as he kicked and struck at them. The trigger-thing sung in Jai's ear, straining against the weight, and couldn't last much longer. Then the whole case of their spare *ilene* blocks tumbled past Jai's head and hit the water's surface.

The water crackled, hissed, steam rushed up. The sealings screamed, high piercing cries. A moment later Flaren cried out and then Jai added to the chorus. It was like invisible fire had rushed up from the water and raced over her skin. She kicked desperately at the only sealing in reach and it let go, falling away. Its fall jolted the next; it lost its grip on Flaren and dropped. Jai and Flaren jerked into motion as the winch hauled them up toward the ship.

They reached the railing and Jai seized it with her one free arm as if she never intended to let go. Her hands were numb and her skin sparked with pain, the fading effect of the *ilene*, and the railing seemed as far they could get. Then Latal leaned over to grab Flaren's harness, planted a small foot on the railing for leverage, and flung her weight back, pulling them both on board.

Jai collapsed on the tilted deck, highly aware they were still a hair's breadth from unpleasant death. She shoved herself up and gripped the railing, looking down.

The sealings had vanished out of range of the sparking *ilene* but the remaining cables attached to the net were still tight with the strain of holding the wind-ship. The water below steamed, but she could see the effect dissipating as the *ilene* expended its energy. "Flaren, get another saw," she croaked as he stumbled to his feet.

"Wait!" Kiev bolted past her, pausing to slam the door to the hatch that Latal had left open. "I have an idea! Everyone hold on!"

Latal grabbed the railing next to Jai and Flaren, and Shiri wrapped himself around the clamps at the base of the mast. Kiev darted into the steering cabin and shut the door. A moment later, the ship's deck tilted further, down toward the water.

"I see," Jai muttered to herself. Without anyone to man the device below, the cables went slack. The way the island heart kept the wind-ship suspended in the air didn't give them many options for maneuvering down toward the ground, but Kiev could roll the ship on its axis.

The weight of the net began to work in their favor as the ship tilted, and it gradually pulled the mass of lines free from the mast to dangle down toward the water. As Jai and the others clung to the railing, Shiri climbed the mast like a treeling and tugged at the edge of the net, finally managing to drag it free. It fell from the ship, taking their cross-saw, a lamp, and a water bucket with it. "That's it!" Jai shouted to Kiev. "Go, go!"

It was a vague command but Kiev interpreted it correctly. The *Escarpment* swung upright, then turned and moved with the wind and away from the sealings' trap.

The ransom box had been drawn up with them, still in the basket, unnoticed as they fought for their lives. Wordless, Jai retrieved it and set it on the deck. The metal was no longer vibrating; whatever spell had protected it had ended once the ransom had been "delivered." She used the prybar Flaren silently handed her to batter the lock open.

They all gathered around to look. Inside were three large water-polished rocks, such as the ships of Issila used for ballast.

"We were the ransom," Flaren said quietly. "The sealings couldn't get to the crew of the trapped sailing ship because they were too heavily armed. They offered to release the ship if they were given a substitute for their prize. So the Issilans offered to send them another ship to take its place."

Kiev took a harsh breath. "They would have been disappointed, when they sat down to eat. Only five of us aboard, for a ship with at least forty crew and passengers."

Latal hugged herself. "They wouldn't know that. They couldn't see our deck."

There was nothing to say, so for once, no one said anything. Jai picked up the box and pitched it over the side.

☾

It took them some while to recover their nerves, but by the time the ship had been restored to order, Shiri had cried a bit on Kiev's shoulder, and they had all eaten some salted fish for dinner, everyone felt much better. Though Jai refused to consider a suggestion to catch up with the freed Issilan vessel in order to dump their garbage on it. She suspected the captive ship had known nothing of the arrangement the pirates had made with Canon Hain. And she didn't think the *Escarpment* could catch the faster craft, anyway.

The sun was setting when Jai found Flaren leaning on the railing. She went to stand beside him. They were passing over a large collection of miniscule rock islands, each capped with a miniature jungle of greenery, and the sun was deepening the sky's blue to purple. Flaren seemed lost in thought, and Jai said, "I am sorry I spoke harshly to you."

Flaren shrugged it away. "You were right to."

"No. If I had been persuasive rather than strident, you might have been more inclined to listen."

"Maybe not." He smiled with somewhat bitter amusement. "Maybe I needed the slap in the face."

Jai differed. "No one needs to be slapped that hard."

After a moment, Flaren said, "My father does."

It surprised a laugh out of her. Flaren smiled. She clapped him on the shoulder, and their little wind-ship sailed on.

THE DARK
EARTH
BELOW

This novella takes place a turn and a half after the events of The Siren Depths.

Jade was having her first clutch at the end of the second rain season, and Moon was beginning to have doubts about his ability to survive the process.

She wouldn't be the first Raksura to clutch in the mountain-tree colony. Three Arbora, Rill, Dream, and Plum, had already clutched, producing eight new warriors and five new Arbora. Moon had been present for each clutching, along with half the court, and had gotten to hold the new babies.

It shocked him that they were small enough to fit into his cupped hands, blinking up at him with half-closed eyes, their scales soft and vulnerable. He had never seen Raksura who were younger than the squirming, climbing toddler phase. At that age they could even shift, though they seemed to do it at random and had little control over it. When he had imagined new babies, he hadn't realized they would be so tiny and helpless. Moon had lived in enough close quarters with groundlings to have seen births before, but somehow he hadn't expected this. It was terrifying.

"They're so small," he told Jade, sitting near the hearth in her bower. "I didn't expect that."

"If they were any bigger, there is no power in the Three Worlds that could make me do this insane thing," Jade snarled, and pushed another cushion under her back.

Jade's belly had been getting gradually larger for a while, but it was only in the past change of the month that it had gotten so big that she had had to stop shifting to her winged form and stay in the queens' level. This hadn't done much for Jade's temper, or Moon's nerves. Though it wasn't as though they had to go through this alone. There were Arbora here constantly, mentors as well as a few dozen teachers and soldiers who took turns waiting outside the bower, braced at any moment to get Jade anything she wanted.

"I just think it's a bad idea to be born all soft like that," Moon said. He had pointed out this obvious fact at Rill's clutching, even though he knew it probably made him sound like an idiot. It was almost as bad as being born into the Raksura's more vulnerable groundling form. That form used less energy and needed less food and water, and meant that part of your body was dormant, which was why it was hard to sleep deeply in a winged or Arbora form. Queens didn't have a groundling form, but their more powerful bodies didn't need one.

Jade stared at him, scaled brows lowered. "And what exactly would you like me to do about that?"

"But how can we take care of them?" Moon knew it wasn't a rational question, but it was the one haunting him.

"There are fifty Arbora out there ready to fight a Fell ruler in a pit for the right to take care of them," Jade said, and threw a cushion at him. "We'll be lucky if we see them for the first month."

At that opportune moment, Stone walked into the bower. Jade growled at him. "Nothing's changed, go away."

Knowing what Stone was here for, Moon tensed. As the court's line-grandfather, Stone was so old the color of his groundling skin and hair had faded to gray, but his senses were far more acute than a normal Raksura, and it was easier for him to hear the babies.

Stone sat down beside Jade. "You want me to check?" he asked her. He had taken an interest in all the court's births so far, but Jade was one of his direct descendants, and this was the first royal birth the court had had since moving back to the Reaches. Though Stone was also cranky and took irascible to a new level, Moon was glad to have him here. He had been the one to find Moon and bring him to the court, and he was the closest thing to a male parent Moon had ever had.

Jade hissed, annoyed. "Fine, go ahead."

Stone put a hand on her swollen belly, leaned down, and cocked his head, listening. Impatient, Jade demanded, "Well?"

Stone nodded. "Still five."

Moon let out his breath in relief. Five heartbeats, Stone meant. By this point, he thought Jade would have felt it if something drastic had changed, but it was still reassuring to know that all was well.

Jade said to Stone, "I'm not doing this again, so there better be five."

"Sure," Stone answered her absently. No one seemed particularly worried about Jade's occasional declarations that she was never having another clutch, so Moon wasn't concerned by it. At the moment, all he cared about was this clutch. He wasn't certain he could stand having another one, either. It had taken nearly a turn to conceive this one, something that Moon had thought was his fault and Jade thought was hers, until they had finally gotten the advice that sometimes it just took a while and they should stop worrying about it. Annoyingly, this advice had proven to be right.

"Where's Pearl?" Jade hissed out a sigh and punched the cushions again. "Is anything going on?"

Weirdly, all conflict between Pearl and Jade had ceased as soon as it became clear the clutch was coming to term. Pearl was the court's reigning queen and Jade's birthqueen, and they had never gotten along. Apparently queens liked clutches, and liked it when other queens had clutches, but just didn't care for the actual process of giving birth to them.

Stone checked the teapot and frowned at the contents. He had been born with one eye partially blinded by a white haze across the pupil, so when he frowned, the effect was pronounced. "Pearl's in her bower, and no, nothing's going on, unless you want to hear about how Snap thinks he's tracked down the drain blockage under the latrines below the moss-flower platform."

Disgruntled was a mild way to describe Jade's expression. She said, "Have we had any more word from Violet Springflower? Are they coming to us or are we going to have to go to them?"

Stone set the tea pot aside. "Sure, there's been a dozen courts in and out of here asking for alliances, we just didn't tell you."

Jade glared. "I wouldn't put it past you."

They had gotten word from Sunset Water that a court called Violet Springflower might be interested in an alliance and trade with them. Violet Springflower was rumored to have extensive garden platforms, some of which had been around since before the Great Leaving, when many Raksuran courts had abandoned the Reaches for more open territory. They were certain to have plant varieties that were native to the Reaches that Indigo Cloud needed. Moon said, "There's plenty of time. It's too late to plant anything new right now anyway."

"Violet Springflower is a ridiculous name for a court." Jade settled back, a grumble of discontent under her breath. "I hate these games. If they want trade, why can't they just come and ask for it?"

Stone said, "You're a queen, you tell me."

Moon rubbed his eyes wearily. He knew Stone was just distracting Jade, giving her something to expend her fluctuating temper on, but it wasn't helping what was left of his nerves.

It wasn't Jade's uncertain temper that was making the whole thing difficult. Moon was pretty certain that if he was the one with babies growing in his stomach, he would be hard to get along with right now too. It was the terror and the protective fury that sat on his chest like a weight when he thought of anything happening to this clutch.

He had thought he had felt protective of the Sky Copper clutch, and of all the children in the Indigo Cloud nurseries, but this was so much more intense. Thinking rationally about it, which wasn't easy, he knew it would lessen as the children grew older and better able to fend for themselves. At least he hoped it would.

"Moon," Stone said, and Moon realized Stone had been saying it for several moments, trying to get him to give an opinion on whether queens were arbitrary all the time or just most of it. "What is wrong with you?"

Before Moon could think of an answer that was a good lie, Jade snarled, "He's nervous about the clutch, what do you think is wrong with him? Leave him alone."

It must have been obvious from his expression. Stone nudged him and said, "Go take a break. I'll be here for a while."

"Yes," Jade said, "Go tell Balm to come in. I want to talk to someone rational!"

❨

Moon found Balm in her bower, a few levels down in the warriors' living area. Balm had a very nice bower, with a balcony looking out on the central well, next to a room with a hot bathing pool. This whole cluster of bowers had been claimed by female warriors and the older males like Vine and Sage. From what Moon could tell, they had all sensibly forced the younger males to go live somewhere else.

He knew Balm had gone down here earlier to sleep, but she was sitting on the furs near her hearth bowl, holding a book but not reading it. She looked up when he ducked in.

He said quickly, "Jade wants you to sit with her," so she wouldn't think anything was wrong.

Balm rolled the book up and tucked it back into its cover. "How is she?" She was in her groundling form, her build slim but strong, with her skin a dark bronze and her hair curly and honey-colored. Jade and Balm had come from the same clutch, and it had taken Moon a while to see it, but Balm's sharp features bore a distinct resemblance to Jade's. In her winged form she had gold scales, close to Pearl's shade.

"About the same," Moon told her. "Mad. Stone said he could still hear the babies, and everyone is acting like everything is fine."

Balm nodded. "How are you?"

Moon shrugged, and said, honestly, "I have no idea. How are you?"

"I didn't think it would be this . . . nerve-racking," Balm admitted. "The Arbora make it look so easy, even when it's their first time." She frowned as she got to her feet. "Part of me is excited and can't wait to see the babies. Another part of me is terrified something will go wrong and I feel like if I have to wait any longer, the top of my head will split. I can't think about anything else."

That was a good description of it. Moon didn't know why everyone didn't feel that way.

Balm took the direct route up the central well to the queens' hall, but Moon knew he did need a break. Flying to expend some nervous energy would make him feel better, but he had no intention of leaving the vicinity of the colony, and a few fast loops around the outside of the mountain-tree weren't very fulfilling. So he went down to the nurseries.

They were deep into the trunk of the mountain-tree, near the teachers' hall. A maze of well-lit, low-ceilinged chambers, with several shallow fountain pools, now comfortably noisy with Aeriat fledglings and young Arbora and the teachers who took care of them. Moon lay on his back on the floor in the main area and let the babies sit on his chest. It helped a little.

Most of his life had been spent in a state of painful anxiety and tension while trying to appear normal—or whatever passed for normal wherever he currently was—on the surface. Waiting for the clutch to arrive should have been easy, or at least no more nerve-racking than he was normally used to. But this tension was almost unbearable.

The other thing the arrival of the clutch would mean was the formal sealing of Moon's position in the Indigo Cloud court; he would be as much a member of the court as if he had been born here. It would be a relief to have it settled, since it would make it next to impossible to throw Moon out of the colony, no matter what happened.

Finding out that he came from Opal Night had taken a lot of the sting out of jibes involving feral solitaries and bad bloodlines polluting Indigo Cloud. It had also given him a place to go if for some reason he did get thrown out. His birthqueen Malachite had only grudgingly let Jade have him, and would have taken him back if asked. But Moon had known that if he ever wanted to leave Indigo Cloud, he would never want to see another Raksuran court again.

Maybe the anxiety came from a combination of the waiting and the responsibility that Moon would be under once the fledglings arrived. He ruffled the frill of the Arbora baby that was currently trying to sink her teeth into his collarbone. It wasn't as if he didn't want fledglings; in many ways he just wanted them to get here so he could get started raising them.

Maybe he had just used up all his capacity to live with constant anxiety over the turns and he just couldn't handle it anymore.

Frost leaned over him. "No babies yet?" The little queen was from the royal clutch who had been the only survivors of the Fell attack on the court of Sky Copper. Since arriving at Indigo Cloud, she and her two consort brothers had been the only royal Aeriat in the nurseries. Moon had wondered if she would be jealous of having to share his attention with a new royal clutch, but she seemed mostly interested in whether there would be new consorts as prospective mates for her and queens for Thorn and Bitter.

"Not yet," Moon told her. "Several more days."

"That's what you said last time," Frost complained. She was in her Arbora form at the moment, her mane of spines still soft and short.

"That's because the last time you asked was yesterday."

Thorn plunked down beside her, and pulled one of the Arbora babies off Moon's chest and into his own lap. "What's wrong?"

"Nothing." Moon started to disentangle himself from the other clinging babies. He should get back to the queens' hall, and he wasn't sure he was up to an interrogation by the Sky Copper clutch. "This is just how long having a clutch takes."

"No, I know that." Thorn was patient with this obtuseness. "What's wrong with you?"

"Uh." While Moon was struggling for an answer Bitter sat down next to Thorn. Moon handed him the last baby. He wasn't sure whether to be honest or not. Maybe not. He didn't want to bring up the possibility that something might go wrong during the birth. The Sky Copper clutch seemed to be looking forward to it with nothing but happy anticipation and he didn't want to ruin that. "I don't know."

Thorn nodded slowly, as if Moon had said something a great deal more meaningful. He said, "When you figure it out, it won't be so bad."

Moon didn't know how to answer that one. Thorn was by far the most perceptive member of the clutch, though since Bitter still preferred not to speak or fly where anyone else could see him and might be concealing an entire second identity as far as Moon knew, it was hard to tell. Bitter patted his arm sympathetically. Frost, queen-like, just said, "Well, hurry up and get over it, and bring us a new royal clutch."

☾

Moon went back up to the queens' hall and found Chime, Root, and Song gathered around the bowl hearth in the sitting area that was usually used for meeting with foreign courts. Many of Jade's warriors had been lingering up there off and on for news, and to be ready to run errands. Raksuran warriors were all infertile, so babies were more a spectator activity for them.

The queens' hall was a big chamber, one side open to the colony tree's central well. There was a fountain against the inner wall that fell down into a shallow pool, and above it a huge sculpture of a queen. Her outspread wings stretched out across the walls to circle the entire hall to finally meet tip to tip. Her scales, set with polished sunstones, glinted faintly in the soft light of shells mounted on the walls. The open gallery of the mostly untenanted consorts' level looked down over the hall.

Ember, Pearl's young consort, had just taken a seat with the warriors. As Moon wandered up, Ember pushed a cushion over for him and said, "No news?"

"No. Stone says everything's still fine, though." Moon sat down, close enough to feel the heat of the stones in the hearth. The other side effect of waiting with nothing to do was a kind of pointless, causeless exhaustion; he felt as if his muscles should be aching even though he hadn't actually done anything more physical than climbing or walking up and down the colony.

"I never got a chance to do a queen's clutching," Chime said, handing Moon a cup of tea. Chime's groundling form had dark bronze skin like Moon and flyaway brown hair, and he was Moon's closest friend in the court. Though he was now a warrior, he had been an Arbora and a mentor before the court had moved to the new colony. Since warriors couldn't be mentors, he had lost his ability to do magic. It wasn't something that happened often, Arbora changing suddenly into warriors, but it was apparently a natural response to a failing court, and the old colony had been on its last legs before Moon had arrived. Chime seemed more reconciled to it now, but the change had had some odd effects on him. "Flower talked a lot about what Pearl was like, and said she almost got some permanent scars."

"It's the consort's duty to prevent that," Ember said. He was still slender, but he had filled out a little and no longer looked like a tall fledgling, too young to be out of the nurseries let alone taken by a reigning queen.

His groundling form was a lighter bronze than usual for Indigo Cloud or for Emerald Twilight, where he was from. He also had a sweet nature which was somewhat unusual for the Aeriat of both courts. He added, "Of course, that's easier said than done." He reached over and squeezed Moon's wrist. "I'm sure Jade won't be like that."

It was pretty clear that Ember wasn't sure of that at all, but it wasn't Jade that Moon was worried about. It wouldn't be any worse than facing a Fell progenitor, or a crossbreed Fell queen, or his mother.

Moon liked Ember, but the only thing they had in common was that they were both Raksura. Their lives had been so different, they might as well have been different species. Except that Moon could think of several members of different species that he had had a much deeper understanding with.

Song sipped tea and said, "Moon's not afraid of Jade." She set her cup down. She had a passing resemblance to Balm, though was much younger. The scar across her throat where she had almost been killed by a Fell was still visible against her dark bronze skin, but it had faded in the past few months. "Moon, what are you afraid of?"

Moon turned his own cup around, looking into the green dregs, debating whether to be honest or not. He finally said, "That something will happen to the clutch."

Root shook the tea pot and everyone else nodded absently, as if he hadn't said anything particularly interesting. "Everyone's afraid of that," Song said. "I mean, are you afraid of anything? I've never seen you seem scared, even of the Fell."

"I'm afraid of a lot of things, especially the Fell," Moon said. It was somewhat disconcerting to speak your secret dark fear and have it discarded as inadequate. His fear for the clutch felt overwhelming, and in a completely different category from the more commonplace fears of being eaten.

"Come on, tell us," Song persisted.

"What is wrong with you today?" Chime asked her, exasperated. He slapped Root's hand away from the tea pot. "Why are you interrogating the first consort?"

"I'm bored," Song admitted. "There's nothing to do but wait."

"It has been boring lately," Root seconded, finally leaving the tea pot alone. He had the reddish-brown hair and copper skin common to some of Indigo Cloud's bloodlines, and the big mouth and lack of discretion that was also sadly common to many of Indigo Cloud's warriors. "No trading, no exploring, hardly any hunting, and all the Arbora want to talk about is babies. Please Moon, tell us things."

Chime eyed Root with disfavor. "He's going to tell you to shut up."

Fortunately at that moment Bead came out of the passage that led to the main stairwell. She shifted to her groundling form because Moon and Ember were in theirs; this was a basic courtesy in formal situations for Raksuran courts, so engrained everyone but Moon did it without having to think. She asked, "Is Pearl in her bower?"

"Yes, she is," Ember said, and Moon asked, "What's wrong?" Because something was obviously wrong. Bead hadn't stopped to wash the gardening mud off her scales and it had transferred to her kilt and her bare feet.

"Something odd happened outside," Bead said. Her expression was a combination of worry and excitement. "We think someone's sent us a message."

☾

Moon followed with Chime and some of the other warriors as Bead led Pearl and Stone outside to one of the colony tree's garden platforms. As Moon flew down from the knothole entrance with the others, it hit him how much a relief it was to be outside. The air was fresh from a recent rain that had heightened the tree's own musky-sweet scent, and his wings felt as if they hadn't been stretched for a month. Maybe a few fast circuits around the tree's clearing wouldn't be as unfulfilling as he thought.

The platforms grew on all the mountain-trees and formed the suspended forest, the multi-leveled midsection of the Reaches, below the overarching canopy but well above the dangers of the forest floor. The trees' thick branches grew together and intertwined in broad swathes, and collected windblown dirt that eventually grew grasses and small forests, collected water, and became home to a large number of the creatures that lived in the Reaches. Including predators. On the colony tree the multiple levels of platforms had been planted as gardens and orchards, fed by the water expelled through the tree's knothole. The waterfall fell from pools on platform to platform, until it vanished in the mists above the forest floor.

Vine carried Bead, who directed them down toward the platform with the large patches of berry bushes. They landed out towards the edge, where Braid, one of the Arbora hunters, stood holding something that looked like a dead bladder fish. He was surrounded by a group of curious Arbora and warriors.

As they approached, Bead continued her explanation, "We noticed it when it floated up past the groundfruit garden. We thought it was an animal, and we were keeping an eye on it to make sure it didn't come at us. But then Needle saw it had that tied to it."

Needle, a young teacher, held up a big leaf rolled and tied with a dried vine, with a purple-blue flower tucked into the knot. "Briar flew out and got it, but she accidentally poked the bladder thing with a claw and all the air came out."

Stone took the dead bladder fish from Braid and held it up. It was actually several smaller membranes carefully sewn together, like the air bladder ships that the Aventerans used, but much smaller. Moon said, "Which direction did it come from?" Stone handed him the bladder, and he handed it to Chime, who spread it out to examine it.

"Up from below," Braid said, pointing down. Several of the warriors went to lean over the edge of the platform, but the mist was rising and Moon doubted they would be able to see anything.

"Hmm," was Pearl's comment. The reigning queen, she was a head taller than any of the Aeriat. Her scales were brilliant gold, the webbed pattern overlaying them a deep blue. The frilled mane behind her head was bigger than Jade's, and there were more frills on the tips of her folded wings and on the end of her tail. She wore only jewelry, a broad necklace with gold chains and polished blue stones. She held out a hand and Needle hurriedly put the leaf scroll into it. Pearl briefly examined the flower, then sliced through the vine with her claws and unrolled the leaf. The warriors and Arbora were too respectful of Pearl and her temper to cluster around. But Stone stepped in to look past Pearl's shoulder and Moon stepped in to look past his.

Scratched onto the leaf's green surface was a series of rough drawings. One was clearly meant to be the colony tree. The second showed a figure that had to be a winged Raksura flying down toward the base of the tree. The third depicted the Raksura standing with several bipedal figures among the tree roots. "That's got to be a message from the Kek," Moon said.

"Did we know the Kek could make these air bladders?" Chime asked, clearly fascinated.

"Presumably," Pearl said dryly. She handed the leaf to Stone. "Did they send messages this way in the past?"

"Maybe. I don't remember." Stone rolled the leaf up and handed it to Bead, who carried it away and unrolled it again to show the warriors. "I'll drop down and see what they want."

Moon took a breath to say he was going too, then thought about how far that was from Jade's bower. No, he couldn't risk it.

Watching him, Pearl said to Stone, "Take him with you."

Moon said, "I need to stay here." It took an effort to keep his spines flat. His temper was suddenly close to the surface. He knew it was just nerves, but knowing it didn't seem to help.

Pearl's expression was somewhere between annoyance and sympathy. It was how she had looked at him for the past month. Which was better than some of the other ways she had looked at him, but still. "It won't happen today. Or tomorrow, for that matter. Just go." She turned away.

"How do you know?" Moon couldn't stop himself from saying it, though he was well aware that Pearl's personal experience with clutching greatly exceeded his.

Pearl didn't answer, but the dismissive flick of her spines was eloquent. She took three long steps and bounded into the air.

Stone gave Moon a shove to the head, but not hard enough to make him stagger. Stone said, "She's right. Are you coming?"

Moon hesitated, but Chime and every other warrior on the platform was watching him hopefully. If he went, Stone would probably let some of them go too. He knew he needed a break from tension. Maybe everyone else did too. It was still an effort not to sound sulky about it. "All right."

$$\left(\right.$$

In the end, Stone only let ten warriors accompany them, including Chime, Root, Song, and Vine, who had all been to see the Kek before. Moon knew half the court would have come if Stone had let them; everyone was curious about what the Kek wanted.

The Kek were groundlings who lived in the eternal twilight of the forest floor among the roots of mountain-trees. They preferred colony trees, and according to Stone, it was a common belief among Raksuran courts that Kek were good for the health of the tree.

Moon and the others followed Stone down the trunk of the mountain-tree, using the updraft of the waterfall, their wings out and cupped to turn the headlong dive into a more leisurely descent. The light under the mountain-tree's canopy was always dim and green, but it grew darker as they dropped past the last of the tree's platforms and into the lower part of the forest. There was a way down inside the tree as well, and doors out to the root area that were always kept securely sealed. But it was better to go this way and not open a passage into the lower part of the tree until they knew what the Kek wanted. The forest floor was far more dangerous than the suspended forest. It wasn't quite as dangerous with Stone here, who as a line-grandfather had a wingspan that was more than three times the size of Moon's twenty pace span. Most predators tended to avoid him.

Moon hoped nothing was wrong, that the Kek weren't asking for help with some disaster. The higher ground among the tree roots was said to be somewhat safer than the deep Reaches, the gorges and rocky outcrops and swamps that formed between the mountain-trees, but it couldn't be that much better. It helped that the Kek had little meat on their stick-like bones and seemed to be more plant than animal. There were few reasons for predators to be attracted to them.

As they passed down through the last layer of mist, Chime said, "I didn't know the Kek could build anything like that air bladder device. They've never done it before."

"They probably don't need them very often," Moon said. It seemed pretty simple to make, just some membranes, probably from snail skin, and a fire to heat the air to fill it. Down here, the fire was probably the hard part.

They landed on the ridge of a giant root, about forty paces above the spongy moss coating the ground. The great wall of the tree stretched up behind them to vanish in the mist. To the west were the ponds and swamps filled with the large snails that the Raksura sometimes harvested, and to the east the Kek village spread out through the roots.

The houses were big round structures woven from sticks, and they hung from the undersides of the roots that arched up off the ground. They were connected by a web of vine rope that the Kek walked along when the ground was too wet even for their light weight. It was a relatively dry day, and piles of grass mats lay under the houses, where the Kek sat braiding vines and doing obscure things with piles of flowers and other vegetation.

The Kek must have spotted the Raksura as soon as they dropped out of the mist; several had gathered around to wait for their arrival. They waved and made noises that seemed to indicate relief and pleasure to see them. Keeping his voice low, Chime commented, "Everything looks all right."

Moon thought so too. He was glad that nothing seemed badly wrong, but it was going to be a little disappointing if the Kek had sent the message just because they wanted to trade snail shells for more interesting flowers, or something similar. Stone tucked his wings in, and jumped to the ground, then shifted to groundling to give Moon and the others room.

The Kek had legs and arms that looked like lightly furred sticks, and their torsos were narrow and flat. Their heads were squarish, the eyes and mouth round, the nose just a slit, and their middles looked like they were all ribs. They wore drapes of vines as clothing, and bits of snail shells, insect carapaces, and flowers as decoration. Moon had never been able to tell what their sex organs were or where they kept them. He thought of the village elder Kof as male, mostly because the white stringy things growing out of his face and body were reminiscent of the beards that some groundlings grew. But the Kek could have had one gender or two or six or a dozen for all Moon knew; it had never seemed polite or relevant to ask and the language barrier kept it from ever coming up in casual conversation.

Kof moved forward to greet them. He was festooned with vines and wore necklaces made of tiny shells, and like the others seemed glad to see them. He gestured for the Raksura all to come forward into the village.

Moon followed Stone. He didn't shift to groundling, mainly because it was easier to get the moss off his scales than his skin. One of the nice things about the Kek was that they genuinely didn't seem to care. They had been a little nervous at the first meeting with the court, since at the time Indigo Cloud had arrived these Kek hadn't seen Raksura for more than twenty turns. But they seemed to like watching Raksura shift, and there weren't many groundlings who felt that way.

As they walked, Kof spoke to Stone, making gestures with the leaf-wrapped stick he carried. The structure of the Kek throat made it difficult for them to speak other languages, and equally difficult for other species to speak their language. They communicated with the Raksura in a kind of pidgin form of Raksuran and Kek that was often woefully inadequate. Moon suspected it was woefully inadequate now, from the way Stone's brow was furrowed in frustration.

When Kof stopped talking, Stone said, "They're asking for help. Some of their people are missing."

"Missing? From the village?" Moon's spines twitched. If some predator was creeping around the tree roots . . .

"No, they were hunters." Stone shook his head impatiently as Chime started to point out that the Kek didn't eat meat. "Plant hunters. That's what took me so long to understand him. We don't have a common word for it. The Kek have hunters who go out looking for new varieties of plants. Or at least that's what I think he means. The hunters were late coming back, and the Kek who went after them found traces where they were supposed to be, but no sign of them, and they couldn't track them. They've been missing for three days now."

Moon winced. This wasn't going to end well. Kof and the others nearby watched them with a hopeful intensity that was obvious even though Moon had trouble reading Kek expressions.

Vine offered, "We can look for them. Maybe we can find—" He glanced self-consciously at Kof, obviously reconsidering the words *their bodies* or *what's left of them*, even though the Kek probably couldn't understand him. "Something to show what happened to them."

Song said, "I'll go," and was seconded immediately by Root, Briar, and Aura.

Stone turned to Kof and said some Kek words. Kof shook his staff in approval and tugged on Stone's arm. Just about any other kind of groundling would never have dared to do that to a Raksura, let alone Stone, but Kof had never shown any inclination to fear them. Maybe the Kek thought Raksura were lucky, or good for the tree, the way the Raksura thought about the Kek. Kof went toward the other Kek, gesturing and talking, obviously filling them in on the conversation.

"Did they say how far it was?" Moon asked. Between the bad light of the forest floor and the uncertain terrain, it wouldn't be easy, but he could see why the Kek had summoned them. Warriors would still be able to move faster and more safely than Kek searchers.

"It's about a day's walk for them," Stone said. He lifted a brow at Moon. "You coming?"

Moon settled his spines. "No." It was too far. They would be away for at least the rest of the day and might stay out all night; he didn't want to be away from Jade that long. "I'll tell Pearl what you want to do." He didn't think Pearl would object to Stone leading a rescue mission. Not that Pearl was particularly fond of the Kek; she was mostly indifferent to their existence.

Stone nodded, accepting Moon's refusal to go with neither approval nor disapproval. He said, "If she agrees, send somebody down with some light stones and other supplies."

"Right. Do you want to take any hunters?" The Arbora hunters were far better at tracking than the Aeriat warriors, but they were used to doing it in the suspended forest, not down here.

"No. The Kek plant hunters are better for this." Stone's expression turned wry. "I don't want to give the Arbora any ideas about hunting expeditions down here."

Moon had to admit that was probably for the best. He leapt back up to the nearest root. There was a scrabble and scrape of claws as Chime followed him. Moon asked him, "You're not going with Stone?"

"No." Chime shivered his spines in mock-horror. "I'm not interested in exploring the forest floor. I feel like it's something that's only going to happen right before I die, so I want to put it off as long as possible."

Moon had to admit, it wasn't pleasant down here, even though the Kek seemed to like it. He crouched and then leapt into the air, and flapped hard to drive himself upward and into the waterfall's updraft. He was a little glad Chime wasn't going, even though the search would be safer in Stone's company. But safer was relative.

And Moon knew he was going to get even less sleep this night than usual, worrying about Stone and the warriors and the missing Kek, added to the now-familiar anxiety over the incipient clutch.

☾

Once they were back inside the colony, Chime went down to the teachers' hall to arrange the light stones and supplies Stone had asked for, and Moon went up to the queens' hall. From the voices, Pearl was in her bower. Moon shifted to groundling and walked in, and she looked up sharply, her spines lifting. "Well?" She was sitting with Ember, Floret, and some of her other warriors. She had clearly been waiting on a report, so Moon was glad he had come immediately. She had been far less critical of him since the clutch had been conceived, but that only went so far.

"It was the Kek asking for help," he told her, and explained what had happened.

By the time he finished the story, the spade-shape at the tip of Pearl's tail was stirring in annoyance. She said, "It's probably too late for these hunters, but tell Stone to go ahead. We might as well be seen to do what we can."

It was grudging, but Moon supposed that Pearl thought that since the Kek had come with the colony tree, she was therefore stuck with them and obligated to help them not get eaten.

Obviously trying to sound casual and not too eager, Floret offered, "I could go with them. If they needed someone else." The boredom of the past few months clearly wasn't confined to Jade's warriors.

Ember said, "I've never seen a real Kek, just drawings." He leaned against Pearl's side. "Maybe you could take me to visit them. It would show concern, over what happened to their hunters."

Pearl's spines flicked and Moon ducked out of the bower before she decided to take it out on him, or he got conscripted to take Ember to meet the Kek.

He made it across the width of the hall and into Jade's bower. Inside was a reassuringly commonplace scene, with Jade and Balm on cushions near the hearth. A kettle and tea cups sat nearby, and someone had brought a plate of flatbread and fruit. This wasn't surprising, as the Arbora had been bringing food continuously since Jade had stopped being able to shift. Balm had an open book in her lap and both she and Jade looked surprised by Moon's sudden appearance.

"What happened? Was the message from the Kek?" Jade demanded.

Moon dropped down beside the hearth. He told them about the missing plant hunters, and Jade hissed under her breath. She said, "The most interesting thing to happen in months and I'm stuck in here."

Balm lifted her shoulders. "It's not that interesting. They're looking for some poor dead Kek. There's little chance of finding any of them alive."

"They found us when we were missing," Jade countered.

"We weren't on the forest floor," Balm pointed out. "It's much more dangerous down there."

That was the sad truth. No matter how dangerous the suspended forest was, the lower levels were worse. *Stone will be with them*, Moon told himself. It wasn't as if the presence of an extra consort would help them find the Kek any faster. He just wished he believed that.

Jade frowned at Moon. "Why are you here? Why aren't you down there finding out what's going on so you can tell me?"

Moon didn't want to explain his reasons for not going, and he didn't want to start an argument by pointing out that Jade had just told him to be in two places simultaneously. "I decided not to go." He added, hoping it would forestall further discussion, "Stone thought I should stay here."

Jade's gaze narrowed suspiciously. "Since when do you listen to Stone? Since when do you listen to anyone?"

She poked at the fruit, as if finding it as wanting as Moon and the rest of the court. "And this is the kind of thing you love to do. It's more like you to sneak off with Stone without telling me."

That was completely irrational. "That is not more like me."

"The one time I want you to do something like that, here you are." She eyed him. "I bet they haven't left yet."

"I am not going." Moon couldn't make it any more clear than that. "I don't want to leave you for that long in case something happens."

"Like what?" Jade asked, apparently genuinely baffled.

Moon rolled backward and lay flat on the floor, exasperated. "Oh, I don't know. Some queen might have a clutch early. Or might have a problem with a clutch, and maybe, just maybe, want a consort around—"

"What's wrong with him?" Jade asked Balm.

Balm grimaced at her. "Jade, stop it. What do you think is wrong? He's worried about your clutch."

Jade made a sound that was half laugh, half snarl. "I haven't had it yet, and right now anything would have to go through me to get to it, and considering how much I really want to kill something, that would be a very bad idea."

None of this was helping. Moon flung an arm over his eyes. "What?" Jade demanded. "What's wrong with you now? If you're going to sulk, go do it somewhere else."

Balm hissed through her teeth in exasperation. "Jade, leave him alone. It's his first clutch too. And I'm worried about you just as much. It's not rational, but we can't help it."

"It is rational," Moon muttered. Sometimes he hated Raksura.

Jade said, "All right, fine, everyone's worried." She slumped over on a cushion. "I understand that, but I'm dying of boredom!"

Moon sat up for one last try. "If it was the other way around, if I was the one having the clutch, you'd feel the same way."

Jade bared her fangs at him. "Right, when you have a clutch in your belly, you get to decide what's dangerous!"

Moon snarled, shifted, and flung himself out of the bower. Jade shouted after him, "If you won't go look for the Kek at least find out what's going on and come back and tell me!"

☾

Moon went with Chime and Floret and Sand to take the light stones and the supply packs to Stone and the others. He wanted to see them off, and despite the fact that he knew he was right and Jade was wrong, and the fact that consorts weren't supposed to go searching for missing Kek anyway, something that seemed to have slipped Jade's mind at the moment, he felt guilty that he wasn't going. He was no more an expert on the forest floor than any other Raksura, but he had a lot more experience at surviving in strange places.

It helped a little that Floret was going, as were Vine, Song, and Root. They had all been on much longer and stranger trips than this.

They found Stone and the others waiting at the edge of the village with the Kek who had volunteered to go along. Moon handed over the pack he carried to Stone, while Chime and Sand passed out the others. "Pearl told Floret she could go with you."

"Good," Stone said, opening the pack's flap to check the contents. The packs contained skins for water, some dried meat and bread, flints, a coil of rope, and some other items that would come in handy in emergencies. One of the packs was heavier than the others and glowing a little. It contained rocks spelled by the mentors to emit light, and Stone took charge of it. He slung it over his shoulder and said, "We'll give it a day, unless we pick up their trail."

The four Kek plant hunters who would be going along carried bags woven out of vines and braided grasses. They also had some sharpened sticks that could be weapons or just useful for poking at plants. They stood near the warriors, clearly anxious to get started.

Moon told the warriors, "Be careful."

Stone added, "And don't get distracted. Root, I'm mainly talking to you."

"Hah, he's joking," Root told the others. "I'm never distracted when we're doing something important. Really," he added, as Song flicked her spines and eyed him deliberately.

"You bring this on yourself, Root," Chime said, and Stone cut off the conversation by shifting to his winged form.

Moon stepped back. In the green twilight, the odd blurring when he tried to look at Stone directly was worse. As a line-grandfather, Stone's winged form had differences other than size, though they weren't always apparent. He never spoke in his winged form, and Moon wasn't sure if he could, and didn't like to ask.

It didn't seem to frighten the Kek. One of them lifted his arms and waved, and Stone wrapped a clawed hand around him and lifted him to his shoulder. Then Stone leapt upward and landed on the arch of the nearest root. Vine, Sage, and Song picked up the other three Kek and all the warriors leapt to follow Stone.

Watching the group move away through the dark foliage, Chime sighed. "I hope they find the Kek, but . . . "

Moon settled his spines. The chances were that Stone and the others would find nothing. The Kek who had gathered to watch the group leave seemed to be equally dispirited. Moon felt they should leave them to their grief. He tugged on Chime's wrist. "Let's go."

☾

When they reached the upper section of the tree, Sand split off to rejoin the warriors who patrolled the clearing under the colony tree's canopy, and Moon and Chime went on inside to the greeting hall. This was the heart of the colony tree, the first thing visitors saw. Two open stairways criss-crossed up the far wall, below the balconies and the round doorways opening into the higher levels, and the big spiral of the central well. The floor was inlaid with polished shell, and a narrow stream of water fell from a channel high in the wall to collect in a pool in the floor. There seemed to be more warriors than usual in the upper level balconies and more Arbora lingering around the pool and the stairway down to the teachers' hall, at least for this time of day. They were hanging around in hope of news, probably.

Balm was waiting for them there in her groundling form. Moon landed and she said immediately, "Nothing's happened. Heart and Bell are with her."

Moon let out the breath he didn't know he had been holding and shifted to his groundling form so Balm didn't have to shift to her winged form. He was going to have to learn to relax about this or he wasn't going to live to see the clutch. Balm continued, "Jade wanted me to find you and tell you she's sorry."

Chime had shifted and was already busy checking his feet for mud and leaf mold. He frowned at Balm. "Sorry about what?"

"Nothing, Jade's mad because she's bored and she wanted to go with Stone," Moon told him. He told Balm, "She's not sorry."

"No, of course not." Balm seemed to feel that should be obvious. "But she wanted me to tell you that anyway."

Moon wondered how consorts like Ember handled these displays of temper. Probably by being conciliatory and solicitous, two things which would irritate the piss out of Jade even if she wasn't carrying five squirming babies in her stomach.

Chime said, "What about a new book? Blossom said Needle found one in the library that she's been re-copying that no one's read in a long time. It's about an expedition that Solace and Sable supposedly took to the mountains on the far edge of the grass plains, where there were groundlings who hung from branches and lived inside fruit."

"Inside fruit?" Moon repeated. Over the past turn, the teachers had been actively trading other courts for books, and so had been digging out damaged and long-forgotten volumes from Indigo Cloud's library and copying them. It had led to some interesting finds.

Skeptical, Balm said, "Solace and Sable got around, for a sister queen and her consort."

"That's why I said 'supposedly,'" Chime said. "I know they did make several trade alliances, but I think some of their Arbora just had over-active imaginations and liked to write travelogues. But Needle said it's a good story."

Balm flicked her spines in acknowledgement. "Go ahead and bring whatever Needle has gotten re-copied up to the bower. Maybe we can get Jade interested in it tonight."

Chime headed off to the stairs down to the teachers' hall. Balm considered Moon. "You look tired."

Moon shook his head. "I'm thinking about groundlings living in fruit."

Balm's lips twitched in a smile. Then she tilted her head toward the outer entrance. "They'll be all right with Stone."

"I know." Moon realized his shoulders were still tense, as if he was holding his wings half-extended. Except he didn't have wings at the moment. He could use a distraction too. Hopefully the fruit-dwelling groundling story was as interesting as it was made out to be.

☾

Fortunately, the story was as good as Needle had said. Chime read the first re-copied section aloud in Jade's bower, to an audience of Jade, Moon, Balm, Heart, Merit, and Bell, and Moon suspected this would be the first of many readings, since everyone in the colony was going to want to hear this at some point. There was enough of it that they didn't finish until late into the night.

Bell went back to the nurseries to take a turn watching the children, but Jade didn't make any sign that she wanted privacy, so the others stayed. She mainly seemed to want to grumble occasionally and listen to them talk, but she was in a better mood.

Moon wished he was in a better mood. He had asked the soldiers on watch in the greeting hall to let him know if Stone and the hunting party returned. Though it was likely that since they hadn't reappeared by sunset, they wouldn't be back until dawn. He still didn't expect to get much rest. And when Balm, Chime, Heart, and Merit all finally curled up on various cushions and furs and fell asleep, Moon was still wide awake.

He thought Jade had drifted off as well, leaning back against a pile of cushions. The hanging bed was no longer comfortable for her, so they used the furs and cushions on the floor that were normally a spot for naps during the day. Then Jade stirred and said, "Come here."

Moon shook his head. "No sex. You decided, no more babies ever."

Jade cocked a brow, amused. "Just come here."

He got up and circled around the cups, cushions, and deeply breathing bodies to sit beside Jade. She wrapped an arm around his waist and pulled him in, and he settled against the warmth of her scales, softer in her Arbora form. Queens and female Arbora had the ability to control their fertility, so sex without babies wasn't an issue, but Jade hadn't been much interested since she had stopped being able to shift. And actually Moon had been too nervous to be interested, with Jade or Chime or anyone else. She said, "Are you really that worried about the clutch?"

"Yes." He wanted to ask *why aren't you?* but knew it would just start an argument. And it was only frustration; he knew why Jade wasn't as concerned. She was a queen and had been raised from birth with the knowledge that she was responsible for the entire court's wellbeing. Every queen was, even the ones who stayed daughter queens all their days. Adding five more tiny lives to the hundreds of others just wasn't that much of a change. Except these five lives came with a great deal of physical discomfort.

The teachers selected to take care of the clutch would do a lot of the work, but the consorts were supposed to make certain a royal clutch knew how to be royal Aeriat. Moon was still vague on the idea of how to be a royal Aeriat; he had no idea how he was supposed to guide five babies. He was hoping a little that they ended up with five warriors, but everyone seemed to think that was unlikely. "I'm worried I won't know how to raise them, among other things."

Jade's sigh stirred his hair. "Well. And there aren't any other consorts to talk to. Besides Stone. And poor sweet Ember, who's useless."

Moon tugged on her frill. "He's not useless." Ember was intelligent and knew a great deal about the relationships, tensions, and trade agreements between the courts of the Reaches, just from growing up listening to the other consorts and the queens of Emerald Twilight. Moon wasn't sure if his birthqueen Tempest had been aware just how much knowledge Ember had managed to soak up or if it was intended to be part of the apology for causing Indigo Cloud unintended trouble. It helped that Pearl was actually willing to listen objectively to Ember, who came without all the turns of past disagreements and bitter arguments of Indigo Cloud.

Jade snorted. "He's useless for this."

That was true. Ember hadn't done this yet and had no real advice. "Stone thinks this is easy." Stone found Moon's anxiety amusing. And Moon had just realized the fact that Stone hadn't made any comment to that effect when Moon had refused to go with the hunting party had just made him more anxious. If Stone, who considered this process so simple, thought it was a good idea for Moon to stay near Jade, that meant that problems were a possibility.

"He would," Jade said, dryly. "Stone fathered so many clutches, it's all routine to him."

At the moment, Moon couldn't imagine this being routine. If he had been raised inside a court, he knew it would be different. He would have been around fledglings all his life, have watched what the teachers did so much it would have been second nature when the clutch came. "I just . . . There's nothing I can do to help now, and I don't know if I know enough to do what I'm supposed to do later."

Jade said, "Telling you that everything will be fine is useless, so I'll just say to try to remember that it won't be too much longer. Then you can stop worrying about me and just worry about raising the clutch."

Moon leaned back to look at her. "That's not helpful."

"Nothing is going to be helpful right now," Jade said. "So go to sleep. No, wait, help me up because I have to piss again, then go to sleep."

Sadly, she was probably right. Moon climbed to his feet, then hauled Jade to hers.

(

Moon woke stretched out on a fur next to Jade, who was sprawled half on her side with a cushion against her back. He had slept erratically and was so bleary it took him a moment to realize Chime was crouched beside him with a couple of female Arbora leaning over his shoulders. "What?" Moon croaked.

"They're back," Chime whispered.

Moon sat up. The two Arbora were soldiers who often guarded the greeting hall, Sprout and Ginger. Ginger added, "Floret came in to tell Pearl, but she said Stone wanted to talk to you."

"So they're all right?" Moon asked, rubbing his face to wake himself up. Heart and Merit were gone, and Balm was awake, sitting beside the hearth and adding tea to a pot. "Where are they?"

"The Kek village," Sprout said. "Floret was in a hurry, didn't say what happened, but she asked for a mentor to go down as soon as possible."

Jade sat up on her elbow and ordered, "Get down there and find out what happened."

(

Moon waited only long enough to hear that Merit had gone to get his simples and the other things he needed for healing and that Floret meant to carry him down to the village as soon as he was ready. Then Moon and Chime went out through the knothole and flew down to the forest floor.

The early morning air was just cool enough to finish waking Moon up. The ever-present dampness had intensified into a light rain at some point earlier, and droplets were caught in the leaves and in the platforms, dripping on his scales. Chime said, "If one of the warriors was hurt, they would have brought them straight into the colony to the mentors. It must be one of the Kek."

It meant the hunt must have been successful after all and Stone had found at least one of the Kek, wounded but alive. It was a much better outcome than Moon had expected.

Moon landed on a root first, squinting to see in the green light. He spotted Kek moving among the waving stalks of ferns, bowl grass, and other foliage at the edge of the village. He jumped down to the mossy ground, Chime with him. Someone called to him in Raksuran, and Moon followed the voice through stands of rushes, under another arching root, and out to a small area of open ground.

Root stood there, but he wasn't the first thing Moon noticed.

Floating above the moss was a giant leaf, light green and gracefully curved, a good fifty paces across and almost as wide. It took a long moment of staring before Moon realized it was a kind of flying boat.

Moon moved closer, caught between admiration and bewilderment. It hovered above the ground, high enough that he could have walked under it without ducking. This close he could see it really was a leaf, and not just made to look like one. The surface was plant fiber with striated veins, and it had clearly grown into this shape. The upper section tented up like a canopy, with long narrow windows all along the midsection. They were covered with something transparent but flexible that clearly wasn't glass. There were puffy mushroom things studding the bottom, and a little moss was growing on it. It smelled like a strange combination of bruised leaves and something sweet, like a peeled fruit.

"We found what happened to the Kek," Root announced. "And," he waved a hand toward the leaf, "That. We can't figure out how to fly it. We just sort of pushed it and pulled it and it came along with us."

"But . . . What . . . Why . . ." Chime's spines flicked in a complex signal of confusion and irritation. Moon sympathized. He was feeling much the same. Chime finished, "Where is everybody?"

Root said, "Stone is in the village, the others are standing guard around us. Is a mentor coming?"

"Floret's bringing Merit," Moon said. "Who's hurt? The Kek? Does this belong to them?" The leaf boat did look like something the Kek might have come up with, if the Kek had made flying boats. But Moon had never seen any hint of anything like this near the village before.

"No, the Kek were dead, we were too late, but the groundlings who were in this thing were still alive," Root said. At Moon's spine twitch indicating that his patience was about to abruptly run out, Root added, "We flew out to where the Kek had already searched and moved on from there. It was getting near sunset, we were about to stop and camp for the night, when Stone caught a scent he thought was groundling blood. We followed it, and then came onto a trail through a bunch of purplevine clusters, where it looked like something had rolled through and crushed them. It was almost dark by that point but we managed to follow the trail to that thing." He jerked his tail toward the leaf boat. "The three Kek were there, but they'd been killed."

"By predators?" Chime asked, still sounding confused. "After the injured groundlings?"

"No. Stone thinks whatever got them got the groundlings too. I think that's what he thinks." Root's spines flicked in frustration. "Better let Stone tell you."

Root led them away from the leaf and toward the interior of the village. They went around some clumps of tall ferns, under a few of the hanging huts, and toward a raised area. It was sheltered by two tall stands of willowy reeds that had been trained to grow in an arch and then woven together. The floor of the raised area was made of dried rushes that had been pounded down and then overlaid with grass mats. Several dozen Kek surrounded it at a distance, murmuring together worriedly. As Root approached with Moon and Chime, they waved stick-like fingers and made urgent gestures toward the shelter. Root said, "There he is. I've got to get back."

The shadowy green light was even dimmer in this part of the village, but as they drew closer to the shelter Moon saw there were people inside.

Stone in groundling form and a few Kek, all leaning over several bundled forms.

Moon stepped up onto the pounded rush floor. There were five shapes lying on the mats in the dimly lit interior, and he could hear rough breathing. Small tent-covers of pounded leaves lay over the bodies, probably to help shield them from insects. Stone glanced up. "Mentor?"

"Merit's coming," Moon said. "What kind of groundlings are they?"

Stone carefully moved the tent-cover away from the nearest body. All Moon could see at first was a mane of gray hair, and he stepped closer. The face was turned to the side, and the skin was smooth and silvery, not scaled or furred.

Stone lifted the cover a little further. "They're all wounded like this, with darts." The groundling wore brief clothing, just a few straps with loops and clips probably meant to hold tools. Its hands were partially webbed, and there were blunt gray claws on the ends of each finger. Moon hissed when he spotted the darts. There were three of them, light green, imbedded in the skin above the right hip. The flesh around them was swollen and dark.

Stone carefully lowered the cover back into place. "We left the darts in because we didn't have anything to stop the bleeding." He gestured to the others. "The rest are a different species." One of the Kek lifted another cover and Moon leaned over to see. The other groundling had dark gray skin, with a waxy texture to it, and something around its head that wasn't hair.

Chime eased forward to look. Moon sat on his heels, the disemboweling claws on his feet sinking into the grass mats. Stone had probably been right to leave the darts in and wait for a mentor. Trying to help wounded members of an unfamiliar species was always chancy, and more so when they weren't conscious enough to tell you what not to do.

Chime said, "Could the darts be from a plant? I mean, they're obviously from a plant, but did they run into a plant that shoots darts at moving things?"

It wasn't a bad idea. There were plenty of aggressive thorn-bearing plants in the Reaches, and some of them preferred to live on meat rather than light and water. But Stone shook his head. "They were all inside their leaf boat. And something tore up the place, searching it. If it was a plant, it was one that could get up and walk around, and if it could do that, it wouldn't have left them in there alive."

Chime hissed in confusion. Stone was right, a meat-eating plant would have finished the job. Moon asked, "Were the Kek killed this same way?"

"No." Stone grimaced. "They were attacked by something, fought it hand-to-hand, all three of them." He added, "And it wasn't one of these groundlings. Their hands don't show any damage."

Chime sat back, tugging a tent-cover back into place over another groundling. "Are you sure? The gray ones look strong enough to break a Kek in half."

Stone's expression showed his patience had come close to its limit with questions, but he said, "The Kek are tougher than they look. And they can't bleed out, their veins close up."

Moon settled his spines again. This whole situation was making his claws itch. "The Kek don't use any dart weapons?" The idea of the Kek attacking anybody seemed unlikely at best, but the groundlings might have threatened them.

"They don't. Not much use to them, as they don't eat meat. And Kek don't attract the kind of predators a dart weapon would work on." Stone looked at one of the Kek, who had brought a snail shell filled with water and was trying to clean the blood away from the face of one of the unconscious groundlings. "Nobody thinks the Kek and some random groundlings got in a fight. Especially the other Kek."

"But it wasn't—" Moon made his spines flat so he didn't accidentally poke Chime. "This doesn't make sense. If the groundlings were attacked by something with a dart weapon, why did it leave them alive? If a predator was drawn by the blood-scent and killed the Kek when they tried to protect the groundlings, why didn't it eat the groundlings? Or the Kek?"

"And when did it happen?" Chime asked, bewildered. "The groundlings must have been out there three days at least, since before the Kek went missing. Why didn't the blood scent draw more predators?"

Stone rubbed his face wearily. With the edge of a growl in his voice, he said, "If I knew, I'd tell you. All I can say is that something happened to these people, and the Kek must have walked up on it either while it was happening, or right after." He looked up at Moon. "I called you down here because I want you to search through that leaf boat. I looked through it but I want to make sure I didn't miss anything. Whoever attacked these people tore it apart looking for something in there, and we don't know if they found it or not."

Moon flicked a spine in acknowledgement and pushed to his feet.

Worried, Chime said, "You want him to make sure there isn't a dart weapon in there. That the groundlings didn't do this to each other."

Stone tilted his head. "That too."

Moon stepped out of the shelter. The Kek who had come close to watch and listen scattered out of his way. Coming toward him through the clumps of fern and clusters of huts were Merit and another Arbora, a young female soldier called Sharp.

Merit had a couple of bags slung over his shoulder and his spines flicked anxiously. As Moon reached him, Merit said, "Floret told me about the groundlings. She's guarding the edge of the village with the other warriors."

"Just be careful," Moon told him. He added to Sharp, "Keep an eye on him. The groundlings don't look like they could do much damage right now, but we don't know anything about these people."

Sharp's spines were reassuringly steady. "I will, consort."

Merit moved toward the shelter, Sharp on his heels, and Moon headed for the leaf boat. Chime caught up with him a few paces later, though he kept glancing back toward the shelter as if he was torn between curiosity about the leaf boat and helping Merit. "It sounds like the Kek have no idea why these groundlings were here in the first place," Chime said. "Were they exploring, trading? Why would they come here?"

"They might be from here. It would explain why they have this." Moon nodded toward the flying boat. It looked bizarre at first glance, but the materials and the way it was put together did suggest it had been assembled or cultivated by people familiar with the forest floor.

Root still paced next to it, keeping watch. Moon went toward what he supposed was the back of the contraption. Instead of being square to hold as much cargo as possible, the body of the leaf boat tapered into a triangular bow at either end.

Most groundling wagons or other transports Moon had seen had an opening in the back, so he jumped up to hook his claws on the curve of the leaf's edge. There was a gap in the canopy here, a door flap with a clump of vines that seemed to act as a way to keep it closed. Moon pulled himself up and crouched on the wide edge, then tugged the flap open and peered inside.

The upper part didn't look translucent from the outside but it and the narrow windows did let light through. Moon saw bundled shapes, and something hanging from the ceiling. He tasted the air, but the damp green scents of the forest floor were too intense for him to detect anything unusual.

Behind him, Chime climbed the stern and hung on with one arm. "Here, Root had one of the light stones." He handed Moon one of the smooth glowing stones.

Moon took it and rolled it into the leaf boat. The white glow of light revealed the width of the interior. Bundles were stacked along the sides, leaving the middle of the space mostly open. Nets hung from the arches that supported the canopy, each of which contained a single bundle or roll of cloth. It seemed an impractical method of storage, until Moon realized the cloth was bedding and the nets were hanging beds.

Moon stepped into the leaf boat, the plant fiber floor giving a little beneath his feet. He was careful to keep his foot claws retracted. Inside, it was easier to detect the scents, a mishmash of unfamiliar groundlings, intense moss odors, rotted fruit, damp grain, and blood. He could see the sticky stains on the floor where the occupants must have collapsed when they were wounded. Most of the blood was a light dull green, but there was also a clear fluid. There was a cloud of gnats hovering, and other insects whizzed around.

A woven reed case lay open on the floor, with rolls of papers, wooden writing utensils, and an ink bottle made of shell. Moon crouched over one of the papers and flicked it with a claw to unroll it. It was a map, drawn in light blue ink on waxed pounded reed paper, marking out a ground level route through a part of the Reaches. At least he thought so, to judge by the huge irregular circles that must be symbols for various mountain-trees. The notations were in a language Moon didn't know.

From the doorway, Chime said, "Is that a map? Can you tell where they came from?"

It looked as if the route started somewhere in the middle of the Reaches. "Sort of." The ground level map did mean that this leaf, unlike Golden Islander flying boats and Aventeran bladder boats, probably couldn't get much higher off the ground than it was now. Moon reached for another roll of paper. "It must be—" He froze, certain something had moved inside the leaf boat. A faint breeze stirred a torn fragment of paper up towards the bow and Moon relaxed, twitching his spines to shake off the tension. They didn't have time to look at the maps right now. He pushed to his feet and continued around.

Stone was right, the place had been searched. Containers and bundles had been dragged around, pulled loose from the vine ties and wooden clips meant to secure them to the floor, and some had been roughly thrown aside. But most hadn't been opened or dumped out, as if whoever had searched hadn't been looking for something that could be hidden inside one. The foodstuffs Moon found were all roots or fruit, and there were several big clumps of mold-looking things, which were emitting the grainy odor. He couldn't tell what they were, but it seemed unlikely that they had produced darts. The contents of the wrapped bundles were either recognizable as the sort of supplies most groundlings needed on a long trip, like cloth made of pounded reed, or utensils or tools made of shell or polished wood, or things like the mold clumps that were completely strange. But there was nothing that looked even vaguely like a weapon that shot thorn darts. So the groundlings hadn't shot at each other, unless they had also thrown the weapons away before collapsing.

Moon climbed back out of the leaf boat and shook his spines. There was something about this whole situation that made the skin creep under his scales, though there had been nothing really odd in the boat. Maybe it was just that five groundlings had lain inside it slowly dying, until the Kek had stumbled on them. And then something else had stumbled on the Kek.

"Well?" Chime said impatiently.

"They might be explorers. There wasn't enough in there for trade goods. One of the groundlings almost looked like a sealing, but I've never seen one come this far inland before." Moon absently dragged his foot claws through the ground moss. "If that boat is going to stay here, we need to clean the blood up before it draws predators."

"I'll do it," Root offered.

"Use some of that hanging moss to wipe it up," Moon told him. "It'll help disguise the smell. And then bury it."

Chime rippled his spines uncomfortably as Root bounded away to get the moss. "We can clean up the boat, but the wounded groundlings are going to attract predators too."

"We're going to have to keep watch on the village, until Merit can get their wounds cleaned and bandaged." Hopefully Pearl wouldn't balk at the necessity.

Chime studied the leaf boat again. "You think they're from the Reaches somewhere."

"They could be." Moon hadn't gotten a good look at the other groundlings. "There's some amphibian species that live down in the deep level swamps." The one that looked like a sealing might actually be some variety of swampling. Moon had never seen one before, but that certainly didn't mean they didn't exist.

Chime flicked a spine in agreement. "And they have to have some sort of magic, to make the boat fly."

"If they had magic, you'd think they could have fought off whatever attacked them," Moon said.

"Or whatever came after them had better magic," Chime said.

Stone appeared, brushing past the stands of fern. Moon started to speak, then stopped as a strange humming sound rose up from the center of the village.

"It's the Kek," Stone said, before he could ask. "Mourning the dead."

Chime twitched uncomfortably. The sound was a little like the hum of insects at twilight, except louder and more resonant. Feeling it echo in his bones, Moon said, "I didn't see anything that could shoot darts like what they're wounded with. Unless they stabbed them into each other—"

Stone growled in annoyance. "This is getting more complicated."

Chime said, "So there must be more groundlings out there."

Moon shook his head a little. "That's a lot of groundlings, even if some of them do come from the Reaches." The Reaches didn't have populated trade routes where groundlings gathered. Unless the amphibians who occupied the lower swamps had trade networks. Now that Moon thought about it, it would be odd if they didn't. He hissed in frustration. They just didn't know enough about all the different species who occupied the forest floor.

Stone favored the leaf boat with an absent glare. "Did you see the map, with the mountain-trees marked on it?"

Moon frowned. "You think they were after a colony tree seed?"

Chime's spines lifted in alarm. Stone shrugged, eyeing the leaf boat. "It's possible. If they knew enough to come for a seed, they knew it wasn't going to be easy."

The groundlings might have thought the colony tree would be empty. The Indigo Cloud tree had been deserted for a long time. But it depended on whether the leaf boat could fly high enough to reach the knothole entrance, and Moon doubted it. And he hadn't seen any climbing ropes or hooks stored inside.

Chime said, "You think someone told them how to find us? Like Negal and the others. Or even one of Ardan's people who survived the trip. Or they could have stolen a map from the Golden Isles—"

Stone growled in irritation, a bone-deep sound that rivaled the Kek's hum. "Too many groundlings know where we are."

"Not that many." Moon just didn't think it was possible. Any ground-lings who had spoken to Negal's people or Ardan's would be coming from a great distance away, including across most of the freshwater sea. The distance from the Yellow Sea was also a long, dangerous trip for anyone without the ability to fly. And he still thought these people were native to the Reaches. "It's just not likely."

Stone's gaze narrowed. "We're not going to know anything until one of them wakes up and tells us."

Moon suspected that was Stone's way of telling them he was tired of discussing it. Root returned with an armload of moss, Briar following him with a waterskin. Watching them climb into the leaf boat, Moon said, "Whoever did attack them could follow the trail here."

Stone turned the narrow gaze on Moon. "I did think of that. That's the other reason why the warriors are on watch."

Moon sensed movement overhead and looked up, his spines lifting involuntarily. But it was only three more Raksura, one of whom was large and gold. Pearl was arriving.

Stone muttered, "Finally."

☾

Pearl met with Kof in the center of the village, not far from the shelter where Merit was tending the injured groundlings. They sat atop a raised dais made of woven reeds. Moon sat behind Pearl, while Chime, Floret, and Sage crouched on the edge. They faced Kof, and three other Kek elders, with a large number of Kek gathered around to listen. Stone sat between them, so he could translate.

Pearl curled her tail around, the color of her scales still vibrant in the perpetual twilight. The Kek in the front were mostly the older members of the village, the ones who were probably Kof's advisors and contributed to the decision-making. The younger ones stood in the back, and many were holding up children so they could see Pearl. It was probably rare for the Kek to see any Raksura except warriors and the occasional hunter. It was terrible that this occasion had to coincide with the death of three of their number.

Pearl turned over a dart with one jewel-sheathed claw tip. It had been removed from one of the groundlings by Merit. "He doesn't know who might use a weapon like this? Or if these groundlings might have some quarrel with Kek?"

Stone translated the questions. Kof waggled and spread his fingers, a display meant to convey complete bafflement, and managed the Raksuran word for "No." Then he added, in the Kek-Raksuran pidgin: "Some other."

Stone said, "He means there's something or someone else involved here."

"Hmm." Pearl's expression conveyed resigned exasperation rather than doubt. A Kek child crept over the edge of the dais and tapped its stick-like fingers on the tip of her tail. Pearl absently held out a hand and let the child tug on one of her claw sheaths. A turn ago this would have surprised Moon, but after so much experience with Raksuran nurseries he knew one thing all queens had to be used to was being tugged on by inquisitive children. She said, "What do they wish to do with the groundlings?"

The answer took more back and forth, but Stone finally said, "They're waiting for them to wake up, to find out what happened to the plant hunters. But they don't think it was these groundlings who killed their people." Stone listened intently to Kof for a time, watching his gestures carefully. Then he sat back. "They think it's a mystery."

Pearl tilted her head at Stone. "That is not helpful."

Unmoved, Stone said, "You asked. We have to wait. And guard the village." Stone had already worked that out with Kof, it was just Pearl who still had to agree to it.

Pearl's spines rippled in irritation. Moon knew why. She wanted to be done with this, a potential source of trouble, but the court was embroiled in it now. They had to consider the fact that the groundlings might have been coming here to try to steal the seed again, no matter how unlikely Moon thought it was. And having offered to help the Kek, they couldn't now stop in the middle and tell them they were on their own. She said, "Very well. Floret will take charge of the warriors to guard the Kek village, until we know if these groundlings are enemies or just unwanted idiot visitors."

Floret stirred. "Can we open one of the doors in the trunk? The one nearest the village? It will be easier if Merit can come and go when he needs to, and the soldiers can guard him and the door."

Pearl considered. "Yes. It will also be faster for you to summon help that way."

Moon managed not to let his spines flick uneasily. He didn't like the idea of opening a door into the tree with these strange groundlings here, not to mention whatever might be following them. But it was safer for any Raksura down here to have quick access and a faster route to get word to the rest of the court.

No one had suggested bringing the groundlings into the colony, and Moon was hoping no one would. Leaving the Kek vulnerable to the higher level predators who might be attracted by lingering blood scent was the last thing he wanted to do, but letting strange groundlings into the colony was also the last thing he wanted to do.

Once arrangements were discussed with Kof, Pearl took her leave and Kof moved away to speak to the rest of the Kek. Floret sent Sage off to bring a new group of warriors, so the ones who had been on the search could go back to the court to rest, and to tell Knell, the leader of the soldiers, about the plan.

Moon told Stone, "I need to get back to Jade. She's going to be getting impatient, especially if she knows Pearl came down here."

Stone tasted the air, his gaze on the point where the nearest root stretched out from the tree and disappeared into the dimness and heavy foliage. "How is she doing?"

Moon said, "The same. She's bored and angry." He tasted the air too, but all he could detect was Raksura, Kek, green plants and damp. There was a trace of blood scent, but far less than before. Merit must have worked quickly to clean and dress the groundlings' wounds.

Chime made his way toward them through the mud and moss, carrying a bag. "I took the maps that had spilled onto the floor of the leaf boat and a book the groundlings were writing in. We might be able to figure out where they came from. Also, I was afraid some of it might get ruined if we left it out here."

Moon told him, "Good idea. Go on up, I'll be right behind you."

As Chime leapt for the nearest root, Moon said to Stone, "You should get some rest, too. Floret can handle it."

"I'll come in when the others do." Stone was still staring off into the heavy foliage.

"What is it?" Moon asked, feeling his spines prickle a little. If Stone sensed something out there . . .

Stone frowned a little. "Nothing. Just nerves."

Hearing Stone admit to nerves was worrying enough. Moon hissed under his breath and leapt into the air. The sooner the groundlings woke up and told their story, the better.

☾

Moon reported briefly to Jade, who had already heard parts of the story from various warriors and Arbora. Then he got sent back down to make certain there was no problem with opening the root doorway.

Moon arrived in time to follow Knell and a group of Arbora soldiers down into the lower levels of the tree, far below the Arbora's work and storage areas. Knell asked Moon, "You're not going out on watch, are you?"

"No." Moon shrugged his spines. "Jade just wants a detailed description of what happens."

Knell didn't question it. He was the leader of the Arbora soldiers' caste and one of Chime's clutchmates, as was Bell, the leader of the teachers' caste. Now that Chime was a warrior, there wasn't much of a resemblance between the three of them, though both Knell and Bell were tall for Arbora, and Knell did share Chime's inclination to be stubborn.

The root levels of the colony were completely unused. The passages and open wells were smaller, the stairs were narrow and woven through and around thick folds of wood. The walls were all undecorated and hadn't even been smoothed down, and the floors were uneven. But it only looked bad if you were used to the lavish living areas in the upper part of the tree. There were still plenty of rooms down here that were dry and had access to clean running water; it was safe and a hundred times more comfortable than living outside the tree.

As they got down to the last stairwell, Thistle, a young female mentor, was going through renewing the light spells on the shells mounted into the walls. The shells down here hadn't been tended in a while and the light spells faded with time.

Moon followed Knell through the little maze of passages to the lowest stairwell. It curved around toward the outer trunk and met the junction where the door was. The opening was large and round, closed by a heavy wooden panel that slid into place and sealed with bolts. There were other doors, but this was the one that was lowest to the ground, and the easiest to get to from the outside. The warriors who were waiting to take over watch duty clung to the walls and ceiling up and down the passage. They stopped talking as Moon and Knell went past but the rustle of scaled wings still filled the air.

Arbora soldiers already waited nearby and Knell nodded to them to open the door. They slid the bolts aside with difficulty and pulled it into the corridor, releasing a shower of dead beetles and dirt. A damp breeze carrying the intense rotted plant scent of the swamps filled the passage.

This door opened into a narrow crevice in the extended roots that formed a cave. The door was about ten paces up the wall of the tree, with narrow steps leading down to the cave floor, which was covered by a layer of dead leaves and windblown dirt. The last time this door had been opened was on their first full day in the colony. This was where they had found the groundling bones, all that remained of two of Ardan's people who had displeased Rift, after he had let them into the tree to steal the seed.

Now the narrow crevice was lit with some of Merit's glowing stones and Briar stood waiting at the bottom of the steps. She turned and called, "It's open!"

Moon stepped away from the door and the soldiers crowded back down the passage to give the warriors room. They flowed outside, most just climbing along the walls and not bothering to drop to the floor. Moon saw River and Drift among them. River had been Pearl's favorite warrior before Ember had arrived, and River had taken a while to adjust to having his place in Pearl's bower occupied by a real consort. He and Moon had hated each other from first sight, but over the past few months they seemed to have come to a mutual truce. Moon still found Drift just as annoying and didn't expect that to change any time soon.

"The others are coming," Briar said from outside.

"Any word from Merit?" Knell asked her.

"None of the groundlings are awake yet," she told him. "Merit thinks there was a poison on the darts."

It crossed Moon's mind that the groundlings might die and take their mystery, and potential dangers, with them, and he winced at the thought.

Then Moon heard a yelp and scrabble just outside the door. Instinct almost made him dive outside when Fair said, "Stop shoving."

"I didn't touch you, idiot," someone else answered. Hissing with annoyance, Briar climbed inside. Following her were Vine, Root, Fair, and the other weary warriors who had been in the original search party. Stone, already in groundling form so he could fit through the narrow cave, came last, and said, "Don't shut the door. We want to be able to get in and out quickly."

Knell lifted his spines in assent. "That's what Pearl said to do. And I'm to send two more soldiers out to Merit."

"Floret's out there, she'll show them where he is." Stone leaned his lanky body against the wall. He didn't look any different, but there was something about the way he was standing that suggested more than the normal amount of weariness for a night spent on the forest floor. Stone wouldn't have been able to fly through the lower forest for much of the search; he would have been hopping from perch to perch, keeping an eye on the warriors and Kek while they went through the undergrowth. He had to be more than usually tired. And Moon would have been willing to bet that despite everything, Stone had been hoping to find those Kek alive.

Moon took Stone's arm and prodded him down the passage. Stone went, which showed that he really did want to go, or there was no way

Moon would have been able to move him, even in his groundling form. "Jade wants to see you." Jade hadn't said so, but it made a good excuse to get Stone upstairs to his bower, to any bower, where hopefully he would rest.

"I need a bath," Stone said, but didn't protest further.

((

Moon couldn't sleep that night. He knew it was just a combination of tension and too much inactivity, but lying on the furs next to Jade, it felt like his nerves were about to crawl out of his skin.

He sat up, slowly, but Jade was curled around a cushion and breathing deeply in sleep. That wasn't a surprise; she had been awake most of the day, anxious about the situation in the Kek village and constantly sending anyone who wandered near the bower down to the roots for reports. She needed the rest and he didn't want to wake her. Everyone else was sound asleep as well, Chime sprawled on a fur on the other side of the hearth, a book unrolled across his chest, and Thistle and Blossom curled up together opposite him.

Stone had sat with them through the early evening, and then gone somewhere to sleep. He might be in his bower, he might be in the teachers' hall or near it, or he might be hanging from the stairwell somewhere. Stone's sleeping habits were not typical even for a line-grandfather.

Moon eased to his feet and walked out of the bower into the queens' hall. Balm and a few teachers sat near the hearth, the teachers all working on stringing copper beads in elaborate patterns. Balm seemed to be occupying herself holding things for them. She glanced up at Moon. "Couldn't sleep?"

"No." Moon sat on his heels beside the carefully sorted piles of beads.

Bark, her lap full of half-braided leather thongs, winced in sympathy. "It'll be a few days yet."

"I know." Moon knew he was about to give into the temptation to stir the beads, just for something to do. He pushed himself upright. "I'm going down to the roots, see if anything's changed."

All the Arbora nodded as if that was a necessary thing to do, and that the soldiers wouldn't have come up to report to Pearl if anything important had happened. Balm just said, "I'll come with you."

((

Moon wasn't inclined to hurry and neither was Balm. They took a leisurely stroll down through the colony's levels, stopping to greet various Arbora and warriors who were awake for different reasons. If there was no pressing task that most of the court was engaged in, then people tended to sleep when they felt like it, or when they had nothing else to do, and some of the Arbora artisans preferred to work late at night. There was more activity when they reached the root area below the Arbora's work rooms and the forges, where the soldiers and warriors were getting ready to change the guard for the Kek village.

They passed a chamber where several soldiers and a few warriors were sleeping, then took a wide curving stairwell down to the chamber where Knell and the others sat near a hearth bowl finishing up a meal. Everyone was in their groundling forms, and looked as if they had just woken up; it was clear the watch had been uneventful so far. Knell glanced up as they arrived, asking, "Anything happening?"

"That's what we came to ask you," Balm said, and took a seat on one of the woven mats strewn around.

Knell set a nearly empty tray of fruit and baked root pieces aside. The soldiers had said no meat was to be brought down here, to keep the scent from drawing the interest of small predators that might be able to work their way in through the open door, a precaution Moon very much agreed with. Knell said, "No, it's been quiet. Merit's out there again, but at the last report he said the groundlings haven't woken."

Root and Song sat nearby, and Moon had noticed Vine asleep in the room above, but he didn't see Floret. "Is Floret still there?"

"Yes, she wanted to take the first two watches, but Sage is about to take her place," Song said. Root yawned and she gave him a push to the shoulder. "We've had a rest and we're going back out."

"Don't let yourselves get too worn out." Balm picked up a piece of fruit from the tray. "I can round up some more warriors if need be."

"I think we have enough so far. But if this goes on longer than a few days, we'll need more help." Knell brushed bread crumbs off his kilt. "It's about that time. Star, go and tell—"

A long sustained yell, muffled through layers of bark and wood, interrupted him: a soldier giving the alarm. Moon shifted by instinct, realized a heartbeat later that so had everyone else. He leapt to the ceiling to leave the way clear for the Arbora and the warriors who charged out of the chamber. All they were thinking about was getting outside to the others; all Moon was thinking about was stopping anything from getting inside the tree.

He swung under the arch of the doorway and jumped from wall to wall until he reached the wide point of the passage where the outer door stood open. Knell and the others swarmed out through it, in orderly but furious fashion. Moon clung to the ceiling above the lintel, a snarl in his chest, ready to murder anything not Raksura or Kek that tried to come in.

Serene, Band, and Fair bounced off the walls below and landed on the ceiling nearby, taking guard positions around the door. Moon was glad that Knell hadn't forgotten this detail. He said, "Where's Stone?"

Hanging upside down from a knob of wood, Serene said, "He's near the teachers' hall, consort. Spring is getting him."

Moon growled an acknowledgement. The Arbora and warriors had cleared the doorway, except for two soldiers who stood ready to slide it shut. Moon heard movement outside, feet on grass and mud, and somewhere distant a crashing through the brush. The high-pitched cries of Kek were woven through it all. Not screaming or cries for help, but the sounds they used to communicate over distances. Then close by, something made a strange low coughing sound, and an Arbora cried out. The soldiers at the door and the three warriors twitched with the urge to respond. Moon snapped, "Stay here!" and swung down and out the door.

He tore through the cave-like passage and out into the open ground just beyond. Arbora had cleared the brush away earlier and a mentor had spelled clumps of moss and flowers in the nearby saplings for light. In the soft glow, an Arbora soldier used a short javelin to fend off something gray, scaled, and four times her size. Another Arbora lay sprawled on the muddy ground at her feet.

Moon crossed the clearing in two bounds and landed on top of the gray predator. Its back was broad, tapering down to a triangular body, its head flattened and jaw wide. He caught a glimpse of at least six clawed feet and a barbed tail. He ripped his claws across its eyes and felt the predator start to roll sideways. Moon leapt into the air and landed a few paces in front of it. The soldier had wisely broken off her attack and now rapidly dragged her wounded companion back toward the root cave. As Moon crouched, sinuous movement in the dark foliage solidified into two more of the gray predators, much larger than the first. There was more rustling behind them; something else was clearly out there.

Which meant Moon had to take care of these three quickly. He shot forward, slashed the first predator across the face again, caught the barbed tail as it jerked toward him and slammed his weight down on top of the predator's head. Then he flung himself backward.

He wasn't certain if it would work, since it depended entirely on how strong the predator's neck bones were, but he was too blind with rage to care. But he felt the snap jolt through the predator's body as he landed. He tossed it aside, just as the second leapt at him. Moon lunged forward and met it with his claws to its open mouth. He stabbed it in the soft tissue inside and jammed one hand and both feet against the open jaws when it tried to bite down on him. It twisted and rolled to dislodge him, and he ripped its tender mouth again with his free hand. The rush of blood and a wild convulsion knocked him loose. As he tumbled free, the creature shot back into the undergrowth, spraying blood.

Moon rolled to his feet but the third predator turned and bolted after the second. He tracked its movement through the darkness, the light reflected off water droplets on disturbed fronds and leaves revealing its progress. There was something else out there, he could tell by the erratic path the predator took. Something out there, and it had hung back, waiting for the three predators to clear the way through to the root cave.

Moon stalked back and forth, spines flared. "Come out!" he yelled toward the darkness, his voice deep and raspy with rage. "Try again, come on!"

He couldn't see movement but he could sense it. Something was out there, considering, gauging its chances. It wanted him to move away from the entrance passage, to come after it in the darkness and confusion of the undergrowth. Moon bared his fangs, dropping his lower jaw to let the full array show. *No, you come to me. Come out here and die.*

Something large went past high overhead, arrowing down toward the village, but Moon knew it was Stone. An instant later he caught a flash of gold in his peripheral vision and Pearl landed in a crouch on the trampled bloody ground. She eased smoothly upright, her spines flared and wings partially extended. She tilted her head and hissed.

Moon tasted the air but there was nothing but the bitter blood scent and stench of the dead predator. He still didn't detect any stir of movement in the dark, but his sense of a presence was gone. "It left," he said to Pearl.

She paced a few steps, her tail lashing. Lights moved in the distance, flickering past the dark shapes of the arched roots. The chorus of cries from the Kek died away. A swish of wings and three warriors landed in the clearing, Floret, River, and Aura. Floret said to Pearl, "There were three attacks at once—" She glanced at the predator with the broken neck. "Four. One was at the opposite end of the village from here, the other two midway between. No one was killed, as far as we know. The

Kek are still checking their own people. Six warriors were injured, and four Arbora."

"Merit?" Pearl asked.

River answered this time, "No, not him or the groundlings. Nothing got into the village."

Pearl inclined her head toward the dead predator. "All the attackers were like these?"

"No. They were different." Floret's spines flicked in agitation as she realized the implications. "The ones I saw were more snake-like."

Aura's spines twitched in agreement. "The ones on our side were bigger than that, with square heads. They fled when Stone arrived."

Predators like this didn't all attack at once. They would feed on each other just as they fed on grasseaters, they would never work together. Something had driven them here, and Moon was convinced it had been out there, watching the passage into the tree, waiting for its opportunity. "Whatever caused this was here. About sixty paces that way, watching. It wanted inside."

Pearl's spines shivered in a way that made all three warriors twitch. She said, "You three. Get the wounded inside." She tilted her head toward Moon. "You. Wash the blood off your claws and go to Jade."

Moon didn't need to be told twice.

☾

"You shouldn't have gone out there," Ember said, pouring tea. "Even though . . . I know you're not a normal consort, but still."

Moon took the offered cup and shrugged a little. He hadn't had a choice, as far as he was concerned. He actually wished that Pearl had arrived a little later. If whatever had started all this had come out of concealment to attack him, she would have been just in time to catch it.

Jade was nursing her cup of tea, her scaled brow drawn down in a thoughtful frown. "If Pearl hadn't been so quick, you might have lured out whatever was hiding in the dark."

Ember looked scandalized. They were in Jade's bower, with Chime, who had slept through everything, Balm, who had also been sent back inside by Pearl, the soldiers Sprout and Ginger, and the hunter Bramble. There were three more hunters and three warriors outside the bower in the queens' hall; Moon had checked the nurseries and the greeting hall on his way up here, and found much of the court guarding those two points. The rest were guarding the root entrance.

Balm handed cups of tea to the Arbora. "I've never heard of anything that could drive predators like that. Could make them do what it wanted and keep them from attacking each other. And that's what was happening out there, there's no other explanation for it."

Chime said, "It's almost like the way the Fell control groundlings. Except I've never heard of them doing it to animals."

That wasn't a pleasant thought. Moon asked Chime, "You haven't . . . sensed anything funny, have you?" Everyone watched Chime, waiting anxiously for the answer.

Chime grimaced in frustration. "No, nothing. Not even the cloud-walkers flying over us." He had been having odd flashes of insight, some sort of side-effect of his change from mentor to warrior and his loss of his mentor's abilities. Sometimes it was helpful, like when he got some warning of strange magic, sometimes it was useless, like knowing an upper air skyling was in the area. "What we should do is search the libraries to see if anything like this has ever happened before, except I don't know when we'll have time. Maybe I should start now while the mentors are busy with the wounded."

"Not tonight," Moon said. "Wait till daylight." The libraries were a little too close to the lower part of the tree, and he wanted Chime where he could see him.

There had already been too many casualties tonight. They were waiting for someone to have time to come up and tell them who was hurt and how badly. So far Moon was managing to ignore Jade's attempts to tell him to go down and get a report; he had no intention of leaving her side. It hadn't escaped his attention that when Pearl had left her bower at the report of the attack, she had told Ember to come in here and sit with Jade while she was gone. Whether it was so Ember could protect Jade or Jade could protect Ember, it was impossible to tell. Pearl might not intend for anything hostile to get inside the colony, but if it did, she clearly wanted all the vulnerable points guarded.

Moon knew Stone was still down in the village, only because Balm had spoken to him briefly before Pearl had sent her back up here. Everyone was concentrated now on getting the colony and the village through the night safely. It would have to wait for daylight before they could look for tracks that might give a clue to what had been out there organizing the attack.

"I looked over those maps and the other papers," Chime said. "I couldn't read the language, but it just looked like a travel log to me. There were characters that looked like numbers, arrows and notations that could be directions. They matched the ones labeled on the map. Whether they were following an established route, or exploring and keeping track of where they'd been, I couldn't tell."

"That's frustrating," Balm said, "If it's a log and we could just read it, at least we'd know why they came this way."

"But the question is," Jade said, "If this thing that attacked us wanted the groundlings, why did it try to get inside the colony?"

It was such a good question, Moon stared at her for a moment. He turned to Balm. "You were in the village. Did it seem like the predators were after the groundlings?"

"That's what we assumed." Balm shook her head a little, clearly trying to remember what she had seen. "There were a lot of predators trying to come in between those two long root sections, to where the center of the village is. But then there were a lot toward the far end of the village, too." She lifted her brows, asking Jade, "You think that was just a distraction?"

"I don't know." Jade twitched her spines. "It's odd. This whole thing is odd."

Moon couldn't argue with that. Chime said, "Maybe the . . . attacker, whatever it was, was after a colony tree seed, like Stone thought the groundlings might be." He gestured in exasperation. "But that doesn't make sense either. It went after the Kek and the groundlings first, when it found them out in the forest. If it was after our seed, why would it do that?"

Bramble, who loved this sort of theorizing, said, "Maybe it was working with the groundlings, and they betrayed each other, and it killed the Kek when they saw it killing the groundlings." Ember looked intrigued, and Ginger and Sprout nodded seriously.

"I don't think even Stone thought Stone was right about something being after the seed," Moon said. He didn't want the Arbora to get started on competing theories. Their capacities for invention and imagination were endless, and they could be at it for the rest of the night. "We're not going to know what happened until the groundlings wake up and tell us. If they tell us."

Jade growled a little. "They had better tell us—" She stopped abruptly and put a hand on her stomach.

Moon froze. "What?"

"Nothing." Her glare was preoccupied. "The little monsters are moving."

"Moving in what direction?" Chime asked. Jade turned the glare on him. He persisted, "Moving down?"

She hesitated, and Moon had to grip a handful of the fur he was sitting on to keep himself from shifting out of pure anxiety. She said, slowly, "I can't tell."

Moon managed to say, "Heart said we had days yet."

Chime was annoyingly calm. "It depends. If the fledglings are large and healthy, and developing fast, they may come a bit early."

"Do you want me to leave?" Ember asked at the same time as Bramble said, "Should I go find Heart?"

"No, everybody just stay where you are, where Pearl told you to stay." Jade eased back on the furs and Balm stuffed another cushion behind her back. "The damn things are still again."

Moon made himself take a full breath. The comment about Pearl worried him more than anything. Jade had been getting along better with Pearl, but Moon had never seen Jade depend on her like this. It made the situation even more nerve-racking.

Pearl would fight fiercely to save the court, Moon had seen her do it. But he thought Jade was better at strategy, that she acted more quickly. He would feel a lot more confident about this if Jade was the one down in the village trying to figure out what was attacking them.

"I'm fairly certain that if you need Heart, Pearl would want us to get her for you," Ember said. He moved the pot off the heated stones, watching Jade worriedly.

Moon asked Chime, "You can't help with the babies?" He didn't like to ask the question, to remind Chime of his lost abilities, but he needed to know. And with the conversation so far, Chime was probably already thinking about his lost abilities. "If you had to. It doesn't take magic, does it?" The other births he had watched hadn't seemed to need any special abilities by the mentors, at least as far as he could tell.

Chime grimaced regretfully. "When it gets close to the time, Jade isn't going to want anybody to touch her except a mentor, a clutchmate, or you," he said. "It's a scent thing. It's something only queens do, probably a holdover from the past, maybe as a protective measure. I don't smell like a mentor anymore." He spread his hands. "But if worse came to worst, I could tell you what to do."

Moon looked at Balm. She said, firmly, "If worse comes to worst, I'll go and get Heart. Ember's right, Pearl will understand."

Jade snorted, and said, "I told you all, it's not happening."

At least, Moon decided, it gave them something else to worry about as they waited out the rest of the long night.

(

After dawn the next morning, Moon went down to the Kek village to try to help the hunters track whatever it was that had come so near the root doorway.

He moved slowly through the undergrowth, ducking under the fern fronds and trailing vines and branches. Bone was right on his heels, Bramble and several other hunters spread out behind him. Moon said, "It was in this area, right around here." It wasn't easy, trying to point out a spot where you had sensed something standing that you hadn't actually seen, but the hunters seemed certain they could find it.

Bone tugged on one of his frills. "Stop there and move back."

Moon edged back behind Bone as the other hunters began to ease forward. They were using rocks spelled for light. It was a clear day above the canopy, but little light penetrated this far down, and it was even darker in the thick foliage. They were about fifty or so paces from the clearing in front of the root door, and the ground was coated with a white mold that felt like you were walking on melon rinds. The ferns and saplings stretched high over Moon's head and clouds of insects hovered.

The hunters searched in silence for a time. Moon stayed where he was, watching a group of what he had first thought were long-petaled colorful flowers make a slow climb up a sapling branch. Then Streak said, "Bone, here."

Moon quivered but resisted the urge to move. The undergrowth rustled as hunters changed position. After a long moment, Bone said, "Good. Go and bring Pearl, now."

Streak reappeared and hurried past. Moon stepped carefully forward until he saw Bone crouched over, and moved up beside him. Bone said, "There was something here, all right."

Moon could barely see the marks in the light-colored mold. Bone flicked it with a claw to show there were loose pieces flaking away from the ground. The mold was hard on the outer layer and soft underneath, and it had cracked where something heavy—heavier than a Raksura and far heavier than a Kek—had stood on it. Bone explained, "It stood here and watched, didn't move back and forth like those predators. Smaller feet, too."

It could have been a smaller predator that had seen the fate of the others and decided not to attack, but it was the only clue they had at the moment. "Can you follow it?"

"Maybe." Bone's head tilted thoughtfully. "We'll try."

Moon glanced back to see Pearl picking her way through the foliage, following Streak. He stepped out of the way.

Moon returned to the clearing, where Stone stood now in groundling form. Several Kek sat on the mossy ground, waiting to hear the verdict, and there were warriors scattered around, crouched on top of the root that led up toward the doorway and perched on the giant gray-brown wall of the trunk. Stone said, "If this thing is stupid enough to stick around after last night, I'll be surprised."

"Nothing it's done has made sense so far, why shouldn't it hang around and wait for us to find it?" Moon tasted the air again, but there was nothing unusual. It was even free of any rank traces of predator scent. "After all that noise last night, most of the predators in this area have probably been scared off, at least for a while. That's going to help a little." He glanced around the clearing. "What happened to the one I killed last night?"

"I ate it." At his look, Stone said, "I was hungry."

"There wasn't anything strange about it?"

"It didn't have any magic bridles stuck in its gut like that leviathan; I looked." Stone grimaced at the movement in the undergrowth, but it was only Plum and Knife, examining the ground at the edge of the clearing. "If this is a groundling sorcerer, he's lived here for a while."

"You don't think it's someone after the seed anymore?" Moon asked. He had never thought it was likely, but he was curious why Stone had changed his mind.

"It's after something. Maybe it's something those groundlings had, and now it thinks we've got it."

"So why didn't it take it from the leaf boat after it attacked the groundlings and killed the Kek?" Moon pointed out. Stone growled and rubbed his face in frustration. Moon sympathized. He added, "I know, this doesn't make sense."

"It makes sense," Stone countered. "We just don't know why yet."

Gold flashed among the deep green ferns as Pearl stepped out of the undergrowth. She said to Stone, "Bone is ready."

Stone gave Moon a shove to the shoulder. "Keep an eye on the place." As he started forward into the undergrowth, several of the waiting warriors dropped off their perches to follow him. Three of the Kek clambered to their feet and hurried after. The other Kek remained behind, and after a moment, Moon realized they were here to help guard the root doorway. The Raksura were watching the village, and so the Kek were watching the colony tree.

Moon thought Pearl would go back into the tree, but instead she stopped and asked, "How is Jade?"

Moon made his spines stay still, though it was an effort. He hadn't forgotten about the clutch, but concentrating on finding the creature who had been waiting and watching last night had provided something of a temporary relief. "She thinks the babies moved last night."

Pearl's brow lifted. "Moved down?"

"She couldn't tell."

Pearl twitched a spine dismissively. "There's still time."

Everyone seemed perfectly confident about this. Moon tried to keep the impatience out of his voice as he asked, "How do you know?"

Pearl tilted her head, but her voice was amused. "When five fledglings all move down together, believe me, she will know."

Someone flapped overhead, then Drift landed in the clearing. "Pearl, Thistle asked for you, she's with the groundlings. One woke up."

Pearl flashed into motion and Moon leapt after her.

He followed Pearl through the low undergrowth and under the arch of the root at the edge of the village. The Kek were clearly agitated, most peering worriedly out of the hanging huts or gathering on the ground and talking anxiously. Moon reached the shelter just a few steps behind Pearl.

Thistle stood in front of it, surrounded by an anxious group of the Kek healers. Thistle was in her groundling form and two of the Kek were patting her on the shoulders and head, apparently trying to commiserate with her. The warriors guarding the shelter all stood at a distance, twitching their spines self-consciously. Pearl demanded, "What happened?"

Thistle's eyes were wide. "Uh, one of the groundlings woke up."

"Which one?" Moon asked.

"The silvery one, who's a bit like a sealing. She's very upset." Thistle glanced toward the hearth that had been dug into the moss and lined with heating stones. The kettle had been tipped off and sat an awkward angle; fortunately it hadn't been full of hot water. "I was moving a kettle, and Drift was there, and we weren't shifted to groundling—" Thistle took a deep breath. She still looked rattled. Moon understood. The first time someone panicked at the sight of you was never easy. "The groundling saw us and she's very upset, and that's made the Kek upset, and Merit went into the colony to sleep, and the groundling doesn't speak Altanic and that's the only groundling language I know."

Pearl started toward the shelter, then stopped and turned to Moon. He fell back a step out of habit, and she flared her spines in annoyance. She said, "You know groundlings. You try to talk to her."

It was only sensible. If the groundling had been frightened by a small Arbora and a warrior, she would be terrified by Pearl, even in her Arbora form. Moon shifted to groundling, and stepped past Pearl into the shelter.

Inside, the groundling was huddled in the far corner, clutching a metal bar used to move big water kettles on and off the warming stones. The other groundlings still lay unconscious on their pallets along the far wall.

It was the groundling who looked a little like a sealing. This was the first good view Moon had had of her face. Her nose was flat and her eyes were completely round, and had a light membrane rather than lashes or fur. Her mouth was lipless and almost square, and looking at her body he wasn't entirely sure she was female, but it was as good a guess as any. She was breathing hard and her silver skin was blotchy, and she trembled from either pain or fear. Though her features were hard to read, Moon thought her expression was probably terrified. They were lucky no one had tried to take the bar away, that there hadn't been an edged weapon available for her to stab someone with, that Thistle and the warriors and the Kek had sensibly fled out of reach instead of trying to wrestle her for it. The last thing they needed now was another injury.

Moon didn't try to go any further into the shelter. He sat on his heels on the edge of the platform, eye level with her. He wished Stone was here. Stone was good with groundlings, and had an uncanny ability to make his groundling form seem non-threatening to a variety of species. But this groundling could answer all their questions. And he was really tired of having unanswered questions.

He heard a rustle behind him and glanced back to see Kof peer through the doorway. Pearl took Kof's hand, clearly being careful of the Kek's stick-like fingers, and urged him to draw back with her.

In Kedaic, Moon asked the groundling, "Can you understand me?" Kedaic was a trade language and Moon had heard it used by groundlings to the east of the Reaches and beyond.

The groundling stared, suspicious and incredulous, as if she hadn't expected him to be able to speak. "What are you?"

Her Kedaic was so oddly accented it took Moon a moment to understand it. "We're Raksura. We're shapeshifters, we live in the suspended forest." There was no point in trying to conceal that fact, since she had already seen Thistle and Drift. He just hoped she wasn't one of the many groundlings who thought all shapeshifters were groundling-eating Fell. He nodded back toward Kof, who sat just within sight of the shelter's doorway. "You're in a Kek village, on the forest floor. We found you, injured, in your leaf boat. Do you remember what happened?"

The groundling blinked her large eyes and her throat moved. She finally said, "I don't . . . I . . . There are two of you."

"Two . . ." He didn't know what she meant. Pearl had taken a seat outside, and from the angle the groundling shouldn't be able to see her.

She said, "You are two beings in one. One is like a land dweller, with soft skin. The other is black and scaled and has wings." Her voice was tinged with suspicion. "You both exist in the same space."

"Uh . . ." That was strange, and as far as Moon knew he had never encountered anything like it before. If any groundlings in the east had been able to see his other form like that, he was pretty certain they would have said something about it. Right after they killed him. "I'm a Raksura, a shapeshifter. Raksura are shapeshifters." Maybe she didn't understand the Kedaic word for shapeshifter. Maybe he was misunderstanding her words. "You're saying you can see both of me at once?"

"Yes." The woman's hands tightened on the bar, a nervous reaction. "It . . . I have very good eyesight."

Moon shifted to his winged form. "What do you see now?"

She flinched and looked away, then seemed to steel herself and faced him. "The same but the positions have changed." She blinked, her pupils widening, the membrane moving back and forth.

That was some eyesight. Moon's first impulse was to call Thistle in, or to send for Heart and the other mentors, as well as Chime. This was bizarre. But behind him, Pearl said, "Moon, get on with it." Kof rattled his staff impatiently.

Right, later, Moon told himself. He shifted back to his groundling form, though apparently it didn't much matter. "I'm Moon. I'm a consort of the Indigo Cloud court. Our reigning queen is Pearl, and Kof is the leader of this Kek village. Who are you?"

She hesitated, then said, "I'm Elastan, of the Sourci of Ildam."

Moon had never heard of the species or the place, if those were what she was referring to. "You're from the Reaches?"

She didn't answer and he added, "That's what we call this forest." The Reaches were vast, and if her species was native to the forest floor, it could easily be possible for her never to have seen a Raksura before. Unless you could fly, it wasn't easy to travel between the suspended forest and the floor, and few species would see a reason to, since it would mean encountering a whole new spectrum of predators. But at least the possibility that these groundlings were after colony tree seeds was becoming even more unlikely than it already had been. If she hadn't known about Raksura then she probably knew nothing of colony trees, either. "You traveled here from somewhere in the forest?"

Finally, she said reluctantly, "Yes, from the mineral basins. Some distance from here."

Moon wasn't sure why she seemed not to want to admit it. It wasn't as if he had ever heard of that place or had any idea where it was. "Why did you come here?"

"I'm here because . . ." She hesitated in what Moon thought was a very telling way. She clearly didn't want to answer the question. That was more than a little suspicious. She finished, "I wanted to explore."

Moon decided to leave it at that for the moment. He wanted her to keep talking, and if he suggested she wasn't telling the truth, the conversation would end. He nodded toward the unconscious bodies of her companions. "Who are they? Are they explorers too?"

She hesitated again, then evidently decided that there was no real reason to withhold that information. "They're called the Amifata. They live in the wet canyons near the basins, and are traders. We—" She stumbled over the word. "They wanted to try to reach a species they used to trade with, who lived deep in the interior. It should have . . . It should have been a forty day trip, at the most. They meant to go no further than that, and turn back if they couldn't find the people they were looking for."

The length of the trip didn't mean much, considering Moon had no idea how fast the leaf boat traveled in a day, but it was a relief she was finally giving him a real answer. He said, "What was it that attacked you?"

The relief was short-lived. She said, "Yes, we were attacked. By a strange species."

That wasn't helpful. It was almost deliberately unhelpful. Just to see what she would say, he suggested, "By the Kek?"

She didn't reply and he thought he read wary incomprehension in her expression. He twisted around and motioned for Kof to come forward. Kof put his staff down, and moved to sit on the edge of the shelter's platform, where the groundling could see him better. Kof kept his movements slow, and didn't rattle, obviously trying not to startle their guest. Moon said, "This is Kof, a Kek. Was it Kek who attacked you?"

"No. Not . . ." She seemed genuinely confused by the question. "I have not seen those people before."

"You saw them at least once before." Moon decided to push the issue a little harder. "Three of them were lying dead by your leaf boat when we found you."

She blinked. "I know nothing of this!"

Moon wished he believed that. Her reactions were so hard to read, he couldn't tell if this behavior was normal for her, or if she was lying to him, or if she was frightened, or if she was just odd. "What did the strange species who attacked you look like?"

She didn't hesitate, but the lids of her eyes shivered. She gestured at the unconscious Amifata. "Like them. But different. They were a swamp species. One I had not seen before."

Moon sat back. This sounded like an attempt to answer the question without accidentally implicating any innocent bystanders. He suspected if he pressed her for details about the "swamp species" their appearance would be so vague as to fit every amphibian in the Three Worlds. He changed direction. "Why did they attack you?"

"Why does anyone attack strangers?" she countered.

"We don't know, we don't attack strangers," Moon said. He gave her a moment to digest that. "But whoever wants to attack you came here last night and tried to kill you again, and hurt some of our people."

She looked away, and her throat worked. That emotion was easy to read—it was fear. *But she isn't surprised*, Moon thought. At least he didn't think so. She said, "I don't know. I don't know." She pressed a hand to her side, where a bandage and poultice covered her wound. She took a sharp breath, and then dug her fingers in and ripped it off.

The wound tore open and blood splattered out onto her skin, the scent pungent in the enclosed space. Moon swallowed back a snarl. Kof made a startled rattle.

Getting angry wouldn't do any good, and she was clearly trying to get some sort of dramatic, distracting reaction out of him. Moon said, "You can put it off, but you have to tell us eventually." He tilted his head. "Thistle."

Thistle stepped in, hissed in annoyance, and reached for the bag of healing supplies.

Behind Moon, Pearl said in Raksuran, "That's enough for now."

Kof scrambled out and Moon turned and followed him. Pearl drew Kof away a few paces, curving her tail to tell Moon to follow her. Her spines were tilted at an angle Moon couldn't quite read. From her expression, he was going to guess it was something like thoughtful irritation. She said, "What good will it do the stupid creature to injure herself and withhold this information?"

Moon shifted back to his winged form. It made him edgy to stand out here in his groundling form. "She thinks we're not going to like it, whatever it is. Which means this group probably isn't just explorers." But having searched the leaf boat and seen their maps, he wasn't sure what else they could be. The story of trying to restore contact with a lost trading partner made sense. But Elastan was clearly concealing something.

Pearl's expression as she inclined her head toward him was not patient. "I realize that. You'll have to try again later." She hissed and flexed her claws. "Explain the situation to Kof. Tell him we need to separate that one from the other groundlings, so we can speak to them without her presence when they wake. If there is no other shelter in the village that will be adequate, tell him the Arbora can build a temporary one." She took a step away and leapt into the air.

The force of her wing flap rocked Moon back on his heels. Kof swayed with the breeze, then turned to Moon inquiringly. In laborious pidgin, Moon went over the conversation, then asked him about moving the conscious groundling to another shelter. Floret landed beside them about halfway through the explanation. She looked weary, her frills drooping, and her scales were streaked with mud. When he got to the part about how the groundling had refused to tell them what might be hunting her and the others, Kof turned to the shelter and shook his staff at it, in an expression of frustration. "That's how we feel too," Moon told him.

They settled the new shelter question readily, with Kof agreeing to the proposition and accepting the Arbora's help. Moon couldn't tell if Kof thought the Kek needed help or was just being nice in accepting it. Whichever, he thought the Arbora and the Kek would be able to work it out between them. And he needed to get back to Jade, because she was going to be seething, waiting for a report.

But Kof launched into his own explanation, and it took Moon some time to understand him. Floret listened worriedly, and finally said, "He's saying they're missing someone? In the attack?"

That wasn't good. "When did you last see them?" Moon asked.

Kof pointed at the curve of the colony tree trunk looming over the village and said the Kek-version of Merit's name.

"He went into the tree with Merit?" Moon asked. Kof lifted his staff in assent.

Floret hissed and clapped her hand over her eyes. "Oh, that's just fine."

"Are they not supposed to be inside the colony?" Moon asked. It didn't seem fair. The Raksura had been all over the Kek village.

"I have no idea," Floret said wearily. "I'm not going to ask Pearl, because if they aren't, then . . . I'm just not going to ask Pearl."

Whether the Kek could visit the colony or not was definitely something they could worry about later. "At least he's not dead," Moon told her. "I'll go get him."

He left Floret explaining to a reassured Kof that Moon would retrieve the lost Kek, and headed back toward the root doorway.

☾

Once back inside the colony, Moon found the Kek with Merit, in the large room at the top of the root area where the wounded had been taken last night. There were only two soldiers and three warriors still resting here, the others having been well enough to go up to their bowers once their wounds were tended. They lay on thick pallets of grass mats and blankets, breathing deeply in healing sleep. The scents of dried blood and sickness still hung in the air.

Heart and Merit sat near the hearth bowl that had been moved into the room, surrounded by bowls and cups holding various simples, and the bags and little bone and horn containers that held the herbs and other materials to make them. They were making notes on reed paper and looked as if they had been awake for hours. Moon couldn't spot the visitor at first, until he realized the bundle of twigs and leaves near Merit was actually a sleeping Kek.

Both the mentors looked up at Moon's arrival, and Heart asked, "Is there news of the search?"

Moon shifted to his groundling form and sat down on the opposite side of the hearth. The radiated warmth of the stones on his skin just made him want to curl up and sleep. "Not yet, but one of the groundlings woke." As both drew breath to ask, he said, "She didn't tell us anything, yet. She said they were attacked by a 'strange species' and she didn't know what had happened to the Kek." He nodded toward the warrior who lay on a pallet a few paces away. "How's Sweep?" Sweep was the most badly wounded. She had gotten bitten by a predator with poisoned spikes on its tongue. Her face wasn't nearly so sunken and hollow-cheeked as it had been last night, but with the healing sleep it was a little hard to tell.

"She's doing well so far." Heart glanced at Sweep and tasted the air, as if it was telling her something about Sweep's condition. And maybe it was; Moon had no idea how mentors evaluated healing patients. "I think we're past the worst. How is Jade?"

"She felt the fledglings move last night and Chime said they might be moving down. But she said they stopped. Pearl said Jade would know."

"Pearl's right." Heart pushed the hair out of her eyes, considering. "They may move off and on for a few days or—"

"Or they might just move all the way down and pop right out," Merit interposed, looking up from his notes. "It's hard to tell—"

"But just make certain someone comes to get me if Jade thinks she's ready," Heart finished, glaring at Merit.

"Right." Moon nodded toward the sleeping Kek. "Who's your new friend?"

"This is Hiak," Merit said, perking up since he had something he was enthused to talk about. "She's a healer, and knows a lot about plants and simples. She was helping me last night before the attack." Hiak, hearing her name, sat up and shook her limbs back into order. "She's really good at making the herb blends, and she has some ideas for new combinations—"

So Merit at least had no idea what he had done, which was pretty much what Moon had assumed. "Merit, the Kek are worried about her. And Pearl doesn't know she's in here."

Heart stared. She turned to Merit accusingly. "You said you had permission for her to be here."

"I did?" Merit frowned, obviously racking his memory. "I may have said that, but I think I was thinking about something else."

"Like what?" Heart demanded.

"Hiak, time to go home." Moon got to his feet with a groan, and motioned for Hiak to follow him. In Kek/Raksuran pidgin he managed, "Back to Kof."

Hiak stood, but waved her arms, indicating the room around them, or maybe the tree.

"I told her I'd show her some of the colony," Merit protested, setting his notes aside and standing up. "There's really nothing that interesting down here. Can I at least show her the greeting hall?"

Moon sighed and rubbed his forehead. He wanted to get back to Jade, but Hiak had apparently worked hard and deserved to have her simple request granted. Of course once the rest of the Kek heard about it, they might want to see the greeting hall too. But that sounded like a problem for someone else. If that happened, Moon could just go up to his bower and pretend he didn't know what was going on; it was one of the few benefits to being a consort. "All right, let's show her the greeting hall."

Moon walked with Merit and Hiak up through the colony, letting Hiak admire the curves of the stairwells and the falls of water and the carved murals along the way. She was the most impressed by the teachers' hall, with the carved trees in the walls with trunks stretching up and their canopies carved in the domed roof. He wondered what the Kek would make of Opal Night's hall of living trees. He hadn't seen any Kek at Opal Night, but that didn't necessarily mean they weren't there. They might have been living deep in the split mountain-tree's roots.

They went up the stairs to the greeting hall, and Hiak pirouetted, staring all around the big chamber. Moon told Merit, "Now you need to take her back to the village. Make sure Floret and Kof know she's back—"

Hiak shook her arms to get their attention and then pointed toward the waterfall. She asked what was clearly a question, but none of the words were in Moon's limited Kek vocabulary. Taking a guess, he said, "That's the water the tree doesn't need. It pushes it out and we use it, and then send it outside."

Hiak looked at him, then looked at the waterfall again, and spoke a little more urgently. Moon shook his head, trying to tell her he had no idea. "Merit?"

Merit said, "I don't know." He spread his hands and spoke to Hiak in stumbling Kek.

She stared hard at him, then waved a hand in front of his eyes, then pointed at the waterfall again. Then she turned to Moon and did the same. Moon couldn't think what question about the water would be so urgent. And she was beginning to show all the signs that the Kek had displayed last night, the shaking and rattling agitation that meant anxiety and warning. *She thinks the pool will overflow? The water doesn't look right?* He couldn't come up with anything that made sense.

Grain, one of the soldiers on watch in the greeting hall, wandered up beside Moon. "What's wrong?"

"We don't—" Moon began, then Hiak grabbed Merit's wrist and tugged him toward the pool. Moon followed.

Hiak went around the pool to the wall next to the waterfall, where the polished wood was damp and had to be cleaned of moss periodically. It had a fine growth of moss now, a light green mound flowing up the wall from the pool. Moon had time to wonder if Hiak was trying to tell them that the moss was dangerous, or helpful, or something similar, when Hiak took Merit's hand and guided it down toward the floor just in front of the wall.

Merit shrieked, shifted to Arbora, caught Hiak around the waist, and leapt backward a good six paces. Moon shifted to his winged form in reaction, even as Grain shifted and stepped protectively in front of him. Hiak patted Merit on his scaled chest, radiating approval.

Merit pointed toward the spot and gasped, "Moon, there's something there we can't see."

Moon took Grain by the shoulders and forcibly set him aside, then crouched and reached out. In the empty space in front of the wall, his fingers touched spiky fur.

He jerked his hand back and hissed out a curse. "Grain, get Pearl. And Heart. And Kof." If this wasn't related to the attack last night, it would be a bizarre coincidence.

Grain bounded off, calling for a warrior. Moon wanted to back away, but he didn't want whatever this was to have a chance to slip past him. Hiak tapped Merit's hands until he set her down, then she scrambled to Moon's side. She spread her hands, trying to show him the shape of the thing. It seemed like it was about the size of a small Arbora, huddled against the wall. Merit crouched beside her and reached out. Moon said, "No, not too close." He stood and urged both of them back a pace. "Is it dead?" he asked Hiak. "Sleeping?" He managed to say the Kek words, or at least close enough for Hiak to understand.

She replied with the Raksuran pidgin for "sick," slurring and clicking the word. She lifted her hands in a gesture of confusion. Moon thought he understood; it looked sick to her, but she couldn't be sure.

If it was sick or injured, that might explain why it hadn't killed anyone yet.

As far as they knew. In the confusion, had someone gone missing and no one noticed?

And was there more than one of these creatures in the colony? *We're going to need more Kek in here*, Moon thought. *A lot more.*

"You know this?" he asked Hiak. "Seen this creature before?"

She made negative gestures, and more indications of confusion and bewilderment.

Staring hard at the creature, Moon thought he could see something. Blotchy patches maybe, small ones, that his eyes tried to say were part of the moss and the brown tones of the wall, but that might actually be hovering in the air in front of it. He wasn't sure if he was looking at something that was using magic, or something with a natural protective coloration, or a combination of both. He leaned close and tasted the air near the creature. It did have a scent, but a subtle one, a faint musk almost disguised by the moss.

Warriors and Arbora, drawn by the commotion, gathered behind them. Grain was back and explaining what had happened, and hisses of disbelief and worried murmurs spread through the greeting hall.

Moon had no warning of Pearl's arrival until she landed beside him and almost flattened him with her left wing. Hiak made an alarmed click and climbed into Merit's arms.

Pearl set Kof on his feet and Moon moved aside so they could both get a better look. Kof crouched, rattled in astonishment, spoke to Hiak for a few moments, then leaned close over the creature.

Watching Kof's reaction, Moon had an idea. He said, "Pearl. The wounded groundling could see me in both forms, groundling and Raksura." Pieces were starting to fall into place. Nothing made sense yet, but the elements that didn't make sense were starting to connect up to each other. Something that couldn't be seen by every pair of eyes, and the groundling who could see both of a shapeshifter's forms . . .

Pearl turned to looked down at him, her spines flared. He could feel the heat off her body, and she radiated fury. "I know. What does—" She stopped, considering. "You think she can see other things as well."

"Maybe that's why she was with the other groundlings, the Amifata. So she could see things for them." Moon looked at Hiak. "And the Kek. Maybe the Kek plant hunters were killed because they could see things too."

Pearl growled deep in her chest.

☾

It was a good thing Hiak had been genuinely interested to see the colony, because she and other young Kek got to see all of it with groups of soldiers and hunters as guides. They examined the nurseries and other most vulnerable points first, then worked out from there. The idea that one creature could slip in, that it might then open one of the colony's root doorways for others, was terrifying. The soldiers were checking all those doors, and the ones in the platforms and canopy, making sure none had been opened or unbolted. At the same time, more Kek systematically searched their own village, looking under every pile of leaves and behind every fernbush, anywhere a small creature like the one they had found could hide.

Moon took Hiak up to Jade's bower personally so she could make certain there was nothing invisible lurking inside. Jade heard the story, growled in frustration, and sent Balm and Hiak out to continue the search. Moon, she ordered back down to find out what was going on. Frantic with thwarted curiosity, Chime asked her, "Can I go? Do you mind? I—"

"Yes, go!" Jade flicked her claws imperatively. "Find out what this thing is! And if there's more of them!"

Moon didn't want to leave Jade alone, whatever she thought. He turned to Ember, who immediately raised his hands and said, "I'm definitely staying here."

Ginger the soldier said, "And I have an idea." She turned to the other Arbora who were guarding the bower. "If we block the door with our bodies, we'll be able to feel if anything tries to get past us."

One of the others said, "Yes, but we need a teacher, because if we had a very thin, light cloth—"

A little reassured by Arbora ingenuity, Moon went with Chime back down through the organized panic of the court to one of the mentors' workrooms, where the still-unconscious invader had been taken.

There, in the center of the room, Heart knelt beside the invisible creature. The only way Moon could tell it was there were the dents in the cushion it lay on. Pearl, Merit, Knell, and Blossom had gathered around, crouching to watch. Kof and some of the older Kek were seated on the floor nearby, listening intently as Merit did his best to translate. Pearl flicked a spine as Moon and Chime joined the group, but didn't comment. Moon asked Knell, "Did the Kek find any others yet?"

"Not so far." Knell was in his Arbora form, and shivered his spines. He was clearly angry, and clearly embarrassed at the soldiers' failure to keep the creature out of the colony. Moon didn't think it was Knell's fault, but he didn't think Knell should feel great about all this, either.

"Its claws are soft and small," Heart reported, handling one not quite invisible hand carefully. She was in her groundling form so her touch would be more sensitive, and the creature's limb was a grayish haze against her warm brown skin. "Not a digger, and not a climber. A tool-user, probably. Unless it can shift, I don't see how it could have gotten in through the greeting hall entrance."

"But how could it have slipped in through the root door?" Knell said, sounding furious. Pearl flicked a spine in his direction, a clear "don't make me have to look at you" signal. Knell hesitated, and said more evenly, "There were soldiers and warriors in front of the open door the whole time. It was never left unguarded, even for an instant."

Moon said, "I wonder if it slipped inside when we first opened the door, when Stone and the others came in. We were being careful, but no one was worried about anything trying to fight its way past us at that point. And there were a lot of tired warriors bumping around in the root passage and right inside. If something had brushed against one, they might not have noticed."

Knell's spines twitched as he thought about it. "Didn't Fair say someone pushed him, and no one would admit to it?"

Blossom glanced back at them. "I'm fond of Fair, but I wouldn't put a lot of faith in what he thinks happened." She had come from a mixed Arbora and warrior clutch, and Fair was her clutchmate. "Could this thing have slipped past Stone like that?"

"Stone was exhausted," Moon pointed out. He was worried about Stone and Bone and the others. The group following the faint tracks found in the undergrowth hadn't returned yet, and finding this creature put a whole different slant on what might be out there. "And this thing doesn't smell like a predator. It smells like a plant, if anything, and the undergrowth scents are heavy in that corridor when the door opens."

"The hard part would have been getting past the Kek," Knell said. "It must have been trying to avoid the village. Maybe that's why it came in here."

"So what are Stone and Bone and the others tracking now?" Chime had edged close to Heart, trying to see the creature better. "And the attack on the village? If this creature—person—was in here—"

"What's wrong with it?" Pearl's deep voice cut through all the speculation. "Is it injured?"

Wounded by a dart weapon, like the groundlings? Moon wondered. Heart said, "It's not breathing well, but I can't find a wound yet. There are places where its fur is matted which might be blood spots. Its skin might have already closed over the punctures, if it was hit with darts like the others. It doesn't seem to have a weapon or anything else on it, either. It might have gotten rid of any clothes and tools so it could conceal itself better." She leaned over what was presumably its head, and did something very gently with her fingers. Moon saw a flash of what looked like eyeballs.

Heart nodded to herself, and drew back so Chime could look too. "It's not invisible on the inside, at least. Its eyes are rolled up in its head."

"Huh," Chime muttered. "How can the Kek see it? Is their vision just more acute than ours?"

Behind them, Merit said, "I think it's got to do with the way they see at different light levels."

Moon had been around enough different species of groundlings to know that his vision in the dark was far better than most. But the Kek were used to the darkness of the forest floor and seemed to see perfectly well in it. The Kek they had met on the shore of the freshwater sea hadn't seemed to have any problem with bright daylight, either.

Merit continued, "I noticed that Hiak could see differences in color and leaf shape between similar herbs in what to me looked like almost complete darkness. But the spell-lights that we put outside and the ones in here didn't bother her. It was like she and the other Kek didn't notice them at all; their eyes just compensate for whatever level of light they're in."

Chime nodded slowly. "If this creature is doing something using light, or the way light works, to conceal itself, then that would explain why the Kek can still see it."

"That could be it." Heart moved her hands carefully, and Moon got a glimpse of gray skin, and what looked like teeth. "Flat teeth. Might be a plant-eater." She lowered its head carefully to the floor. "Merit, someone, get me some water."

Moon moved back to give them room as Merit jumped up to get a bowl. He said, "Something else was trying to get in here last night. Maybe whatever it was knew this creature had gotten inside, and it was trying to get in after it."

"Two of them trying to get inside," Pearl muttered. "At least."

"So far as we know," Knell added darkly.

Chime sat back on his heels, shaking his head in frustration. "And which one attacked the groundlings and killed the Kek?"

"This one was so desperate to hide that it came in here," Blossom said. Pearl lifted her brow and Blossom explained, "Well, think about it. Small groundling like this, uses camouflage to protect itself, we have to look like terrifying predators, even if it knows what Raksura are. Sneaking in here was desperate. How was it planning to get out?"

It was a good point. Chime turned to Blossom and said, "If it was hurt, sick, it might have come in just looking for a place to hide, to die in peace."

Moon hissed to himself. Blossom and Chime were right, this creature had behaved like something that was hunted. "So we have one groundling, Elastan of the Sourci, who can see things we can't, who might be able to see this creature. And she said the Amifata were looking for a species that they used to trade with. If this is the species, then why not tell us that?"

Knell said, "Maybe it wasn't trade they wanted. Maybe the groundlings with her came to the Reaches to . . . capture this thing? But something else wanted it too, and it followed them."

Blossom nodded grimly, and Chime added, "The something-else attacks the groundlings in the leaf boat, but the invisible creature hides from it. Maybe the invisible creature is injured and trapped in the leaf boat and can't get out, or is afraid to get out. The Kek come along and they see it. Maybe it asks them for help . . . "

Blossom leaned forward. "Or not, but then the Something Else realizes the Kek can see the invisible creature, and it thinks they want to steal it, and it kills them. But it still can't get the invisible creature, because it can't see it either. Then we come along and bring the leaf boat here, and it follows, and the invisible creature sees its chance to hide in the colony, but it's hurt or sick from being trapped so long—"

"Possibly," Pearl said, and stood up. "We have to wait until we know whether there are any more of these hidden in the colony or outside it. And until we hear what Bone and Stone and the others have found." Her tone made it clear she wanted an end to the speculation. She added, "Now tell Kof and the other Kek what we know so far—know, not suspect. Knell, Blossom, I want word from the soldiers and the teachers of how the search goes." She stepped out of the room with an elegant swish of her tail.

Knell and Blossom scrambled to follow Pearl, and Moon turned to the patiently waiting Kof, and started to try to explain. When he had finished, Kof just sat there a few moments, rattling thoughtfully. The other Kek watched him with worried intensity. Kof said finally, "Predators, driven as leaves."

Moon followed that. Predators had been driven into the village, like the wind driving leaves. He said, "It can't do that again. All the predators have been frightened away." They hoped, anyway. Having Stone moving through the undergrowth outside the root area most of the day with Bone and the hunters might keep any new ones from coming into range tonight.

Kof gestured in assent. "Then what night?"

Moon didn't get that one. Chime, who had been listening closely, said, "He means 'what happens tonight?'"

It was a good question. This thing that was stalking the groundlings, it had powers, whatever it was. Moon wasn't looking forward to how it might choose to use them.

Moon left Chime with Heart and Merit and the teachers who would be guarding and caring for their mostly invisible guest, and walked Kof and his advisors back down to the root doorway. It would have taken longer, but Kof was anxious to get back to the village and kept urging the other Kek to stop looking at the carvings and hurry.

River found them in the stairwell that opened into the root level, moving so fast he leapt past them at first and had to turn and tent his wings to drop back down. "Moon, one of the other groundlings is awake."

☾

It was two of the other groundlings, the ones that Elastan had said were called Amifata.

When Moon shifted to his groundling form and stepped inside the shelter, one Amifata was sitting up, blinking uncertainly, and the other lay on its side, hunched up in pain but with its eyes open. Their dark gray skin gleamed in the spell-light of the moss draped around the shelter. They looked far more like amphibians than Elastan had. There were round spots with feathery feelers on their necks and cheeks that must be for breathing, because they didn't have noses at all. Their faces were smooth and triangular, with a sharp slope down to their small mouths. Their eyes were round and encircled by heavy lids, and Moon had no idea what the halos of loose gray tissue around their heads might be for. He just hoped they could speak a language he knew. He also hoped that they didn't have too acute of a sense of smell; it had been a while since he had had time to bathe and he had forgotten to change his moss-stained clothes today.

As he took a seat on the edge of the platform, Thistle and the Kek healers moved away to make room. Kof took a seat just outside the door to listen. The Amifata who was sitting up turned its head so its left eye was more directly regarding Moon. He noticed the right eye had rolled to watch Thistle and the Kek. Moon said in Kedaic, "Do you understand me?"

"Yes." Its voice sounded raspy and almost metallic. Its lips opened a little and Moon had a view of a strange vocal apparatus. It was like seeing the part of a throat that made noise but without any skin covering it. Moon couldn't tell if it was a part of the creature's body, or something that had been made. It said, "The others will recover also?"

Moon recalled suddenly that Elastan hadn't asked that. It was another point against her. In Raksuran, he said to Thistle, "He wants to know if the others will be all right."

Thistle said, "We think so. I hope so. At least now that we know what we were trying to do worked on these two, we have a better chance with the others. We've had to be very careful with the simples we've been giving them, since we can't tell what sort of poison was on the darts."

In Kedaic, Moon told the Amifata, "She thinks they will." From what he could see, this one didn't look that recovered. Its left eye seemed to have trouble focusing on Moon and its movements were still sluggish.

The Amifata made a breathy noise, then said, "What has happened to us?"

It sounded almost plaintive. Moon said, "We found you on the forest floor. You were attacked in your leaf boat. Do you remember?"

The Amifata lowered a hand to its bandaged wound, then looked down at the others. The one that was still hunched up miserably didn't move, but made that same breathy noise that might be a sigh, or maybe it was how their actual, unaltered speech sounded. The Amifata said, "A projectile weapon. I was outside when I was struck. I remember nothing after that. The others were also wounded that way?"

"Yes. We think there was a drug on the darts. You have no idea what attacked you?" Moon decided that trying to read expression and intention off the face of a species who was so different, and only half-awake, was useless. But his impression of this being was that it was far more straightforward than Elastan. And it had woken up surrounded by its wounded companions and being tended by strangers, and its reaction hadn't been panic or fear. It was assuming good intentions on their part, possibly because if the situation had been reversed, its intentions would have been good. Elaston's reaction might have been what Moon was used to, but maybe it had been sparked by more than just fear of a strange species. "You were found by Kek plant hunters, but something attacked and killed them. The Kek asked us to help find them, and we found you, too."

"Kek? Kek were killed? When did this happen?" The Amifata's head turned to let the left eye see the Kek healers. It was almost as if each eye had different functions.

"When you were attacked, or not long after," Moon told it.

"We have met Kek, in the southern climes of the great forest, the dryer areas among the root-hills." It stretched out its hand to the nearest healer. She held out her hand, and it touched the stick-like fingers gently. It sat up and turned the left eye back toward Moon. "What are you?"

"We're Raksura," Moon said. By this point, he thought it very unlikely the Amifata would react with fear at the name, and he wasn't disappointed. It held out its hand to him the way it had to the Kek.

Deciding this was a greeting, Moon got up and moved closer, sitting near enough so the Amifata could touch his hand. Its long narrow fingers had multiple joints and suckers along the underside. Its skin felt soft and a little damp. It rubbed gently at the groundling skin on the top of Moon's hand. "We know of Raksura. Stories only, of the life of the mid-forest, high above." It leaned down to study his skin more closely with its left eye, then started to fall over sideways.

Moon caught it by the shoulders and lifted it carefully upright again. "Thistle, just what kind of simples have you and the Kek been giving them?"

"We've had to try different things," Thistle said, an air of protest in her voice. "It's hard, when you can't put someone in a healing sleep. The Kek have a lot of simples and some of them were stronger than we were really expecting and—We didn't want them to be in pain."

"I don't think it's in pain." Moon steadied the Amifata until it could hold itself up again. In Kedaic, he said, "Do you know anything about a small groundling, a small creature, maybe a pace and a half tall, who can camouflage itself so it's almost invisible to many species?"

It turned the eye to face Moon again and its gaze sharpened. "Yes, we call them the Onde. We were sent here to find them."

"Sent here?"

"By a trader of the mineral basins. Some number of turns ago, the Onde traded with both the mineral basins and the moss canyons. But one turn they failed to appear, and as far as anyone knows, nothing has been heard of them since." The Amifata tried to move, and let out a half-groan, half-gasp. Its vocal apparatus almost fell out, and it lifted a hand to awkwardly tuck it back in. Thistle leaned forward to watch curiously, and Moon just sat there. At least that answered the question of whether it was a natural part of the Amifata's mouth or not. At least, he thought it did. It adjusted the apparatus, and continued, "We were asked to find them again."

That matched Elastan's version well enough, though Moon didn't understand why she had been so reluctant to speak. The Amifata didn't seem to consider it a secret. "So you found them?"

"Yes, though it was difficult, and a longer journey than we had believed. We reached the old trading ground, where we were told to go, and put out the trading signal. It is a plant device, that releases a specific scent. Some time later, an Onde appeared. Elastan saw it through its concealment." It looked down at the others. The one that had seemed conscious had closed its eyes again. Then the Amifata seemed to realize that one of the group was missing. "Where is Elastan?"

"She was hurt too, but she's in another shelter." Moon asked, "Why is she with you?"

The Amifata angled its left eye toward Moon again. "She brought us the offer to search for the Onde, and gave us the map and the old trading signal. We don't normally venture to these dry spaces, among the roots. We are of the moss canyons. We trade with the mineral basins, but we met her in the trading assemblage of the moss routes."

And Elastan didn't mention any of that. "She said you were explorers."

The Amifata's left eye rotated. "We explore and study the territories around the moss canyons." It tapped its mouth. "We use translators, and carry speech between species who cannot understand each other. We help them to trade with each other. We have not come so far before, but it seemed worth it, to find the Onde again."

Elastan had been oddly cagey about whose idea the trip had been. Moon still didn't understand why, unless it was some matter of territory between the mineral basins and the moss canyons that no one outside those two places would understand or care about. "What happened after Elastan saw the Onde?"

"We tried to speak with it, then Elastan cried out . . ." The left eye blinked slowly. "That was when I was struck down." It turned its eye down on the others again. "I remember nothing else."

Moon set his jaw and didn't hiss. If Elastan had had time to cry out, she must have seen what had attacked them. "We think the thing that attacked you came here last night, and tried to get inside our colony. You don't have any idea what it is?"

"I did not see." The Amifata's left eye went unfocused and the right eye started to rotate. "I did not see the others struck down . . ." It started to lean over sideways. Moon caught it and steered it upright again. As if it hadn't noticed, it said, "I hope we will see home again."

"We'll help you all we can," Moon said. "We'll make sure you get back there." He had no idea where the moss canyons were, but as long as it was somewhere in the Reaches it should be possible to get to it relatively easily, if they ended up having to fly the Amifata back. But there didn't seem to be anything wrong with the leaf boat. If the Amifata recovered fully, they might be able to make their way home on their own.

Its left eye rotated again. "That is ... That is ..." The Amifata started to fold over and the Kek healer jumped up to help Moon guide it down to the pallet.

As Moon got to his feet, Thistle moved around to sit next to the Amifata. She handed the Kek healer a small container made of woven leaves and asked Moon, "Did you find out anything?"

"I found out I was talking to the wrong people," Moon said. He climbed out of the shelter into the clearing. Clouds must have moved in somewhere high overhead, because the dim light had faded almost completely and the chorus of insects and treelings rose and fell in waves of sound. There was movement all around, but it was mostly Kek, shifting their stores of plant matter around, herding smaller Kek toward the center of the village. The air about five paces above the ground was filled with small flying lizards and frogs, catching the insects drawn by the moss-lights.

A little distance away, Kof stood with another Aeriat in groundling form; it took Moon a whole heartbeat to realize it was Stone. "You found something?" Moon said, too startled and relieved to make a better greeting.

"Not as much as you found," Stone said. His clothes were covered with mud and moss stains; he must have had to shift to fit into some narrow places. "Sage says the colony was invaded by an invisible groundling? I was only gone for half a day, what's wrong with you?"

Kof rattled his staff at Stone and headed off, presumably to get the full story from the Kek who had gone along on the hunt. Moon said, "Are Bone and the others all right?" Stone's tone never gave away much, but Moon didn't think the hunt had been successful. A dramatic find would have meant an earlier return; he suspected that they had returned now because the change in weather had made it too dark for further searching.

Stone stretched and rolled his shoulders. "Everyone's fine. I sent the others inside, and Bone's gone to tell Pearl about it, if he can find her." Moon knew that last part wasn't a criticism. Considering how Pearl had behaved when Moon had first come to the court back at the old colony to the east, the idea of her taking an active part in anything must still be a welcome relief to Stone. He continued, "We tracked whatever it is to a lair in the roots of the next mountain-tree to the south. It must have hidden there after it saw us move the leaf boat into the Kek village. We didn't find much evidence of a camp, just a place where something slept for the night. We kept looking, but we couldn't pick up its trail. Then the clouds came in and Bramble says her bad shoulder is predicting heavy rain."

That wasn't encouraging. Moon doubted the thing had given up after all this effort; the idea of what it might be doing out there as the light failed made his groundling skin creep. He said, "We know why the groundlings were here now. And I think I know why the thing—whatever it is—wanted to get into the colony last night. It was after the Onde." He told Stone what had happened while the hunting party was gone, and what Elastan had said and her account's key differences from the Amifata's version.

Stone looked up at the flickers of color flashing through the air, as the lizards fed on the insect cloud. He said, "This Onde must have been hiding in the leaf boat. When we found it, the Kek plant hunters were too upset about their dead to pay much attention to it, and none of them looked inside."

Moon thought Blossom and Chime were right. Whatever was after the Onde hadn't been able to see it either, so after searching the boat unsuccessfully it had just sat there with the dying groundlings and the Onde trapped in the leaf boat, waiting for the Onde to give in or die too. The Onde's faint scent, mixed in with the scents of all the plant matter, the leaf boat itself, and the Amifata's blood, must have been indistinguishable even in the confined space. The creature had killed the Kek who had happened on it, then must have fled when Stone and the others arrived. It had followed when they had brought the leaf boat here, the Onde still hiding inside. The Onde must have realized it couldn't avoid a whole village of Kek, and had left the leaf boat and hidden in the brush. When the Arbora had opened the root doorway, the desperate Onde had slipped inside, using the noisy tired warriors as cover. And whatever was after it had somehow tracked it to the colony. "And Elastan is lying. She did see what attacked them."

Still watching the flicker of the lizards' wings, Stone's eyes narrowed. "So let's have a talk with Elastan."

☾

The Kek and the Arbora had built the smaller shelter for Elastan about a hundred paces further into the village, closer to the trunk. Moon and Stone picked their way among the Kek's arrangements of plant matter under the hanging huts to reach it. The shelter was lit by moss spelled for light as well, and now that Moon knew to look, he could see Merit was right, the Kek seemed completely indifferent to the brighter light.

The shelter was smaller and with a different design, with the reeds woven to form a circular structure, though the platform base was the same. It was guarded by a group of Kek and Arbora hunters. There were a couple of warriors as well, and Moon asked Stone, "You want to send someone to tell Pearl?"

"I want to send someone to tell Pearl after we know what this ground-ling's lying about and why." At Moon's look, he said, "What, is she in a good mood about all this?"

He was right, it was probably better to wait until they had something definite to report.

One of the hunters, Blaze, came forward to meet them as they crossed the foot-trampled mold in front of the shelter. She asked, "Did something happen?"

"Maybe." Moon looked toward the lit doorway of the shelter. "Has she tried to get away?"

Blaze flicked her spines in agitation and followed his gaze. "No. She hasn't really done anything, except eat a little fruit and sleep. She hasn't tried to tear her bandage again. Thistle warned us about that. I can speak Kedaic, but she won't talk to me."

"Hmph," Stone commented.

Moon ducked under the reed cover and stepped into the shelter. Elastan sat in the center, on a pallet of cushions and blankets brought from the colony, softening the Kek's grass mats. There was a water skin and a plate of half-eaten fruit and bread, and a covered jar that from the smell was acting as a temporary latrine. It was still hard to read expression on her face, but she didn't look happy to see him.

When Stone stepped in behind Moon, she gasped and covered her eyes. "What is that?"

"That's our line-grandfather." Moon sat down on a mat, folding his legs under him. Stone had to be a strange sight for someone who could see both Raksuran forms at once. His winged form was too big to fit into this shelter. "He's been out hunting the thing that tried to kill you."

Elastan lifted her head a little, looking away as Stone sat down in the doorway. Blaze and a couple of the Kek peered in behind Stone, crouching on the edge of the platform, and Moon didn't tell them to leave. Maybe Elastan would be more intimidated by a bigger audience. He said, "The Amifata are awake."

That made her look directly at Moon. He wondered if her strange sight could tell her if he was lying. Since he didn't need to lie, that wasn't a disadvantage. "The Amifata say you were the one who wanted to come out here, you had the map, you had the old trading signal."

She wasn't surprised or angry to hear it. She said, "They lie. They are afraid of you."

Moon had thought he had plenty of patience for this, but suddenly he found it rapidly draining away. It was growing darker and a breeze scented with rain moved through the reeds. If Bramble's bad shoulder was right, the weather would turn worse, ruining what little visibility they had tonight. "We found it."

Her pupils got smaller. It might or might not mean shock, but it was a dramatic reaction. After a betraying hesitation, she said, "Found what?"

"The Onde. We're like the Amifata, it's almost impossible for us to see it. But the Kek are like you; they can."

Her eyelids fluttered and she took a sharp breath. Moon made sure none of his relief showed. *We were right to believe the Amifata. She is the key to this.* He added, "Is that why the three Kek who found your leaf boat are dead?"

"I don't know." That answer came quickly. At least she had decided not to dispute the existence of the Onde; Moon didn't think he could have sat through that without doing something drastic. She moved her hands restlessly. "I didn't see what happened to those Kek. I told you I was injured, dying."

"So the thing that attacked you was waiting while you and the Onde and the Amifata were slowly dying in the leaf boat, and when the Kek stumbled on you and tried to help you, it killed them. Why won't you tell us what it is?"

Elastan said, "I don't know—"

"We know you saw it."

Elastan looked away. Then she reached for the bandage at her waist. Moon said, "Touch it, and I'll rip it off myself and throw you out in the undergrowth for the carrion eaters."

Elastan went still, except for the flutter of her eye membranes. She cautiously snuck a look at him. Whatever she saw must have convinced her. She carefully removed her hand from the bandage.

Moon had to take a deep breath and let it out, managing not to hiss or growl. Getting angry wasn't helping. He was beginning to think Elastan wasn't very intelligent, or at least not very good at thinking her way out of difficult situations. She had revealed her strange eyesight when she had said she could see two of him; if she hadn't done that, no one would have realized her connection to the Onde. "Tell me what that thing out there is. It tried to kill you once already. You have no reason to protect it." If she couldn't see a way out for herself, he had to find one for her. "The Amifata still think you're their friend. If you tell us what we need to know, you can leave here with them, and they can take you back home."

Elastan made a choking sound. She pressed her hands over her face for a moment. "I did not mean for them to be injured. I didn't mean for myself to be—I did not think this would mean anyone would be hurt. It wasn't what I was told. I thought we were meant to ask the Onde for trade again, that was all."

She shuddered, but Moon almost thought it was from relief. Maybe the idea that she would be trapped out here, that the Amifata would abandon her, was what had frightened her more than the thing stalking her. "Who told you what to do?"

"He was a trader called Tsgarith. He is a Kithkal, and he came to the trading port at the mineral basins and found me. I was not . . . I am separated from the pods of the basins and was alone. I work where I can, hauling bundles for traders up the walls of the third basin. It isn't good work. He needed a Sourci to see something for him. This isn't uncommon; our vision is meant for the sea deeps, where we first came from. We can see things other species can't. But I am not reputable so none of the other traders have ever wanted to hire me for seeing. But this was a long journey into the forest depths and no one else would go." She choked again, and swallowed it back. "I didn't want to go out of the basins, into the swamps and the gorges, but he offered me great wealth."

"To find the Onde?"

"To hire the Amifata and travel with them, and tell them where to go with a map he gave me. The Kithkal do not trade with the moss canyons. He wanted the Amifata to be occupied, away from the markets, so he could take their trade contacts. I thought it would not hurt them, and if we did find the Onde, then the Amifata would profit anyway." She rubbed her palms together anxiously. "But the map wasn't wrong, and we did find the Onde. It was concealing itself but I could still see it, though the Amifata couldn't. I tried to speak to it. Then I saw Tsgarith in the undergrowth. He had a weapon. I called out, but he fired on us and two of the Amifata were struck by darts. We ran for the leaf boat, dragging them with us, and the Onde was trapped in the clearing and ran after us. But Tsgarith kept shooting and I was hit. I don't remember anything after that." She took a deep breath, and there was a gurgle in her throat. Her voice thick, she finished, "I did not know he intended this. I do not know why. It makes no sense. I feared . . . I feared the Amifata would blame me, and leave me out here. I am not one of them."

Moon realized he had been leaning forward and sat back. He accidentally elbowed something warm and scaly; Blaze had moved forward until she was right behind him. She wiggled back a little. He said to Elaston, "Describe Tsgarith."

"He is like all the Kithkal. They are a swamp species, like the Amifata, but their limbs are different." She made a waving gesture. "More joints."

Moon was glad he didn't have to pick Tsgarith out of a crowd of other amphibians based on that description. "Can his species make forest predators avoid them? Are they shaman?"

Elastan blinked. "No."

"So . . . He followed you here through the forest? On foot or did he have a leaf boat like the Amifata?"

"I don't know." Elastan spread her hands as if that was obvious. "He must have, he was here."

This didn't make sense. Moon wished he thought she was lying now, but he had the terrible feeling she was telling the truth. "If he wanted to hurt the Amifata, why wait till now, why not do it when you were a few days travel away from your settlements?"

"I don't know!"

Stone leaned forward then, and Elastan flinched and looked away. His voice even and calm, Stone said, "When he came to you at the trading port in the mineral basins, was that the first time you had seen him?"

"No." Elastan couldn't look at him, but she answered readily enough. "Tsgarith comes to the port a great deal. He trades with many."

Moon turned to Stone and said in Raksuran, "Whatever's out there, it's not Tsgarith."

"No." In Raksuran, Stone told Blaze, "Stay here, talk to her, be sympathetic. Try to get more detail out of her." He jerked his head at Moon and slipped out of the shelter.

Moon climbed out after him and said, "She didn't imagine all that, not unless she's out of her mind. Something made her think she saw this trader."

The Arbora, warriors, and Kek gathered around all watched them intently, though the Kek probably weren't understanding most of the Raksuran, and the Kedaic conversation must have gone over everyone's head except Blaze's. But it was clear that something important had been uncovered. Stone said, grimly, "I know what it sounds like."

So did Moon. "It can't be. We'd scent it." Fell rulers had the ability to convince most groundlings of almost anything, to influence their minds.

If one had gotten close to Elastan and told her it was the trader Tsgarith who had tried to kill her, she would have been just as certain as if she had really seen it. But even the heavy scents of the forest floor couldn't conceal Fell stench, not from Raksura. And as Chime had said, Moon had never seen or heard of Fell making animals do what they wanted, not grasseaters or predators or anything else. The Fell had no reason to; the only prey that satisfied them were sentients.

Stone spared him a glare. "I didn't say it was, I said that's what it sounds like."

Moon ignored the glare. "So this isn't something that followed the Amifata. This is something that was here. It was after that Onde." Thunder rumbled somewhere high overhead, and Moon twitched involuntarily. He hated storms. At least it wasn't as bad down here as it was in the suspended forest; with the heavy mountain-tree canopies and so many layers of platforms between him and the sky, the thunder seemed a little more distant. "I should have asked the Amifata if the Onde could influence predators. Maybe the thing out there is another Onde that doesn't want traders looking for them."

"Maybe," Stone said. "But with camouflage that good, why would they need to be able to influence—"

Moon caught a scent that made him shift without conscious volition. His winged body formed around him, his spines already flared and extended. The scent was predator, rank and strong and moving this way. The Arbora growled in startled chorus.

Stone snarled, a deep reverberation in his chest. "It's big; warn the Kek," he said, and shifted in a smooth flow of black scales. He leapt up onto the nearest root arch.

Moon said, "Tell Blaze, tell the warriors, the Kek." As the Arbora and the Kek healers scattered, Moon whipped around and bounded back into the village. He landed near the first group of Kek and said in pidgin, "Tell Kof predator coming!" He lifted his arms and wings. "Big predator!"

He wasn't sure all of them understood what he had said; most of the Kek didn't know the pidgin, but they knew an urgent warning when they saw it. Three of them stepped back and let out the high-pitched warning cries while the others bolted into the village calling for Kof.

Moon turned just as Balm bounded past, headed toward the root doorway. "I smelled it," she called back to him. "I've warned Thistle!" He followed, dodging under the hanging houses of the village outskirts and through the undergrowth toward the looming wall of the trunk.

Balm reached the clearing in front of the root cave first and landed among the Arbora and Kek there to guard it. "Inside!" she shouted. "Now!"

Moon took one more bound and partially extended his wings to bounce up to the top of the root ridge. He looked outward and for an instant saw nothing in the diming light but the heavy greenery of the ferns and trees and vines, laced through with rising mist, shadowed by the platforms of the mountain-trees. Then several hundred paces away, beside the trunk of the mountain-tree at the edge of the colony tree's canopy, there was movement.

Foliage stirred, ferns bent aside and spiral trees leaned. Moon spotted a dark-colored mass moving through the green leaves and shadow. His heart started to pound in earnest and he thought, *Oh yes, it's big.*

Below him, an Arbora said, "What about the Kek?"

Moon called down, "The Kek too. Get inside, now, and bar the door!"

The Arbora had been moving to obey, but whatever they heard in Moon's voice encouraged them to move faster. Urging the Kek to come with them, they climbed up into the root cave. Balm leapt up to land beside Moon. She saw the movement in the forest and hissed.

Moon said, "Thistle and the others?" The Amifata, Elastan, the rest of the Kek . . .

"No time to get everyone over here. They're going to dig in, get under the roots." A growl rose in her throat. "It'll be coming for this door, won't it?"

Moon twitched his spines in agreement. "This is what the thing that's been after the Onde has been doing all day. Looking for a predator big enough to handle us."

"The what?" Balm said, but River and Drift curved in from above and landed further down on the root ridge. More warriors landed on the trunk behind them, clinging to the bark with their claws. A little breathlessly, River said, "We saw Stone, he's trying to get around behind it."

That was typical of Stone. Moon said, "He can't handle it alone."

"Maybe he can." That was Drift, who had to argue about everything, especially in stressful moments.

A shape moved out of the greenery, a big limb that wrapped around the arch of a root. It pulled forward a long, oddly-shaped body that was a mottled color, hard to discern in the worsening light. It was draped with giant capes or tarps, like bottom-dwelling river creatures used for camouflage . . . Moon said, startled, "It's from the swamps." He had heard the descriptions, read from old books in the court's libraries, of the deep gorges of the forest floor, with swamps at the bottom, and channels that connected under the earth and rock.

More limbs appeared, writhing out of the crushed trees to drag the big body along. It was moving fast for something so big, so out of its natural element, but then it must have to get through the forest on occasion.

As it pulled itself out of the clump of smashed spirals and fern trees, Drift said in small voice, "Oh. It is too big for just Stone."

Pearl dropped onto the ridge in front of Moon so abruptly he almost flung himself away in pure reflex. He heard a flustered rustle from the warriors behind him but they all managed to stay on the root.

More warriors landed on the trunk and the ridge. Moon spotted Floret, Vine, Sage, Root, and Song, and there were others landing further up. He ducked as Pearl furled her wings. She said, "Stone is out there. Is there a plan?"

"Uh, no." Moon thought, *we probably should have had a plan.*

Pearl hissed something under her breath. The only word Moon caught was "consorts." She said, "Sage, keep five warriors with you and watch this door. Make certain nothing tries to break through it, and that no one opens it from the inside." She lifted her spines. "The rest of you come with me when Stone—"

A dark shape exploded out of the undergrowth, arched up and then dropped down onto the predator's back. Moon had an instant to be appalled at how small Stone looked compared to this swampling. Then Pearl snarled, "Now!" and flung herself into the air.

Moon leapt after her, snapped his wings out and flapped hard. As they crossed the short distance toward the swampling he made out more details: the skull was narrow with a long snout. Its mouth seemed to take up most of the lower part of its head but he couldn't see any teeth, just a rippling curtain shielding its lower jaw. He couldn't see any eyes either, but the gray spots mottling the slope of its head might be sensory organs. It was still dripping muddy water and its back was dotted with moss clumps and other plants growing in the dirt caught in the folds and loose flaps of skin.

Stone had landed at the junction of the swampling's neck and body, normally always a good point of attack. As Moon dropped down for a view from the side, he could see Stone's fangs and claws digging into the swampling's hide but there was no blood or fluid.

Pearl and the other warriors darted in to slash and tear at the swampling's head. A heavy limb swung toward Moon and he snapped his wings in and twisted and dropped. The limb passed overhead to wrap around another tree and drag the swampling forward. Moon caught the top of a bent fern tree and climbed down, trying to see what the swampling's underside was like.

It was too dark to see detail but the drapes of tough skin extended down the sides, rippling as the swampling moved. There were lower limbs too, that crashed down through the undergrowth to support it. Then the swampling lifted up and surged forward. Another limb, this one much wider, slammed toward Moon and he dove off his perch. He landed on a lower branch and saw the dark shape of the swampling's underside looming over him.

Knowing he might just be making his last mistake, Moon took a breath and leapt upward. He sunk his claws into the skin of the swampling's belly and held on.

For a few heartbeats he was too disoriented to do anything else. It was too dark to see anything and the body writhed like a snake, twisting violently from side to side as its lower limbs carried it through the forest. He had hoped for a soft point of attack but the skin under his claws felt like the toughest major kethel hide. He climbed up toward the neck area, treetops scraping at his back and furled wings, and searched blindly for a vulnerable spot.

His spines sensed something looming just under him and he flattened himself to the swampling's skin. Rough wood brushed his scales and he looked down into the glow of light and hissed in dismay. They had just passed over a root arch, with a clump of spell-lit moss stuck on it; they were near the village already, near the trunk of the colony tree.

He stretched up for another claw hold. He had to get up to the head area, there had to be a vulnerable point there. He had lost track of all the others and just hoped none of them were dead; the swampling had never seemed to pause long enough to kill anyone, so maybe it was just so tough it could ignore them.

Then the whole world whirled around suddenly and he realized the swampling had just lifted up on its rear limbs. Moon glanced over his shoulder and saw the dark wall of a mountain-tree's trunk coming at him. He scrambled frantically upward.

Moon reached the folds of skin below the lower jaw just in time. The swampling's belly crashed against the trunk with crushing force as it started up the tree. Its limbs found holds on ancient branch stubs and gripped the rough bark. Moon huddled under its chin, with just enough room to keep from being squashed. Sick fear settled into his stomach. *It's heading for the knothole*, he thought.

But there was no way something this big would fit through the knot-hole. The entrance passage at the back was filled and carved down to be just wide enough for a large queen. Stone had to shift to groundling to get through it. And the twists and turns would keep this creature from even being able to work a limb down it. The passage had been designed and carved and grown just to prevent this sort of incursion. But maybe this swampling didn't know that.

Moon clawed at the looser folds of skin here, but the hide was far too tough. And the intense mineral stench of plant rot and mud was about to smother . . . *Plant rot and mud*, Moon realized suddenly. Mud laden with sulfur. Non-sentient predators, and some sentient ones, smelled of rotting meat and dried blood that they never cleaned from their claws or hide; the flesh they ate permeated their bodies and fouled their scent. This swampling had smelled like predator from a distance, but maybe that had just been the odor of something that lived in the bottom of a swamp among rotting plants and dead creatures. Was this thing even a predator? Was it just a distraction? *I have to see if it has teeth.*

Moon tried to scramble further up the swampling's neck but the big body twisted sideways and he had to huddle back as a huge branch scraped past. Wood snapped and groaned and crashed somewhere against the trunk below; he hoped that platform hadn't had anything too important on it.

Then the skin under his claws twisted and a violent shake flung him sideways. Moon lost his grip and tumbled. He thought he was falling through open air and turned to unfurl his wings. But he smashed face first into wet grass and earth. He lay there a heartbeat, stunned; he had struck the platform so hard the interwoven branches beneath the layers of sod and grass creaked. Gritting his teeth, Moon shoved himself over onto his back and looked up.

The swampling had hooked its lower limbs over the edge of the platform and stretched for the knothole. It turned its head sideways to avoid the spray of the waterfall and Moon had a clear view of the side of its jaw under the flaps of concealing skin. *No teeth*, Moon thought, still dazed. Its mouth was lined with bristles, a natural filter to draw in and consume small plants and smaller fish, like some skylings fed on clouds of tiny air dwellers. *Another distraction.* Whatever had driven the predators into the village last night had driven this thing out of the swamp and straight up the side of the tree. So was the real attempt to enter the colony happening below them, at the root doorway?

Warriors darted frantically through the air, Pearl's gold form flashing among them. Stone had released his hold on the swampling and clung to the trunk above the knothole. Moon struggled to sit up, watching as the swampling reached the knothole. The edge of the waterfall washed over its side and it let out a bellow that echoed off the mountain-trees. It pulled away from the knothole and started back down the trunk without turning around, moving as readily as if it had a head at each end. Stone pushed off from the trunk and dove past it like a sharp shadow. Pearl swung in a tight circle and led the warriors in a steep descent.

But if the swampling was a distraction, why was it leading everyone back down? And why had it come up here in the first place? Moon clawed his way to his feet and managed to extend his wings. He jumped and flapped, fell back to the platform, staggered up for another go, and made it into the air this time. He might be wrong, but he wanted to check something first, just to be on the safe side.

If he had ridden the swampling all the way across the clearing and up the colony tree without it or anyone else noticing, something else could have managed it too. Especially if the something else was an Onde.

Moon landed at the edge of the knothole. From the spell-light of the snail shells mounted on the inner walls, he saw that the swampling must have slammed a limb down in here. Water from the stream that fed the waterfall had splashed out of the channel and dripped down the walls, and the floor was awash in mud, obscuring the polished shell inlay. And there were tracks in it, the tracks of something too big to be an Arbora.

Moon furled his wings and stepped forward, staring at the marks in the mud. *Something fell here, went toward the edge of the stream, then toward the passage into the greeting hall . . .* Moon flung himself toward the passage. He had really thought he was wrong about this.

He shot through the defensive twists and turns far too fast, bouncing off the smooth wooden walls. Halfway along he heard snarls of alarm from the greeting hall, eliminating any last chance that this was a mistake.

He burst out through the doorway and slid to a halt, his foot claws tangled in something. It was the remnants of a light cloth drape that must have been fixed over the doorway, as a means to warn the guards if any camouflaged beings tried to get in. Something had ripped right through it. Grain and three other soldiers lay sprawled on the floor near the stairs down to the teachers' hall. Moon scented blood.

Moon shook the shredded cloth off his claws and reached them in one bound. Grain struggled to sit up. He had a dart embedded in his shoulder, another in the scales above his knee. He gasped, "Consort, something got inside! It was like the other one, we couldn't see it! It went down there!"

Down the stairwell. *Toward the nurseries.* A pulse of pure rage made Moon's vision go white on the edges. He dove for the stairwell and whipped down it into the teachers' hall.

He couldn't see the intruder but it was obvious it was here. Arbora blocked the doorways leading away from the hall and two huddled back against a wall, wounded. The one in groundling form was Strike, bleeding from a dart wound in the shoulder. But a big wooden projectile weapon lay shattered on the floor near Strike, a stock of darts scattered beside it. The Onde's weapon would have been visible even against its camouflaged fur; the Arbora must have been able to disarm it.

From the opposite doorway, Merry shouted, "It hasn't gotten past us! It's in here somewhere."

"We think it hasn't gotten past us," Sprout countered grimly.

"Quiet," Moon snapped. Everyone shut up, leaving the only sound the ragged breathing of the wounded. This was bad. Most of the Arbora were probably down in the bottom of the tree, making sure nothing tried to come through the root doorways, and the bulk of the warriors were out with Pearl and Stone.

Moon moved forward slowly from the stairwell and extended his wings, raised his spines to their fullest extent. They were right, the creature was still in here; he could sense movement, a trace of foreign scent, foreign breath. Any gaps in the camouflage were impossible to see against the wall carvings and the falls of light and shadow from the shell-lights. Broken pottery and a spilled kettle lay near the bowl hearth in the center of the room, but there was nothing on the polished wood floor to show tracks.

Other senses told Moon that whatever was in here was moving, that it was larger than the other Onde, maybe much larger. He wondered if the smaller Onde was a child, but if it was, this was no parent trying desperately to retrieve an offspring. The small Onde was fleeing this creature, had been willing to die in hiding rather than be caught by it.

Something gray flicked at the edge of his vision and he half-turned toward it. He sensed the swing before it connected only because his wings were so sensitive to air movement and there was no breeze in the teachers' hall. He ducked by instinct, snapped his wings in and rolled.

Moon came to his feet a few paces away and pounced at where the creature should be. His claws caught rough spiny fur. Something made a low grunt of effort as it whipped out of his grasp. The Arbora snarled in chorus.

Moon landed facing the stairs up to the greeting hall. For an instant, he froze. Standing on the steps was a Fell ruler. Moon's heart contracted; in the next instant he realized there was no Fell stench and the Arbora weren't reacting. Now he knew why Elastan had been so certain she had seen Tsgarith. Air moved near his spines and he dropped and lunged sideways, felt the blow pass just overhead.

Moon said to the Arbora, "Careful, it can make you see things that aren't there."

There was no reaction for a startled moment, then Braid said from somewhere behind him, "Well, that's all we need."

The next blow caught Moon in the chest and knocked him backward. He hit the floor and slid. The Arbora started to surge forward and he snarled, "Stay where you are! It wants you to move so it can get past you!" If it got out through one of these passages, it could get anywhere in the court. The nurseries would be guarded, but it might find the workroom where Heart and the others had the little Onde.

The Arbora scrambled back into position and braced themselves. Moon came to his feet and dodged as something slammed past him toward the nearest passage. He leapt after it before it reached the Arbora there, caught fur in his claws and tried to clamp on. It twisted away and threw him off. Moon bounced back to his feet, thinking, *it understood what I said*. It had stopped making him see things, knowing it couldn't fool him, and it had charged the Arbora, knowing it wasn't going to be able to trick them into moving now. And Moon had been speaking Raksuran.

He ducked another blow and a familiar voice said, "Moon, get ready, we have an idea."

Moon managed an appalled and furious glance toward the passage up from the nurseries. Jade stood in the doorway behind the Arbora, a nervous Ember on one side and Chime on the other. For a heartbeat he thought it might be another illusion. But the Arbora were staring too, appalled. He said, "Have you lost your mind?"

She said, "Shut up. Chime—"

Chime caught Moon's eye and lifted a light-colored bundle. He started to say, "It's—"

He didn't know the creature could understand him. Moon shouted to cover whatever Chime was about to say and snapped his wings out. He felt the creature brush past on the right and flung himself at it. He hit it across the body, felt sharp-edged fur and rock-like muscle against his scales. He clawed at it, tried to grab on, but he couldn't get his claws through the metallic fur. Big hands gripped his neck, the Arbora howled in unison and something wet splashed over him.

The hands released his throat and Moon scrambled back, his neck aching where the creature had nearly snapped it. He could see it, it stood barely four paces in front of him, a big amorphous shape outlined in dripping red fluid.

Behind it, Chime dodged back behind the Arbora. The bundle he had thrown at the creature was broken on the floor, a sack made out of membrane. It had been filled with red dye and water. Jade growled in triumph.

The shape that was the creature's head moved, as if staring down at itself. Moon bared his fangs and hissed in amusement. He said, "Have you ever fought anything that could see you?"

"I've fought many," it said in Raksuran, the words distorted by a throat not meant to form them. "Including little insects like you."

Moon moved sideways, hoping it would pace him. He wanted it further away from the stairs. If it got away again, got out through the knothole, they could be living in fear of this thing for a long time. "But they couldn't see you. What are you, an overgrown Onde?"

It matched his steps. Behind it, the Arbora moved in concert, watching it with a growing intensity. Ember tugged at Jade's wrist, trying to get her to withdraw, and she shook him off. Moon figured he only had a few moments before the Arbora's patience snapped and they swarmed. He didn't want them to leave their positions in the doorways until this thing was down. Then it said, "I am their god."

Moon went still for an instant and thought, *Oh, that's nice.* An overgrown Onde, gone completely mad. No wonder the little one had tried to hide in a Raksuran colony.

All around the hall, the Arbora twitched and flinched and hissed. Moon caught a dozen dark flashes in his peripheral vision, and ignored the display. The creature was trying to distract them with visions again; the dye was dripping off its fur and it must realize that if it could break free and get to a pool or a water channel, it could wash it off and disappear into the colony. He said, "So how long have you been a god?"

It said, "You have one of my people prisoner; give it back to me."

"It came in here to hide from you," Moon countered. "It would rather bleed to death in here than be caught by you. We know you killed the Kek because they could see you. Why'd you try to kill the traders?"

It said, "The Onde don't need traders, they have me."

Stalling is not going to work, Moon thought. The dye was running off and he could only see about a third of its body now. The Arbora on the right side of the room cried out and shied away from something only they could see. Chime twitched backward, his spines flared. Moon figured the creature was going to break in that direction, toward the back passage.

It started to say, "I will let you live if—" and Moon leapt.

This time he saw the arm that swung at him. He ducked under it and slashed across the body, felt his claws glance off the metallic fur. It grabbed for his neck again and Moon twisted away, but the other fist connected and he slammed down into the floor.

The nearest group of Arbora charged. Three hit it in the back and two went straight for its head, another three lunging for the legs. It spun and threw them off like they weighed nothing. Moon came to his feet as Braid flew over his head. He knew it would run. He shouted, "You're not a god, you're an idiot, a joke!"

It wasn't brilliant, but it did the trick. The creature surged toward him instead of the doorway. Moon bounced into the air and landed on its head. Teeth glanced off his scales as Moon wrapped his body around its head and neck and twisted all his weight sideways and down. He felt bones snap as they both hit the floor. A dozen very angry Arbora landed on top of the creature, tearing at the metallic fur.

"Consort, are you all right?" Merry panted. He pinned a big arm down with his body, two hunters piling in to help.

Moon felt the thing twitch under him, then the rattle of a last breath in its throat as its muscles went limp. He could feel the wrong angle of its neck, and probed with his claws. Bone moved under his hands in a way he was pretty certain it wasn't supposed to, even in an unfamiliar species. "I think it's dead." He let go and disentangled himself. The body was gradually becoming visible, but most of the Arbora were on top of it now, so Moon couldn't make out much detail. Easing backward, Moon braced to jump back in if he was wrong, but the creature didn't move.

"Good," Jade said, matter-of-factly, "Now someone get the wounded down to the mentors. It'll be quicker than trying to get the mentors up here."

"There's wounded in the greeting hall, too," Moon told them.

Arbora ran up the stairwell, others went to carefully lift the two injured. "I'm fine, I can walk," Strike objected, and was shushed.

Moon said, "Merit and Thistle know what those darts are poisoned with now. And that dye was a good idea." His voice came out a little strained from the near strangulation.

"We thought it might be." Chime came forward to warily circle the dead creature. "We'd been talking about things to use against chameleons, so when Wake came running to tell us what was happening, dye was the first thing we thought of."

Jade had stayed back in the doorway, and was now leaning against the carved frame. She added, "It's a good thing the teachers had planned to dye the new cloth today or there wouldn't have been any made up."

Moon glared at her. "What are you doing down here?"

"What, I was supposed to hide up there while all this was going on?" Jade shrugged her spines, clearly indifferent to Moon's opinion. "Everyone was busy outside, someone had to come down here and check on things."

"Jade—"

Bone appeared in the doorway, more Arbora behind him, and growled at the sight of the dead Onde god. "I hope this is all for the day, because this court's had enough excitement."

The Arbora satisfied themselves that the creature was dead and backed away. It looked like a big inert heap of metallic fur, the color mostly gray but with green patches. Moon leaned closer to examine one of the patches and realized it was moss. Onde forest gods must not be partial to bathing or grooming. Bone said, "Do we know what it is?"

"It said it was the god of the Onde," Moon said. Bone stared at him, scaled brows and spines lifted incredulously, and Moon said, "I know." He turned back to Jade. "Are you going back to your bower anytime soon?"

"Probably." She didn't sound as if it was likely. "Where's Pearl?"

That was a good question. Moon asked Bone, "Do you know what happened outside?" The swampling had seemed as if it was heading down to the roots and the village, but if this creature hadn't been there to drive it, it might have fled back to its home.

Bone said, "They kept it off the village, and it turned back and left the clearing. We were lucky."

Chime was still staring down at the creature. He sat on his heels and tugged gently at the fur. It seemed oddly loose. He pulled harder, and with a faint ripping sound, it lifted away from the body. He said, "I thought so."

Startled, Moon hissed. He dropped to the floor beside Chime for a closer look. Chime pulled the fur piece back so Moon could see that it had been sewn into the exposed skin of the body beneath. The scent coming up from it was foul, like rotted meat. The skin itself was a mottled gray, hard and slick, but bruised dark and swollen where the sinew had been pinned through its flesh. Kneeling beside the creature's left leg, Braid pulled back another piece of fur, exposing more lacing to hold it against the skin. Some of the wounds where the fur had been sewn in were old, others relatively new, as if the coverings had been patched and replaced over a long period of time. Moon said, "But this is Onde fur."

"But this isn't an Onde." Chime pulled more fur away from the torso. "The other one isn't like this." He moved down toward the creature's head. "Braid, help me here."

Watching Chime and Braid work at the heavy roll of fur around the neck, Moon didn't know what to think. Blossom stepped up beside him and squeezed his wrist. Everyone who hadn't helped carry the wounded to the mentors had gathered around, staring in baffled silence. Then Bone said, "I think I know what this must be. But . . . "

Chime and Braid lifted the covering off the head. As Braid held it up, Moon saw it was a combination of a mask and helmet, made of more Onde fur, some sort of bone, and eye pieces of a clear material. The head that Chime was examining had a round bulbous skull and ragged hanks of hair. With no need to be careful of the broken neck bones, Chime turned it so they could see the face. The dead eyes were round, and unlike the amphibians it had a nose. The mouth was wide and hung open, revealing a startling array of fangs for a groundling with a head this small. From the doorway, Jade said, "Bone? What is this?"

"I think it's a hunter. It took the Onde hide and attached it to itself, so it could use the camouflage." Bone grimaced. "The fur concealed its scent, too."

"But the fur was alive," Braid protested. Other Arbora nodded. "You can't just cut a body part off and attach it to somebody else, that doesn't work—"

"It doesn't work for us, or most groundlings." Chime's tone was grim. "It worked for this species, whatever it is."

"There are species back in the east who can do this," Moon added. He had heard some pretty horrific stories, but then for such peaceful people, the Hassi had loved telling frightening tales, the more grotesque the better. "But only to each other. They take the heads of their enemies and sew them onto their bodies, and they're still sort of alive."

"That's disgusting," Jade commented. Then she muttered, "Uh oh."

Ember said, "Moon, get over here now."

Moon reached the doorway in one bound, not consciously realizing he had moved until he had hooked his claws on the wall carving. Ember stared worriedly at Jade, who had one hand on her belly and a preoccupied frown on her face. Two Arbora stood on either side of her, Ginger the soldier and Dream, a young teacher, watching her intently. Jade looked at Moon and grimaced. She said, "The fledglings moved down."

Moon shifted to groundling and reached out. Jade gripped his wrist. She didn't look upset or worried, just annoyed. Moon said, "Ember—"

"I'll get Heart," Ember said, and bolted down the passage.

Dream said, "We need cushions, and blankets. Come this way."

"There's some good clean ones just above us in that store room off the back passage into the greeting hall, we use them for visitors." Ginger motioned to Moon to follow Dream. "There's a room down here that's good, there's a water channel."

Still frowning, Jade said, "The mentors need to take care of the wounded."

Moon pulled gently on Jade's arm and steered her after Dream. Ginger said, "The wounded are with Merit now, with Copper and the others to help him."

The teachers had their bowers on this level, but there were plenty of unused rooms. Dream led them down a couple of short passages until the noise from the hall faded, and then into a large room that was a common area for several attached bowers. She said, "We use this when trade goods come in and we need to sort the plant cuttings." It had been swept out recently and the shells spelled for light, but the bowl hearth set into the floor was empty. There was a small bathing pool but the drain in the bottom was open, so the water was running from the wall channel into the basin and out.

Moon opened his mouth but Dream stepped into the pool to close the drain, and Ginger must have moved blindingly fast because she was already coming through the door with an armload of cushions, followed by Rill with blankets and Bell hauling a metal carrier filled with warming stones. It was obvious nobody needed instructions about how to prepare the room. Moon said instead, "Can someone find Balm? She was with Pearl."

"Then she's busy," Jade objected. She paced in a small circle, a highly annoyed glare directed at her belly.

"She wants to be here. And she can tell you what happened down there," Moon told her.

Jade transferred the highly annoyed glare to him. "Do not treat me as if I'm a delicate idiot."

Moon said, "Fine. Then just shut up and have the damn babies." Jade bared her fangs at him, and Bell, dumping the warming stones in the hearth, flashed his spines in approval.

Moon was aware of more Arbora moving into the rooms around them, taking up guard positions or just wanting to be close by. It was reassuring, but all he could look at was Jade.

Heart walked in then, and that was even more reassuring. She was in her groundling form, her skin and hair wet and dripping a little onto the light shirt and pants she wore. Breathless from excitement, she said, "Sorry, I had to wash first."

Moon didn't care what she had to do first as long as she was here now. Still pacing, Jade asked her, "Who's with the wounded?"

Heart told her, "Merit and Thistle are taking care of them. I need to check on the babies." She threw a glance at Moon.

Moon caught Jade's wrist and steered her around to face Heart. "You need to stand still."

"I don't want to stand still, I want to move," Jade said through gritted teeth.

"That's a stupid thing to want right now," Moon said, and as Jade growled at him, Heart stepped up to her and lightly put her hands on Jade's stomach.

After a moment of concentration, Heart stepped back. "Shouldn't be long now." She looked around at the preparations the other Arbora were making. "She might be hungry afterward, so make sure there's something ready for her."

Moon looked down and realized he had swampling mud on his clothes, though some of it had shaken off during the fight with the Onde-skinning creature. Moon started to move away, but Jade took his wrist and pulled him back. He said, "I need to clean up, I have giant swampling mud all over me."

Bell turned to the other Arbora. "Someone go up and get Moon fresh clothes."

Jade hissed out a curse. "You were fighting the giant swampling? Where were Pearl and Stone?"

Then Stone slipped through the doorway, snagged a spare cushion, and sat down. "Fighting the giant swampling too." Moon felt such a wave of relief to see him, he almost swayed. After Bone's report, he hadn't been worried so much about what had happened outside, or at least he thought he hadn't. But for some reason he couldn't articulate to himself, having Stone here caused his heart to unclench just a little.

"What happened out there?" Jade demanded.

"It was a trick so that thing with the Onde skins could get in through the knothole," Stone began, and started to describe the swampling.

Warriors were joining the Arbora in the adjacent rooms, and Moon saw Vine and Floret peek in through a doorway. He couldn't keep track of who all was here; the only thing he could really focus on was Jade. He turned to Bell, who was sitting on his heels beside the hearth. "Everything that needs to be guarded is still being guarded, right?"

Bell said, "Bone and Knell and Sage are taking charge below and in the greeting hall. There's not that many people up here, it just seems like it. Everyone's taking turns, coming in for a little and then going back out."

Someone appeared with a clean shirt and pants for Moon. He managed to get Jade to let go of his wrist and Rill and Chime helped him with a rapid wash up and change of clothes in the next room. Chime said, "Moon, you need to relax. Just take deep breaths."

That was great advice, and of course, impossible to take.

When Moon returned, Jade commented, "Good. You smelled terrible."

Thistle slipped in next, also dripping from a recent wash and carrying a couple of bags of mentors' supplies. "Grain was the only one who needed a healing sleep," she reported. "We've got their wounds bandaged up and Merit and the others are making simples in case those darts were poisoned too. And Balm is on her way."

Balm appeared next in her groundling form, her hair wet and her shirt on backwards. Her face was tight with tension, her jaw set, and Moon hadn't seen her look this nervous since the last time something had tried to eat them. She sat beside Stone and leaned against his arm. Stone was the only one who looked calm and as if he was actually enjoying the whole thing. He patted her knee reassuringly.

Watching Jade with intense concentration, Heart gently touched her belly again. Jade said, "Tell me about the battle, Balm."

Balm tried to smile. "It wasn't as much fun as it sounds."

Then Heart said, "It should start any moment. Everyone who isn't a mentor or in the direct line, out." Bell squeezed Moon's shoulder and made for the door. Chime leaned in to nip the back of his neck and whispered, "It's fine, it's going very well, I can tell," and followed Bell. Everyone but Stone, Balm, and Thistle scattered for a doorway. Moon could tell they were all still nearby, in the other rooms, but no one was peering through the doorways. Then Pearl stepped inside and settled onto a cushion.

Heart told Jade, "You need to crouch down. It'll be easier."

Jade grimaced and gripped Moon's forearm. He helped her down and knelt beside her. Sitting on her heels in front of them, Heart gave Moon a glance that was all nerves. A bead of sweat was already making its way down her brow. This was the first time Heart had supervised a royal birth, though she had done all three recent Arbora births here. Moon recalled his job was technically to keep everyone calm, and told her, "It's fine. You're doing great."

Heart nodded, and said, "This should be it."

Hissing between her teeth, Jade said, "Finally."

Moon actually saw the scales on Jade's stomach ripple and move as the babies changed position.

Heart scooted closer, up between Jade's knees, and muttered, "Here we are." Then she added, "The first one is a little turned. That's normal, but I'll have to turn it back a bit so it can come out right."

Heart leaned down and Jade's other arm snapped up. Moon intercepted it in mid-reach, catching her wrist. He said, "Don't."

Jade relaxed and hissed in dismay at her own lack of control. It was a good thing she didn't really want to hurt Heart, because there was no way Moon could stop her if she hadn't wanted to be stopped. Heart, her face tense with concentration, hadn't even noticed. Jade said, "I hate this."

"Me, too," Moon agreed, evenly. His pulse was pounding in his temples and he hoped he didn't black out.

Heart did something that made Jade snarl.

Balm crept a little closer, craned her neck to see, and winced in sympathy. Pearl just flicked a spine.

Then Moon caught a glimpse of a little dark bundle, streaked with blood, as Heart handed it off to Thistle's waiting towel. The blood gave him a moment of heart-stopping terror, but the bundle was squirming in Thistle's gentle hands. She wiped the blood and fluid away, then passed it to Stone, who said, "Hah, female," in a pleased tone, and showed it to Balm.

Moon felt so dizzy with relief, he almost swayed and fell over. Then the next one started to come, Jade reached for Heart again, and Moon caught her wrist again.

The next two babies were slightly twisted, but Heart, gaining confidence with each successful birth, freed them without trouble. The fourth came out smoothly, but the fifth had to be turned completely around. Listening to Jade's growls, watching Balm's expressions of horror and Heart's teeth-gritted efforts, it was all Moon could do not to die of anxiety. He remembered the stories of difficult clutches, all the turns of troubled births in the old colony. Then Heart sat back with a tiny wriggling shape in her hands and an exhalation of exhausted relief.

Jade let go of Moon and stood up immediately. Moon tried to but his legs failed to work and he just slumped in a heap instead.

Jade demanded, "How did we do?"

"A mixed clutch," Stone reported, taking the fifth one from Thistle. "Three female and two male."

Pearl said, "Very good." Taking that as a signal, the warriors and Arbora in the surrounding rooms burst into happy talk. There was no way to tell yet if the babies were queens and consorts, but the chances were good. Everyone had told Moon that single gender clutches were the ones most likely to have warriors.

"Good," Jade said. She leaned down and grabbed Moon by the back of the neck and bit him in the shoulder, almost but not quite hard enough to draw blood. He said, "Ow," but it was more of a comment than a protest.

Then Jade stepped over to crouch beside the nest and examine the new babies. Standing up again, she told Balm, "I really need a bath. And I'm starving."

Balm was grinning with joy and relief. "Come on, they've been warming a pool in the next room, and they were going to bring some food up." They went out together.

Moon, who found he had gone almost numb from the waist down from kneeling in the same position too long, crawled over to Stone to look.

They were all curled in the soft blankets, tiny shapes, their scales a very dark bronze, their eyes black, blinking sleepily. He knew they would change color as they developed, and take on more individual characteristics. Pearl came to look over his shoulder and said, approvingly, "And they're all the same size, too."

"What does that mean?" Moon asked.

"It means they were conceived at the same time," Stone told him, and ruffled his hair.

"So it turns out you are good for something," Pearl said, almost fondly, and left.

Moon was too overwhelmed to care. He touched one little belly cautiously, reverently, and got a wriggle in response. The baby wrapped a little hand around his finger. Despite its claws still being soft, the fledgling's grip was solid. He stroked another little back, feeling the soft spines. The scent, a strange combination of groundling baby and Raksura, he had expected from the other new babies he had held. But these babies also smelled like Jade, and it made his chest go tight. "Who's going to feed them?" Queens didn't feed babies from their breasts, like most mammalian groundlings, though mentors' lore said they had at some point in the distant past, before the Aeriat joined with the Arbora. Female Arbora did, but only for the first few days. Raksura were born with teeth and like their claws, they hardened over time.

Washing her hands in the basin Thistle had brought her, Heart said, "Bead and Needle will take turns. Then we switch them to meat broth for a while, then solid food."

Jade wandered back in, still dripping from a quick bath. She was in her winged form, as if she had missed it and hadn't been able to wait to shift. After the past month of fast growth, it was odd to see her belly back to its normal size, as if nothing had happened. And she clearly had all her energy back. She sat on her heels beside Moon, and said, "Ready to name them?"

Surprisingly, Moon was. A large part of his terror for the future seemed to have inexplicably receded. He stretched out on his side with his head propped on his hand so he could see the babies at eye level. "Go ahead."

Jade touched each baby in turn, starting with the girls. "Solace, Sapphire—"

"Fern," Moon interposed. It had been the name of the Arbora who he had thought of as his sister, who had been killed by the Tath with Swift and the others, all those turns ago.

"Fern," Jade agreed. She touched the first boy. "Cloud."

Moon nodded. Indigo Cloud should have a Cloud. As Jade touched the last boy, to tease her, he said, "Puffblossom."

"Not Puffblossom." Jade was firm on that point. She hesitated. "Dusk? Or do you think Malachite would mind?"

It was the name of Moon's father, who had been killed by the Fell. Moon considered that. "She might not be able to look at him." Malachite had had trouble looking at Moon, who apparently closely resembled his dead father. If this little one turned out to be a consort and closely resembled Moon, it might be even more difficult for Malachite.

"Hmm. What about Rain?"

Rain was the name of Pearl's previous consort, the one who had fathered Jade and Balm. He had died several turns before Moon had come to the court. He asked, "You don't think Pearl would mind?"

"I think she'd like it," Stone said.

"Rain," Moon agreed. Then he laid his head down and fell asleep.

☾

Moon woke abruptly, already sitting up. He would have thought he dreamed it, except he was looking down at five sleeping babies cuddled in a carefully arranged pile of blankets. He blinked and rubbed his bleary eyes. No, he hadn't imagined it.

"Are you all right?" Chime asked, handing him a cup of tea. "Do you need something to eat?"

Chime, Bell, Rill, and Bark all sat nearby, watching him expectantly. The room was empty except for them, though there were hunters and some other teachers sitting in the doorways. Moon drank the tea, which stung his dry throat. He coughed, and heard the distant rumble of thunder, cushioned by the thick wood of the trunk. The air smelled of heavy rain now, carried on the drafts coming down from the greeting hall. Someone had stuffed a cushion under his head without waking him. He must have been sleeping like the dead. He could tell it was night, that was all. "How long?"

"It's past the middle part of the night," Rill told him. "Jade said we should let you sleep."

"She said she'd kill anyone who woke you, actually," Chime said, taking the cup back and refilling it from the pot.

Sleeping for the rest of the night was a nice idea, but Moon was pretty certain he still had things to do. He had left a dead predator in the teachers' hall that could turn invisible by sewing another species' skin to itself, for one thing. "Where is Jade?"

"Jade's with Pearl and Stone and the others, trying to figure out how to help the Onde." Bell winced in sympathy. "It's been getting worse, and the simples aren't working on it. They brought in one of the other groundlings to try to talk to it and get it to tell the mentors what to do."

"That wasn't going well, the last we heard," Chime said. "That thing you fought—the Onde calls it a skin-hunter—has been preying on the Onde in this area for turns, and there aren't many of them left. The skin-hunter wouldn't let the Onde have any contact with other species. As if the skin-hunter wasn't just hunting them, but herding them, the way some groundlings do with grasseaters." He grimaced in distaste.

Moon shook his head. If it was true, it was a horrible situation. All this had been happening just a few days' walk from the colony tree, but it might as well have been all the way across the Three Worlds. The Onde hadn't even asked the Kek for help. It would never have occurred to them that the local Raksuran court might have been perfectly willing to kill the creature that was tormenting them. Well, Pearl might not have been willing, but could probably have been talked into it, just to remove a potential threat.

Moon downed the second cup of tea and felt more coherent. He wanted to go to Jade, and he might be able to help with the Onde, though he wasn't sure how. He looked around again. Apparently he was in charge of the babies for now. Or until they grew up. It was still a daunting thought. He looked at Chime and the three teachers and said, "I have absolutely no idea what to do now with . . ." He nodded toward the babies.

"Oh." Bell glanced at Bark and Rill. "We don't want to move them to the nurseries just yet."

Bark said, "For one thing, it would wake them up, and wake up all the babies and fledglings, and it would be chaos for the rest of the night."

Rill added, "Usually we just keep them where they were born for a few days, so everyone can come through and see them. We were planning to do that in Jade's bower, but since they're down here, it's actually more convenient to be near the teachers' hall. And we can make it comfortable for you and Jade to sleep here until it's time to take them to the nurseries."

Bell finished, "But it's your decision."

Moon's decision. He wished Bell hadn't put it like that.

Chime leaned forward, eyeing him sharply. "When I asked if you were all right, you didn't answer. Are you all right?"

"Uh." Moon rubbed his eyes again. He was confused and overwhelmed, but he didn't want to admit it out loud.

Bark said carefully, "Why don't you go see Jade and then come right back? We'll be here." Rill nodded and patted Moon's knee.

That Moon could handle. "I'll do that."

Chime had to steady Moon when he stood up.

As they went to the passage that led to the lower stairwell, Chime said, "You should get something to eat soon. And you have bruises all around your neck."

Moon had almost forgotten about that. The muscles of his shoulders and chest ached and he had a scatter of painful spots all over. Whatever it was, the thing with the Onde skins had been brutally strong. "Thanks for staying with me, when . . ." He couldn't think of a way to end that sentence that didn't sound wrong. Something more interesting had been going on, and it had involved a little groundling dying, and maybe Chime would have preferred to be there to try to help save it. "Watching me sleep is not all that exciting," he finished, feeling inadequate.

Chime shook his head a little. "I got to hold the royal clutch before most of the court has even had a chance to see them. But I do wish . . ." He hissed in frustration. "I should just stop talking about not being a mentor anymore. Even I'm tired of it, you all must be exhausted by now."

"We used to be, but now we just ignore it," Moon said, and got a shove to the shoulder.

They shifted to their winged forms to drop down the stairwell to the lower levels, and Moon saw some of the warriors and Arbora standing just outside the doorway of the workroom where the Onde had been taken. They were all watching something inside. He swung down onto the walkway and shifted back to groundling, Chime following him.

Blossom saw them, slipped away from the doorway, and came to meet them. "Are you all right?" she whispered to Moon. "You look terrible."

"I'm fine. Is Jade in there?"

Blossom's spines signaled dismay and frustration. "Yes, she's in there with Stone and Pearl and Balm. The Onde's dying. We brought one of the Amifata in to talk to it, but it still won't tell us where the others are so we can get help. It's too afraid."

If the story about the skin-hunter and what it had done was even partly true, then Moon could understand why the Onde wouldn't reveal its people's location. But that didn't leave a lot of options for helping it. "Did it tell you what happened at the leaf boat?"

"Yes, it was willing to talk about that. It said it caught the scent from that trade-beacon the Amifata had and went to warn them. But it didn't realize the skin-hunter could detect the beacon too. The Onde was hit with a dart but pulled it out, and ran into the leaf boat with the others. The amphibians all collapsed once they got inside but it was awake and managed to hide. The skin-hunter searched for it, but it couldn't see past the camouflage like a real Onde; the skins didn't give it that ability. So the skin-hunter just sat outside, talking to the Onde, telling it to give up." Blossom rolled her shoulders, releasing tension so her spines would drop. "It was entertaining itself, I suppose, waiting for them all to die in there."

Chime leaned in to ask, "Were we right? The skin-hunter killed the Kek plant hunters because they could see it?"

Blossom gave him a grim nod. "The Onde said it didn't see the Kek arrive, but it heard some disturbance and then looked out and saw the Kek fighting the skin-hunter, and saw it kill them."

"But what was the skin-hunter?" Chime asked, "What species?"

"The Onde didn't seem to know. The Amifata said it had never heard of anything like it. Since the skin-hunter spoke Raksuran to Moon, the hunters are trying to find out if it had any . . ." Blossom bared her fangs briefly in disgust. " . . . Raksuran parts on it."

Chime hissed, appalled. Moon's skin twitched with the urge to shift. It was a sickening thought, but all too possible. Chime said, "The hunters are trying to find this out?"

"The mentors are all busy, so they have the skin-hunter down in their tanning room taking it apart to try to figure out how it works."

"If they miss something . . ." Chime twitched, apparently at the idea that the hunters would bungle the job. "Maybe I should go down there."

"They could probably use the help," Blossom agreed.

Moon nudged Chime. "Go. They need you."

Chime squeezed his wrist gratefully, shifted, and bounded down the walkway.

Moon followed Blossom to the workroom, where she elbowed a couple of warriors aside to make room for him to slip up to the doorway. Jade, Balm, and Pearl stood a few paces inside the room, but Moon didn't want to go in any further and risk interrupting. Jade didn't even look tired. It was as if she had stored up a great deal of energy while being unable to shift, and now it was time to expend it.

From here he could see the Onde. It had dropped its camouflage, or was too weak to maintain it, and lay propped up against a pile of cushions. Its long metallic fur was a blue-tinged white. The fur made its features harder to distinguish, but it had a long nose and a pointed jawline. Its eyes were large and luminous, taking up much of the space on the upper part of its face. Each ear wasn't a single piece, but were multiple folds and fans, like feathery fur-covered spines. It was blinking at the lights in the chamber, even though a few had been removed. It might be nocturnal, or just unused to any light that wasn't filtered through the forest.

An Amifata knelt beside it, and from its injuries, it was the same one Moon had spoken to earlier. It seemed far more alert than it had before. It spoke to the Onde in another language, filled with clicks and stops. It held out its hands as if pleading with it, and its leftward eye was focused intently on the Onde's face.

Stone sat a few paces away from them, watching, and Merit was nearby, along with Copper. Also present were Hiak and some other Kek who Moon recognized as the healers who had helped the Amifata. They were surrounded by a litter of water jugs and containers for simple ingredients, bowls and bone cups and wrapped leaves.

Blossom whispered, "It looks a little like it's related to some of the treelings we've seen."

Weave whispered back, "I wonder if there are treelings we can't see."

The Amifata stopped speaking. The Onde replied, almost too softly for Moon to hear. The Amifata's eye swiveled back to Stone and it said in Kedaic, "It will not tell me. It asks again, if the skin-hunter will return?"

Jade leaned over to whisper to Balm. Balm turned and, as the warriors and Arbora hastily made way for her, slipped out through the doorway.

Pearl, her spines twitching impatiently, asked, "What's this?"

"A demonstration for our guest," Jade said.

After a few moments, Balm reappeared, followed by Bramble. Bramble carried a bundle wrapped in an old piece of cloth.

The warriors and Arbora moved aside for them and Bramble stepped just inside the room. At a nod from Jade, she pulled the cloth aside to reveal the skin-hunter's head.

It didn't look much worse dead than it had alive. The punctures and bruising where the Onde hide had been sewn into its scalp stood out against the mottled gray skin. The eyes were dull and glazed over with a white film, and the mouth gaped open.

The Onde stared, its eyes widening and the multiple layers and fans of its ears spreading. It leaned forward. Then it sat slowly back and its body relaxed. It spoke to the Amifata, whose right eye rotated in response, possibly a reaction to show consternation. The Onde lay down on a cushion, curling up as the Amifata spoke agitatedly.

"What is it?" Pearl demanded. "What did it say?"

The Amifata turned its left eye to Pearl and said in Kedaic, "It thanks you and says it believes you now. And it wishes to rest."

"What?" Stone stared at the Onde, clearly not understanding. Jade hissed in dismay. Pearl flicked her tail impatiently, and the Kek rattled worriedly, wanting a translation.

The Amifata said, "It will not tell us where its people are, or how to help it. This behavior is not clear to me."

Moon said, "It's too much." He wasn't sure why he understood, but he did. Everyone turned to stare at him, and he tried to explain, "It's too tired. It can't run anymore, and now it doesn't have to. And that thing being dead isn't going to bring back any of the dead Onde." He turned and pushed past a few warriors not fast enough to get out of his way. He didn't want to argue with anyone while they translated what he had said, and there was nothing he could do to help. It had been too late for that long before the Amifata and Elastan had decided to come here.

☾

Moon went back to the clutch, curled up next to their nest, and fell asleep again. He was conscious of teachers moving around in the room occasionally, or going in and out, but it was comforting and not enough to wake him. He woke briefly when Stone came in. Stone said nothing, just shoved Moon over a little and fell asleep beside him.

When he did wake, Jade sat beside the nest, letting a couple of the sleepy babies chew on her fingers. She was in her Arbora form again, her scales and spines softened, her wings gone. He could tell that outside the great tree the sun was just moving above the horizon. He felt completely rested for the first time in days.

Jade said, "The hunters and Chime found parts for a dozen different species on that thing. No Raksura, though. It had a sort of voice device down its throat, like the Amifata have. They're grown in the moss canyons by their version of mentors, but the Amifata said other species make them too. The skin-hunter must have taken it from some trading species that used it to speak Raksuran."

Her expression was preoccupied and a little sad. Moon asked, "What about the Onde?"

"It died."

Moon sat up on one elbow and put his hand in the nest. A little warm body wrapped around it. No one else was in the room, but he could hear Blossom and Bead talking nearby, then Chime's voice, and Balm's.

Jade's brow was furrowed in thought. "How did you know . . . How were you so sure you understood how it felt?"

Moon hadn't been sure at the time, but the badly needed sleep had focused his thoughts. "It stayed in the leaf boat. Maybe it didn't want to leave the Amifata and Elastan, maybe it was giving them water, hoping enough Kek would show up to make the skin-hunter leave. But it could have slipped away if it really wanted to. So it must not have wanted to." That was one reason. The other was that Moon knew what it was like to live with that sort of tension for turns at a time. The combination of that and the near-mortal dart wound must have been hard to struggle against. And they didn't know how old the Onde had been, how many of its family and companions it had lost.

Jade's mouth twisted in resigned agreement. "It didn't try to help itself until the leaf boat was brought here. Then it just slipped into the tree and found a place to die."

The baby was trying to gnaw on Moon's thumb. "At least we saved the Amifata. And Elastan. They wanted to be saved."

Jade shook her head a little. "I wish we could have saved those Kek plant hunters. Kof asked us for help and all we did was bring them trouble."

"They helped bring the trouble," Moon pointed out. The thing he had learned from all this was that the Kek were shy and gentle and nervous, and when threatened, utterly fearless. And from what he had understood from Kof and the various healers, they had had no intention of leaving the groundlings to die out in that leaf boat.

From behind him, Stone said, "I'm beginning to think the Kek like trouble. That's probably why they live under Raksuran colonies."

Jade didn't look reassured. "I wish I'd been able to help."

Fern was crawling away from the others, and Moon scooped her up and set her in Jade's lap. As nerve-racking as this whole situation had been for Moon, he knew it had been worse for Jade, unable to shift and stuck inside the colony. "Me too."

Jade stroked Fern's soft frills, and smiled a little. "We decided to put off the celebration until the Amifata recover and leave, just in case anything else happens."

"That's when I get gifts, right?" Moon asked, partly to distract her further from thoughts of the poor dead Onde, partly because he really wanted to know. He had been given one new armband already for the successful conception, but from what he understood, there was more coming.

Jade lifted a brow. "I thought you didn't care about gifts."

Stone snorted. Moon considered elbowing him but he didn't want to be knocked unconscious. He said, "This was rough. I want gifts."

"Then we should get started." Jade put Fern back with her brothers and sisters. "Most of the court is waiting to see this clutch. Our clutch." Jade's smile was whole-hearted this time. "Are you ready to let them in?"

Moon was ready.

APPENDICES

Appendix I

THE COURT OF INDIGO CLOUD

AERIAT

Queens

Pearl—Reigning Queen.

Jade—Sister Queen.

Amber—former Sister Queen of Pearl, now dead.

Azure—the queen who took Stone, now dead.

Frost—a fledgling queen of the court of Sky Copper, now adopted by Indigo Cloud.

Indigo—the Reigning Queen who originally led the court away from the Reaches to the east.

Solace—a Sister Queen in an earlier generation of the court, who was the first to visit the Golden Isles.

Cerise—a past Reigning Queen; Indigo's birthqueen.

Consorts

Stone—line-grandfather.

Rain—Pearl's last consort, now dead.

Moon—Jade's consort.

Thorn and *Bitter*—fledgling consorts of Sky Copper, now adopted by Indigo Cloud.

Cloud—the consort Indigo stole from Emerald Twilight.

Sable—Solace's consort.

Dust and *Burn*—young consorts given away by Pearl when Rain died. Dust became the second consort to the reigning queen of Wind Sun.

Warriors

River—leader of Pearl's faction of warriors. A product of one of Amber's royal clutches.

Drift—River's clutchmate.

Branch—River and Drift's clutchmate, killed in a Fell ambush.

Root—young warrior from an Arbora clutch; a member of Jade's faction.

Song—young female warrior; a member of Jade's faction.

Spring—fledgling female, one of only two survivors from Amber's last clutch of warriors.

Snow—fledgling male, Spring's clutchmate.

Balm—female warrior, and Jade's clutchmate. Jade's strongest supporter and leader of her faction.

Chime—former Arbora mentor, now a warrior; a member of Jade's faction.

Vine and *Coil*—male warriors of Pearl's faction, though they chafe under River's rule.

Floret—female warrior of Pearl's faction.

Sand—a young male warrior of Jade's faction.

Serene—a young female warrior of Jade's faction.

Band and *Fair*—young male warriors of Pearl's faction.

Sage—an older male warrior of Pearl's faction.

Serene—a young female warrior of Jade's faction.

Briar and *Aura*—young female warriors, inclining to Jade's faction, but currently unattached. Aura came from an Arbora clutch.

Sorrow—female warrior who took care of Moon as a fledgling, believed to be the last Aeriat survivor of his court, killed by Tath.

Arbora

Mentors

Flower—leader of the Mentors' Caste.

Heart—young female mentor, one of the Arbora rescued from the Dwei Hive by Moon.

Merit—young male mentor, rescued with Heart.

Copper—a young male mentor, still in the nurseries.

Thistle—a young female mentor.

Teachers

Petal—former leader of the Teachers' Caste, killed in the Fell attack on the old Indigo Cloud colony.

Bell—new leader of the Teachers' Caste, and clutchmate to Chime.

Blossom—an older female, one of only two teachers to escape during the Fell attack on the colony. Later learned to pilot a Golden Isles Wind-ship.

Bead—a young female, she escaped the colony with Blossom.

Rill, *Bark*, and *Weave*—female teachers.

Gift, *Needle*, and *Dream*—young female teachers, rescued from the Dwei Hive by Moon.

Snap—young male teacher, also rescued from the Dwei Hive.

Dash—a very old male teacher.

Gold—an older female teacher, and the best artisan in the court.

Merry—a younger male teacher, and Gold's student.

Hunters

Bone—leader of the Hunters' Caste.

Braid, *Salt*, *Spice*, *Knife*—young male hunters.

Bramble, *Blaze*, *Plum*—young female hunters.

Wake—an older female hunter.

Strike—a very young hunter, male, who volunteered to test the Fell poison.

Soldiers

Knell—leader of Soldiers' Caste, and clutchmate to Chime.

Grain—the first Arbora to speak to Moon and to order him to leave Indigo Cloud.

Shell—Grain's clutchmate, killed in the Fell attack on the colony.

Sharp, Ginger, Sprout—young female soldiers.

THE COURT OF EMERALD TWILIGHT
AERIAT

Queens

Ice—reigning queen of Emerald Twilight.

Tempest—senior sister queen, Ash's birthqueen.

Ash—youngest daughter queen.

Halcyon—another sister queen, Tempest's clutchmate.

Consorts

Shadow—first consort to Ice.

Fade—second consort to Tempest, now dead.

Ember—consort sent to Indigo Cloud, from Tempest and Fade's only clutch.

Warriors

Willow—a female Warrior who greets visitors at Emerald Twilight.

Torrent—female warrior, from a queen's clutch with Tempest and Halcyon.

Beacon, Prize—female warriors of Tempest's faction.

Dart, Streak, Gust—male warriors of Tempest's faction.

THE COURT OF OPAL NIGHT
AERIAT

Queens

Malachite—reigning queen of Emerald Twilight.

Onyx—sister queen.

Celadon—daughter queen, of Malachite's line.

Ivory—another daughter queen, of Onyx's line.

Consorts

Dusk—first consort to Malachite, killed after the attack on the eastern colony.

Umber—first consort to Onyx.

Shade—young consort, son of Malachite's consort Night.

Warriors

Rise—female warrior of Opal Night, of Malachite's faction.

Saffron—female warrior, clutchmate of Ivory.

Sorrow—female warrior who took care of Moon as a fledgling, killed by Tath.

Horn, Tribute—male warriors of Ivory's faction.

Gallant, Fleet—female warriors of Ivory's faction.

Dare, Rime—male warriors of Celadon's faction.

ARBORA

Mentors

Lithe—female mentor, young but powerful.

Tear—older female mentor, now dead.

Reed—young female mentor.

Auburn—an older male mentor.

Teachers

    Feather—female teacher, survivor of the eastern colony.

    Russet—female teacher, survivor of the eastern colony.

    Twist, Yarrow—two male teachers killed in the eastern colony.

    Luster—a male teacher.

    Moss—a young male teacher.

Hunters

    Fair—a female hunter killed in the eastern colony.

THE COURT OF VERIDIAN SEA

Amaranth—reigning queen.

Flint—her first consort.

THE COURT OF SUNSET WATER

Zephyr—a sister queen, daughter of an Emerald Twilight consort, Shadow's clutchmate, who was given to the reigning Sunset Water queen.

THE COURT OF OCEAN WINTER

Flame—a sister queen.

Garnet—a daughter queen.

Venture—a female warrior, clutchmate to the reigning queen.

Violet—a female mentor.

Appendix II

EXCERPT FROM OBSERVATIONS OF THE RAKSURA:
VOLUME THIRTY-SEVEN OF A NATURAL HISTORY BY
SCHOLAR-PREEMINENT DELIN-EVRAN-LINDEL

The Two Breeds of the Raksura

ARBORA: Arbora have no wings but are agile climbers, and their scales appear in a variety of colors. They have long tails, sharp retractable claws, and manes of flexible spines and soft "frills," characteristics that are common to all Raksura. They are expert artisans and are dexterous and creative in the arts they pursue for the court's greater good. In their alternate form they are shorter than Aeriat Raksura and have stocky, powerful builds. Both male and female Arbora are fertile, and sometimes may have clutches that include warrior fledglings. This is attributed to queens and consorts blending their bloodlines with Arbora over many generations.

The four castes of the Arbora are:

Teachers—They supervise the nurseries and train the young of the court. They are also the primary artisans of the court, and tend the gardens that will be seen around any Raksuran colony.

Hunters—They take primary responsibility for providing food for the court. This includes hunting for game, and gathering wild plants.

Soldiers—They "guard the ground" and protect the colony and the surrounding area.

Mentors—They are Arbora born with arcane powers, who have skill in healing and augury. They also act as historians and record-keepers for the court, and usually advise the queens.

AERIAT: The winged Raksura. Like the Arbora, they have long tails, sharp retractable claws, and manes of flexible spines and soft frills.

Warriors—They act as scouts and guardians, and defend the colony from threats from the air, such as the Fell. Warriors are sterile and cannot breed, though they appear as male and female forms. Their scales are in any number of bright colors. Female warriors are usually somewhat stronger than male warriors. In their alternate form, they are always tall and slender. They are not as long-lived generally as queens, consorts, and Arbora.

Consorts—Consorts are fertile males, and their scales are always black, though there may be a tint or "undersheen" of gold, bronze, or blood red. At maturity they are stronger than warriors, and may be the longest lived of any Raksura. They are also the fastest and most powerful flyers, and this ability increases as they grow older. There is some evidence to suggest that consorts of great age may grow as large or larger than the major kethel of the Fell.

Queens—Queens are fertile females, and are the most powerful and deadly fighters of all the Aeriat. Their scales have two brilliant colors, the second in a pattern over the first. The queens' alternate form resembles an Arbora, with no wings, but retaining the tail, and an abbreviated mane of spines and the softer frills. Queens mate with consorts to produce royal clutches, composed of queens, consorts, and warriors.

Appendix III

EXCERPT FROM ADDITIONS TO THE LIST OF
PREDATORY SPECIES BY SCHOLAR-EMINENT-POSTHUMOUS
VENAR-INRAM-ALIL.

Fell are migratory and prey on other intelligent species.

The Known Classes of Fell

Major kethel—The largest of the Fell, sometimes called harbingers, major kethel are often the first sign that a Fell flight is approaching. Their scales are black, like that of all the Fell, and they have an array of horns around their heads. They have a low level of intelligence and are believed to be always under the control of the rulers.

Minor dakti—The dakti are small, with armor plates on the back and shoulders, and webbed wings. They are somewhat cunning, but not much more intelligent than kethel, and fight in large swarms.

Rulers—Rulers are intelligent creatures that are believed to have some arcane powers of entrancement over other species. Rulers related by blood are also believed to share memories and experiences through some mental bond. They have complete control of the lesser Fell in their flights, and at times can speak through dakti and see through their eyes. (*Addendum by scholar-preeminent Delin-Evran-lindel: Fell rulers in their winged form bear an unfortunate and superficial resemblance to Raksuran Consorts.)*

There is believed to be a fourth class, or possibly a female variant of the Rulers, called the *Progenitors*.

Common lore holds that if a Fell ruler is killed, its head must be removed and stored in a cask of salt or yellow mud and buried on land in order to prevent drawing other Fell rulers to the site of its death. It is possible that only removing the head from the corpse may be enough to prevent this, but burying it is held to be the safest course.

ALSO AVAILABLE
FROM MARTHA WELLS
AND NIGHT SHADE BOOKS

THE CLOUD ROADS

Moon has spent his life hiding what he is — a shape-shifter able to transform himself into a winged creature of flight. An orphan with only vague memories of his own kind, Moon tries to fit in among the tribes of his river valley, with mixed success. Just as Moon is once again cast out by his adopted tribe, he discovers a shape-shifter like himself . . . someone who seems to know exactly what he is, who promises that Moon will be welcomed into his community.

What this stranger doesn't tell Moon is that his presence will tip the balance of power . . . that his extraordinary lineage is crucial to the colony's survival . . . and that his people face extinction at the hands of the dreaded Fell!

Moon must overcome a lifetime of conditioning in order to save and himself . . . and his newfound kin.

"Martha Wells' books always make me remember why I love to read. In *The Cloud Roads*, she invents yet another rich and astonishingly detailed setting, where many races and cultures peacefully coexist in a world constantly threatened by soulless predators. But the vivid worldbuilding and nonstop action really serve as a backdrop for the heart of the novel—the universal human themes of loneliness, loss, and the powerful drive to find somewhere to belong."
– Sharon Shinn, bestselling author of *Archangel* and *Troubled Waters*

$14.99 trade paperback • 978-1-59780-216-1

THE SERPENT SEA

Moon, once a solitary wanderer, has become consort to Jade, sister queen of the Indigo Cloud court. Together, they travel with their people on a pair of flying ships in hopes of finding a new home for their colony. Moon finally feels like he's found a tribe where he belongs.

But when the travelers reach the ancestral home of Indigo Cloud, shrouded within the trunk of a mountain-sized tree, they discover a blight infecting its core. Nearby they find the remains of the invaders who may be responsible, as well as evidence of a devastating theft. This discovery sends Moon and the hunters of Indigo Cloud on a quest for the heartstone of the tree—a quest that will lead them far away, across the Serpent Sea.

In this follow-up to *The Cloud Roads*, Martha Wells returns with a world-spanning odyssey, a mystery that only provokes more questions—and the adventure of a lifetime.

"A starring light of the fantasy genre recaptures her mojo by going in a new direction."
– *SF Signal*

$14.99 trade paperback • 978-1-59780-332-8

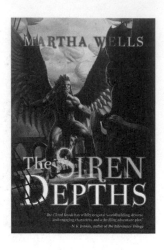

THE SIREN DEPTHS

All his life, Moon roamed the Three Worlds, a solitary wanderer forced to hide his true nature—until he was reunited with his own kind, the Raksura, and found a new life as consort to Jade, sister queen of the Indigo Cloud court.

But now a rival court has laid claim to him, and Jade may or may not be willing to fight for him. Beset by doubts, Moon must travel in the company of strangers to a distant realm where he will finally face the forgotten secrets of his past, even as an old enemy returns with a vengeance.

The Fell, a vicious race of shape-shifting predators, menaces groundlings and Raksura alike. Determined to crossbreed with the Raksura for arcane purposes, they are driven by an ancient voice that cries out from . . . The Siren Depths.

"Martha Wells writes fantasy the way it was meant to be—poignant, evocative, and astonishing. Prepare to be captivated 'til the sun comes up."
– Kameron Hurley, author of *God's War*, *Infidel*, *Rapture*, and *The Mirror Empire*

"Riveting storytelling."
– Steven Gould, author of *Jumper*

$14.99 trade paperback • 978-1-59780-440-0

STORIES OF THE RAKSURA
VOLUME ONE: THE FALLING WORLD
& THE TALE OF INDIGO AND CLOUD

In "The Falling World," Jade, sister queen of the Indigo Cloud Court, has traveled with Chime and Balm to another Raksuran court. When she fails to return, her consort, Moon, along with Stone and a party of warriors and hunters, must track them down. Finding them turns out to be the easy part; freeing them from an ancient trap hidden in the depths of the Reaches is much more difficult.

"The Tale of Indigo and Cloud" explores the history of the Indigo Cloud Court, long before Moon was born. In the distant past, Indigo stole Cloud from Emerald Twilight. But in doing so, Indigo and the reigning Queen Cerise are now poised for a conflict that could spark war throughout all the courts of the Reaches.

Stories of Moon and the shape changers of Raksura have delighted readers for years. This world is a dangerous place full of strange mysteries, where the future can never be taken for granted and must always be fought for with wits and ingenuity, and often tooth and claw. With two brand-new novellas, Martha Wells shows that the world of the Raksura has many more stories to tell . . . .

$15.99 trade paperback • 978-1-59780-535-3

About the Author

Martha Wells was born in Fort Worth, Texas, in 1964, and has a B.A. in anthropology from Texas A&M University. She is the author of more than a dozen fantasy novels, including *The Wizard Hunters*, *The Ships of Air*, *The Gate of Gods*, *The Element of Fire*, and the Nebula-nominated *The Death of the Necromancer*. She has also had short fiction published in *Realms of Fantasy*, *Black Gate Magazine*, *Lone Star Stories*, and the Tsunami Relief anthology, *Elemental*, and has articles in the non-fiction anthologies *Farscape Forever* and *Mapping the World of Harry Potter*. Her books have been published in seven languages. She lives in College Station, Texas, with her husband. Her website is www.marthawells.com.